I0625105

Trouble Brewing

In Ashwood, Volume 2

Kinney Scott

Published by Kinney Scott, 2017.

TROUBLE BREWING

First edition. September 15, 2017.

Copyright © 2017 Kinney Scott.

ISBN: 978-1950800094

Written by Kinney Scott.

Also by Kinney Scott

In Ashwood
Inheriting Trouble
Trouble Brewing
Chasing Trouble
Addicted To Trouble
Trouble Undone

Watch for more at https://kinneyscott.com.

To Lia, Mercedes, and Keke - I hope we can all meet soon
and have a pint.

ONE

Wade leaned into the weight of the dolly. His arms flexed as he pushed another keg of Double Deet IPA behind a long, temporary bar. He narrowed his eyes to bring the details of the party into focus.

Damn, do I need glasses already?

The radical changes he inspected were perfect. Just about everyone in Ashwood had worked to transform the massive shop at Whitewater Homes into a surprise party venue. And that was no small feat.

This morning, Seth's employees—Rick, Kent, and Carlos—had come in early on a Saturday to clear the construction equipment from the industrial space. In place of tools and lumber stood Mosquito Creek Brewing's portable bar, a dance floor, and a massive sound system ready to shake the ancient timbers of the old lumber mill.

Kelsey's shrill whistle halted buzzing conversation. "Hey, listen up!" she yelled over everyone's heads. "Ben's having trouble stalling Seth and Natalie in Portland. We've got less than three hours to get this surprise party ready—so move!"

Confident he could handle the hundred-plus invited guests, Wade tested the taps for his popular IPA. No problem. He turned to check in with Iris.

Once she secured the lid on an ice-filled cooler, she stretched to ease her tired back. Iris lost herself in a distracting overhead feline stretch, and Wade couldn't help but admire the slender muscle running the length of her thigh.

When Iris caught him looking, she grinned. "I tried to kill myself with yoga this morning."

"Yoga? I thought that was all about relaxing and meditation," he teased, unable to recall a time when he'd seen Iris wearing a skirt.

"Not if you do it right." Her eyes danced with a wicked gleam.

This flirty version of Iris intrigued Wade. He reminded himself that she was a good friend and a valued business connection, but damn, his body wouldn't submit to his logic. They knew each other well, and he appreciated her support. Her bar, north of town, promoted his brewery each time he launched a new beer.

"Thanks for shutting down Northside Grill for this event," he said." We couldn't have pulled it off without you."

She shrugged off the compliment. "Seth and Natalie's engagement party is exactly where I want to be. I love helping out, especially when it keeps me in my happy place—behind a bar." As her knuckles rapped the wooden surface, her jade green eyes danced, and Wade couldn't look away.

When Iris turned and opened another package of napkins, he finally asked. "Do you need any help?"

"Could you slice a little more fruit?"

"On it." He grabbed a paring knife and went to work. Together, they finished the prep, promising their guests a proper drink and a proper buzz.

An hour later, Kelsey shouted, "Seth and Natalie are only a few miles away!"

Bodies scrambled and the lights were doused. Behind the bar, Wade huddled in his hiding spot next to Iris, ready for the surprise. In the dark, he tucked a little closer to her intoxicating scent—lavender shampoo and a delicious trace of orange. His mouth watered.

Iris giggled and squirmed. "Oh, no—my leg's cramping." She stretched and contorted like a circus performer. When the bendy move pressed her warmth against him, a bead of sweat trickled down Wade's spine. He closed his eyes and swallowed hard.

Outside, car doors slammed. Wade turned his head and whispered, "It won't be long now."

Electric anticipation pulsed through the inky room. Quiet murmurs ceased, then a nervous giggle floated through the dark. Amanda whispered, "Stop it, Kent."

Wade huffed and gritted his teeth. Those two were always messing around.

A door squeaked, and a moment later the couple of honor crossed the threshold. Thousands of tiny white lights suddenly flipped on.

A deafening "Surprise!" bounced from the lofted ceiling. "Kiss–kiss–kiss," arched in crescendo as Seth took his bride-to-be in his arms. He bent her into an iconic embrace—kissing her senseless. The pair rose from their amorous public display to thunderous applause.

Dragged to the stage, Seth and Natalie blinked, stunned by the throng. Their trembling hands grasped flutes of golden champagne as they smiled for pictures and waited for a toast. Natalie's older brother, Ben, jogged across the dance floor and joined them in front of the noisy crowd. After he tapped the mic, Kelsey slid a glass of champagne into his hand.

"Thanks, Kels," he said, then cleared his throat. "I guess it's my job, as Natalie's brother, to make the toast and get this party started."

Cheers and applause broadened Ben's nervous grin. He gripped the mic tighter, eyes glistening with emotion, and said, "Natalie discovered her happily-ever-after when she hired Seth to build her tiny home. Seth secured their future when he got down on one knee and proposed. Let's celebrate that moment when fate brought this couple together to create enduring love."

"Congratulations!" bounced from the rafters. Flutes clinked and everyone joined the toast. Moments later, heavy bass thumped from four massive speakers. Dancers flooded the floor with laughter, bright dresses, and wiggling hips.

It didn't take long before every thirsty guest had a drink. Wade couldn't resist the temptation and pulled Iris to the floor.

"I don't know if I've ever seen you dance. You're always working the bar at Northside," he said as she followed him into the crowd.

"I'm happy to dance with you tonight." The bluesy music drummed a sensual rhythm. Her lithe dancer's body, draped in a silky skirt, floated naturally to the nuanced beat.

Mesmerized by her movements, his body responded to her gentle sway. Wade let his hands explore, and he kept her close until a line coaxed him back to the bar.

Iris didn't stay behind the bar serving drinks for long. Wade wasn't the only man who had noticed this surprising change in the woman they all knew well. Sexy music, white lights, and her long legs stretching from a short skirt inspired a continuous queue of suitors.

Jealous heat flicked Wade's eyes to the dance floor where Iris spun with five different partners in a row. The first few were locals, regulars at Northside Grill. The latest, a newcomer to Ashwood, held her close for a slow rock ballad. From Wade's vantage point, it seemed like Iris appreciated the close attention. When she lifted her head and smiled, her dance partner bent close to whisper something in her ear.

Whatever passed between them stopped their dance. Instantly, Iris went stiff, her shoulders hitched, and tattooed arms caged her.

Wade took quick action, but before he rounded the counter, Iris had already peeled herself away from the tattooed man. For a moment, she stood unmoving in the center of the dance floor, then on a swift turn she landed with an oomph against Wade's solid chest. She caught her breath as he wrapped his hands around her arms, possessing her briefly.

Wade smothered the desire to claim more than just her time. "Do you feel like another dance," he asked. "Or would you rather grab something to drink?" He studied her carefully, trying to measure her shifting expression.

Iris blinked up and said, "I'd love one more dance." Seeming to need human contact, her arms slipped around his neck. Her torso shuddered as she inhaled a shaky breath and blew it out again. Warm and sweet, the light exhale tickled his skin. In a few beats, she'd settled herself into an easy rhythmic sway.

"Did you invite that guy to the party?" she asked.

Wade nodded, regretting that invitation. "Yeah. Seth did some renovation work at Lincoln's place. He's opening a pizza shop in town."

Her lips rolled in, then she forced a smile. "That's what Lincoln told me, out there on the floor."

Wade squeezed her waist. "Don't worry, you can handle the competition." She relaxed in his arms, but he sensed she still needed more from him to feel completely at ease. "He only has a small place planned. You won't even sense a change at The Grill. Sorry I invited him," he whispered on a closer lean.

"Don't be silly. Lincoln might be new to Ashwood, but he's part of the town." Iris stared past Wade's shoulder for a long moment and his hand spread across her back, nestling her closer, wanting to keep her to himself. Their thighs brushed and pushed, prickling with provocative heat.

On a long sigh her spine straightened, and Iris tipped away to look at Wade up-close. Gold flecks in her jade-green eyes mesmerized him until she asked, "How many of these people are part of your family?"

Scanning the heads in the room, he spun Iris on the dancefloor to give her a specific view. "That entire side of the room is filled by the Michaels' clan. Those are my parents sitting with Seth's mom and dad. They drove in from the family hop farm with two of my sisters.

Linnea and Sylvia are here. Brooke and her husband stayed in Yakima to keep the farm going."

Iris glanced from the parents' table to him and studied his features. "You look a lot like your dad."

He nodded. "Unfortunately, I inherited his stubborn side, too." Wade spun her to the center of the dance floor. The maneuver shifted the subject to safer territory while blending them into the crowd.

"Do you come from a big family?" he asked.

"Not really. My brother was military. Mom lives in Texas."

With no mention of her dad, Wade chose not to press her for more. Not here, not yet. After spinning one last time around the floor, he spotted a short queue forming again for drinks and reluctantly returned to his post. Iris wandered to visit with friends at a nearby table.

Once the line disappeared, Seth stopped by for another IPA and a glass of champagne for Natalie. "Thanks for everything—this party will go down as one of Ashwood's greatest."

Wade reached across the bar and squeezed his cousin's shoulder. He'd do anything for this guy and loved him like a brother. "Happy to help, and happy for you. I hope to find what you have someday, but I'll give it a few years."

"When you least expect it," his cousin warned with a sly grin.

Iris returned and surprised Seth with a quick peck on the cheek. "Congratulations," she said, as she slipped past to claim her spot behind the bar.

Seth thanked her with a chuckle before he headed toward Natalie, a drink in each hand.

Now that this temptation had returned, her subtle lavender scent teased Wade's senses, and he began to love the tight space behind the bar. Her perfume left him guessing the flavor of her soft lips. Would she taste spicy like the delicious fragrance that radiated from her warm skin, or sweet like champagne?

A hip-bump amplified the gentle flirtation as she swayed, still under the spell of the music. "I'd forgotten how much I loved to dance. Thanks for hauling me out there."

His eyes feasted on the swing of her hips as she blended a fruity cocktail. With each tilt, he imagined grabbing hold to press his length against her contours. "Why haven't you gone out on the floor a little more at Northside Grill?"

One shoulder shrugged. "For the same reason you don't drink at brewing festivals—someone has to be in charge."

"True. I don't know who's in charge tonight, but I know it *isn't* me," he said with a raised brow.

"You can't fool me, Wade Michaels. I know you're happiest with your feet planted near those kegs." Her fingers lingered on his arm as he pulled another beer.

She understood him. They had similar passions—independence and hard work, but tonight she seemed to be hinting toward something more. "At least the numbers are thinning," he said. "It won't be long before Seth drags Natalie home to give her a preview of their honeymoon." His comment drew Iris closer, touching shoulders, hips, and thighs.

"You picked up on that, too?" Iris' eyes gleamed with an intensity that sent a clear message.

Wade reached around her for a lemon and added it to the beer he'd just poured. The maneuver planted his front to her back, and nestled Iris against the bar.

"Hard not to notice," he growled close to her ear.

"That's what she said." She laughed, pressing her spine against the muscled plane of his chest.

Both knew where this sweet seduction could lead. Iris swayed her ass against his groin and didn't pull away from his solid, enthusiastic response.

Suddenly, Wade wanted Iris alone and was tempted to push everyone out the door. Bad timing killed the moment. Across the room, a few couples stood and pulled on coats. At the same time, his sister aimed for the bar. With a groan, his body left Iris. He was thankful to have the bar between his lower half and Linnea's eyes.

"What can I get you?" he asked, tight-voiced.

"Nothing for now. Mom and Dad are taking off with Aunt Sandy and Uncle Bill. They wanted a head count for breakfast in the morning. Are you in?" Linnea's eyes pleaded *yes*. He knew his sister didn't want to go home to Yakima without spending more time with him.

"Sure. I'll be there. Are you staying for the rest of the party?" Wade knew his sister often ditched these things to curl up with a book instead.

"I guess so. Sylvia asked me to hang around." Linnea smiled and leaned forward. "And tonight, I don't mind. This party's a great way to meet everyone in Ashwood." Her blue eyes sparkled. Wade could see in an instant that she looked forward to running his taproom. Once the new location for Mosquito Creek Brewing was finished, she'd leave the family farm and begin a new job—a new life in Ashwood.

The imminent move had created another rift with Dad, but Wade desperately needed her help with the taproom, and she wanted off the hop farm. Wade counted the days until she could start.

"Why don't I help you and pour a few drinks right now?" she asked. "I gotta start sometime."

"Not tonight, Sis. We've got it handled. Soon you'll be trapped around kegs so much you'll be sick of the smell of hops. Go, enjoy." He waved her off and she turned back toward her seat with a sigh. Hugging the perimeter of the room, Linnea avoided the dance floor.

Wade dreaded that family breakfast tomorrow morning. He hoped his father would keep his opinions to himself. Not likely.

Lately, every conversation ended in an argument about the costly expansion of Mosquito Creek Brewing.

No matter how much his father protested, Wade never intended to return to Yakima and run the prosperous five-generation family hop farm. His future was in brewing, no matter the cost.

With contracts signed and notarized, money now flowed in freely from the Chicago-based investors. In the past few weeks, Seth and his construction crew had accelerated the pace of Mosquito Creek's expansion. The transition now progressed at a ferocious pace, like an avalanche rolling down Mount Adams' steep slopes.

TWO

From behind the bar, Wade's gaze followed his sister's path as she edged the dance floor. He noted another person tracking her progress. If Rick kept studying her that way, he'd have to meet with the guy and have a talk. Linnea was shy and didn't recognize the power she held over the men in the room.

Seated among her family and new friends, she already seemed to fit in. He hoped Linnea would end up loving the job she planned to tackle at his brewery—the success of his taproom depended on it. So, if she got a little attention from one of Seth's employee's, he'd deal. At least Whitewater Homes was right next door, and he could keep an eye on his sister. From the way Rick was acting, it looked like he would need to do just that.

Wade huffed as Rick made his move, closing in on Linnea's table. The muscle-bound guy had begun his prowl moments after Ben asked Kelsey to dance. When Kent pulled Amanda onto the floor, Rick rushed in.

Somehow, Linnea hadn't noticed. She sat smiling, watching the floor, bobbing her foot to the beat of the music while taking another sip of champagne. Rick relocated himself behind her, took a big breath, and tapped her shoulder.

Wade chuckled to himself when Linnea's quick pivot put her eyes on Rick's belt. His sister blushed crimson as her eyes panned up, locking in on a nervous face. When Rick held out his hand and asked her to dance, she smiled, nodded, and followed him to the dance floor just as a slow song came on.

***

Wade glanced at the clock. It was half-past midnight and loud music still echoed through the shop. Four couples clung to each other on the dance floor, determined to stay until their feet shuffled holes through the wooden planks. Among those still dancing, Wade spotted his sister, Linnea, trapped in Rick's heavily muscled arms.

Cleanup progressed around the swaying hopeful romantics. Iris tossed Kent a trash bag and thanked him for his help. After filling it, he grabbed another stuffed-full bag and headed toward the giant dumpsters behind the shop.

Out of her heels, Amanda dashed in flip-flops to catch up. "Let me get the door for you," she said.

Kent grinned as she yanked on the massive bay door until it gave way with a metallic groan. The moment that door ground open, Amanda jumped up and down, clapping her hands.

"Snow!" She squealed and dashed outside, lifting her face to thousands of tiny flakes falling in a cascading snow globe descent.

All heads in the room turned toward the wide-open bay door. Groans mingled with profane complaints. In a few seconds, the magic of the party vanished when the music turned off and the bright overhead lights flicked on.

Hugging her body for warmth, Amanda caught a snowflake on her tongue. "Kent, isn't it beautiful?"

"Not as beautiful as you, sunshine." Kent laughed and jogged to the dumpster to get rid of the bags. His boot skidded across the pavement as he returned.

"How bad do the roads look?" Rick asked, while releasing Linnea from his embrace.

"Not too bad, yet," Kent answered then raised his voice, "If anyone needs a ride, I've got a four-wheel drive."

Within minutes, nearly everyone plodded out to the parking lot in the swirling snow. They shared rides, abandoning less storm-worthy cars in the lot until morning.

Wade was in no hurry to leave. As usual, he intended to stay on-site at Whitewater Homes. When the work next door had begun on his brewery expansion, he spent most nights in the tiny home sitting right outside the shop. His cousin, Seth, kept the demo on site for his potential customers. For now, the compact place was his.

He missed his home on Mosquito Creek, his bed, and his original brewing operation, but it didn't make sense to make the commute an hour north of Ashwood over winding roads to reach the remote location.

Under the care of his head brewer, *Old Mosquito* operated just fine without him. Erik and his wife, Trish, kept the original brewery running smoothly.

The other member of his crew, Dillon, a long-time friend, bounced between the old location and the new one in Ashwood. His employees saved Wade's ass from the time-sucking commute.

When the last truck pulled away, Iris finally shrugged on her winter coat. "Are you staying here on a cot in the office?" she asked.

"Not a cot. Seth keeps a tiny house on property. I've been there more often than not during the brewery expansion."

"How convenient. Is it nice?" she asked with a hopeful, flirty smile.

Heating with possibilities, his body responded to her not-so-subtle hint. "Yeah, would you like to take a look?"

He watched her green eyes go from steamy to molten. What he offered, she seemed willing to sample, but he had to be sure. Until today, their professional contact had never hinted at anything more than friendship.

"Show me the way," she said, her voice darkened by longing. Leading her to the side door of the shop, the breadth of his hand spanned the sway of her back. Just a few steps away, his home welcomed Iris, where the glow from the porch light illuminated the falling snow.

"Wow, it's really coming down." She held out her hand to catch a few fat flakes.

Wade led the way, and Iris stepped into his large deep footprints to save her delicate silver shoes. The pair climbed the steps onto the covered porch and turned to watch the snow. Her gaze lingered on her lime green Volkswagen Beetle parked across the lot. A three-inch blanket of white already covered the hood. That car wasn't going anywhere tonight.

"I think you should stay." He reached and swung the door open. The move pressed his torso against hers.

"Are you sure?" she asked. "I think I can make it home if I leave now. Or, I could borrow one of Mosquito's trucks." She stroked her hand over his bicep, letting him decide.

A shake of his head shut down her protest. Wade wrapped one arm around her waist and eased her over the threshold with his body. "Don't you think you would be safer here with me?" he said as his palm nestled against the nape of her neck, and he stroked her lips with his.

"Safe isn't exactly what I had in mind," she murmured against his kiss while closing the door with her foot.

While nipping her tempting mouth, his hands explored, sliding from her waist to the swell of her ass. Locking her body in place, he pressed his arousal against her, and she moaned at the sensual contact. The muscular length of his thigh eased between her legs, inching them apart, teasing. Her pleasure vibrated his lips and transmitted the sensation straight to his cock.

Iris tugged his shirt from his jeans, eased her hand underneath, and explored the ridges of his stomach. Her gentle caress teased his pecs first, the nails scraping lightly across his small nipples. Wade hissed in a breath on a shiver.

"Mmm, you like that?" she whispered.

Instead of answering, Wade reached behind his head, fisted the fabric, and tugged his shirt off. Iris stepped back to study the

13

contours of his chiseled physique. Her eyes lingered on the black and gray mosquito tattoo covering his rib cage.

"Nice ink." Iris bit her lip and eagerly reached for his belt.

Wade shook his head, "Not yet." He wanted to savor her. To slow the momentum, he covered her hand with his own.

Her disappointed whimper got a smile, and he gently tugged her up the narrow stairs, into the lofted bedroom. Teasing her blouse away, he lifted it over her head but left the filmy skirt in place. No need to rush, he planned to appreciate her body one inch at a time.

Her bra, the deep color of melted chocolate, matched her glossy hair. His fingers traced the decadent silk. Edged with fine strands of gold lace, it glimmered in the low light. He loved when women splurged on lingerie, decorating their already beautiful forms with deserved attention.

"Stunning," was the only word he uttered as he followed her to the mattress. In a fluid movement, his body bent to worship her soft breasts. He nibbled a line where her tantalizing skin spilled over the shimmering gold.

The tip of his tongue wound a path down the valley of her chest, where he found a trace of the lavender scent she'd applied to that spot and licked it. Inhaling, he trailed kisses over the pale swell. His hand snuck up to caress the other breast over the delicate lace. She arched in pleasure, seeking more, giving his fingers room to search for the clasp. When Wade released her breasts, she sighed and the need to explore took over.

Stretching each arm over her head, Wade encouraged her to grasp the rails of the bed. Her eyes flared when she recognized his need for control. She held on tight and gave him full access. Wade rewarded her patience, licking his way across the swell of her stomach, while his hands lifted the delicate skirt.

After inhaling the scent of her arousal, he laid his lips over her lace-covered mound. The moment he made contact, her desire turned molten and Iris bucked. He slid the lace thong down her legs, and set it aside, but left the skirt bunched around her waist for now.

He grasped her slim hips and lifted, bending to her. His tongue invaded slowly, deliberately, and deep. She gave him a desperate moan. Needing to hear that again, Wade repeated the path once, twice, three times. With each measured repetition, he pressed harder, moaning as he lapped her delicious arousal.

"Please," Iris cried, unable to reach the peak that was just out of grasp. His chuckle vibrated against her, as he grabbed a pillow to keep her hips where he wished. Now that his hands were free, he used first one finger, then a second to swirl the rim of her entrance. Slick, hot, and ready—he pulsed his fingers in and out until her body quaked.

Hands clasped tight onto the bed, her knuckles white with coiled tension, Iris gave her body over to him. His fingers curled, pressing against the spot she craved. Firm lashes from his tongue danced over her sensitive bud, and her body flexed as her breathing fractured.

Wave after wave crashed, and the arc of her orgasm echoed her satisfied cries. It ebbed and peaked while he circled her channel with deep, soft kisses. His lips lavished attention across her thighs landing, warm and soft, on the inside of each knee. Her body quivered, savoring the final ebbing pulses.

Dark and sexy, his voice pulled her back. "You with me, Iris?"

Her eyes went wide, landing on his jeans. "Poor man, you look ready to explode." She reached for him and added, "Wade, you have many talents, but I'll be damned if that wasn't better than your beer."

"Not as easy to bottle and sell," he said on a chuckle.

"I won't let word get out. *You're my secret.*" She stretched and seized his waist with her calves, urging him forward.

"If that was the warm-up round, I can't wait to get started with the main event," she said as he prowled over her body to claim her mouth again. He shared the taste of her arousal on a kiss, getting a purr as his denim trapped erection pressed against her center.

Iris inched away, eyes dancing as she pivoted from the bottom to the top. Wade's sexy smirk invited her to seize control.

She shimmied out of her skirt, then went to work, tugging off his jeans and boxers. As he sprang free, she paused to enjoy a leisurely, decadent view.

"We'll need something from your wallet," she said.

"Top drawer." He motioned toward the built in bedside table.

On a slow crawl across the bed, she gave him an unapologetic view of her supple ass. With a giggle, Iris settled again over his hips. Her heated gaze scorched his body like tinder-dry wood. She tickled the dusting of hair on his chest and slowly followed the trail down.

Tortured too long, he warned, "Babe, I'm so ready to impale you. Too much foreplay, and you may only get a floor show. Just saying."

"Will I have another chance to explore *all this* later?" she asked gesturing with her hands and eyes. Iris took in every spot she intended to lick and nibble, especially the detailed tattoo that stretched over his ribs.

"I'm counting on it, but..."

"Get on and ride?" she laughed aloud.

"Now."

She grabbed the condom, tore open the package, and rolled it down his length. Centering her torso, she teased with wet heat, taking in the wide smooth crown.

With a low growl, Wade grabbed her hips and impaled her in one solid stroke. "Fuck me," he groaned when her body clamped his cock as tight as a fist.

Iris took over the rhythm, encouraging him with satisfied moans. He kneaded her breasts and teased the tip between his finger and thumb.

Beads of perspiration glistened as she accelerated the pace. Her hips rose and slammed down with increasing force. The unrelenting cadence increased, and his jaw clenched, fighting for control. With each writhing descent, her hips circled and pushed.

"Nearly there," she moaned, eyes half-mast basking in the first surge of sheer pleasure.

They broke together, and wave after wave of molten release took hold. He lifted her with the force of his groin, keeping her centered in his expansive grasp. Each fulfilling thrust that shot from his body shook her breasts in an erotic display. An all-consuming climax left them wholly spent, sated, and completely satisfied.

After Iris drained the last ounce of bliss, she collapsed forward, resting on his expansive chest, giving him her weight.

Gentle fingers stroked her nape, mapped the spot between her shoulder blades, and finally spread over the swell of her firm behind. He hated to move, but he rolled and eased from her body to take care of the condom.

Returning from the bathroom, Wade discovered Iris already sleeping on her stomach. Stretched out like a work of art, she was on display for his eyes to admire. He grinned when he spotted the tattoo. Beautiful and perfect, she'd chosen a delicate blue iris to decorate her right shoulder blade. Carefully, he covered her with a blanket. She stirred for a moment as he climbed next to her warmth. For the first time in weeks, Wade found tranquil sleep. Even the stress of the brewery expansion could not override his sated bliss.

THREE

Iris woke early, out of sheer habit more than feeling completely rested. After that satisfying night, she ached in all the best places. Good God, the stunning man snoring next to her definitely knew how to please a woman. Just the sight of him tempted her resolve to leave before he woke. Gathering her belongings, she slid silently into yesterday's clothes, hoping the buildings nearby would be prying-eye free.

When she glanced out the window a quiet groan escaped her lips. Deep snow covered the ground and hung heavily from the stoic Douglas Firs that surrounded the parking lot. Damn, it was early March, and winter refused to release its stubborn grip.

Iris kneaded her lip while staring at the shoes near the front door. She decided to borrow a pair of boots to save her pale silver flats from certain death. Wade's boots reached nearly to her knees, and her small feet swam in the leather expanse. Pulling the door closed silently behind her, she trudged outside and crunched a path of giant footprints across an undisturbed blanket of cold.

After scraping the snow from her windshield, Iris crept slowly home in a car she loved but regretted on days like today. Snowplows often ignored these late winter blasts, as the sun would likely melt all evidence away by noon.

A quick shower and a change of clothes put Iris back into work-mode, but she couldn't stop thinking about the brewer with the long hair who had touched her in all the right places. Once she made it to the safety of her office, she sent Wade a short text to explain his missing footwear.

Snatched your boots for the trek to my car. Thanks. I owe you breakfast.

***

Wade rolled to the side of the bed that still held Iris's spicy warmth. Propped on his elbows, he stared from the small loft window and spotted the sleek lines her tires had carved into the snow. Too early to move, he lay back to think about the previous night.

A grin stretched across his face. He couldn't understand how Iris had escaped his notice for so long. A pulse of need shot to his groin, his hand wandered down, and he coaxed his shaft. While he recalled every decadent detail of the previous night, his pleasure surged with the memory of Iris writhing above him. Release crashed quickly, forcing him out of bed to deal with the mess.

Wade staggered from the loft wondering why Iris left without a word. If he could roll back time, he'd have kept her tangled between his sheets all morning.

While the coffee maker sputtered, he scrolled through his emails. Each new message destroyed his morning. He closed his eyes to shut out another daunting day. With a flinch, he opened his calendar and groaned at his color-coded system. The tasks he'd plotted fuzzed into a mess of red, orange, and green distress signals. His brilliant organization method had failed him.

The phone vibrated in his hand, signaling a text. Iris' words stretched a smile on his face. She thanked him for the use of his boots and mentioned breakfast.

He read that word again. *Breakfast?*

"Ah, shit." He was supposed to have that meal with his family.

After gulping the last of his coffee, he brushed his teeth, found a clean pair of jeans and a shirt, and grabbed his keys. While dashing out the door, he nearly tripped on the little silver shoes Iris had left behind when she pulled on his boots. A special delivery would give him the perfect excuse to see if Iris craved a repeat of last night as much as he did.

On the drive, work pushed thoughts of Iris out of his mind. He needed a clone to share the load.

A clone? Linnea looked nothing like him, but his sister worked harder than he did.

All at once, Wade decided to ask Linn to move to Ashwood a few months early. With her steadying presence she'd be perfect, and he trusted his sister more than he trusted himself. He took a deep breath, finding relief in a solution that would solve everything. Eager to talk with her, he pressed the accelerator and fishtailed through an icy turn, closing in on his aunt and uncle's home.

Peals of laughter filled the air as he eased into Bill and Sandy's driveway where a grinning snowman welcomed him to the craftsman style home. From the safety of the cab, he watched his cousin, Amanda, streak across the yard. She ran away from his youngest sister, who carried a snowball in each hand. In the center of her back, Sylvia's coat was decorated by a large white blotch, a clear sign of a recent snowball hit. Following Amanda, Sylvia skidded out of sight. Payback was inevitable.

Wade climbed warily into the warzone, his breath white puffs in the crisp morning air. Amanda came around the house again, and he leaned against the fender to enjoy the battle.

Amanda, with three older brothers, had a definite advantage in all games of war, but Sylvia lettered in track and volleyball.

This should be good.

A snowball flew from his sister's hand landing right in the middle of Amanda's butt. His roaring laugh didn't last long. During the fray, Linnea had snuck from behind and tried to stuff snow down his coat. He spun and snagged his sister's wrists before she succeeded.

"Where did you come from?" Wade asked past a lingering chuckle.

"I stayed outside, watching for you." Linnea's smile begged for mercy, but there was something more. When she dropped the snow in her hands, he released her wrists.

"Dad's in one of his moods," she warned with a glance toward the house.

"Great. Why don't we sneak away now?" he suggested with a hopeful grin.

Linnea shook her head. "I don't' know what you're complaining about, I'm the one that has to ride home with him to Yakima."

Their mother burst through the front door, killing Wade's chance to talk with his sister about changing her plans. His mother's voice rose over the snowy-warfare. "Hey, Wade! Get in here. We didn't have time to talk with you last night."

Climbing the steps to the welcoming front porch, Wade stamped hard to clear snow from his boots, then stepped inside where the smell of bacon and onions surrounded him.

"Breakfast won't be long," Aunt Sandy called from the kitchen.

Wade peaked his head into the dinette and asked, "Do you want me to round up the troops?"

Sandy's smile welcomed him. "Please, that would be terrific."

Dad followed him out, and Wade pierced the air with a whistle. When he shouted "Breakfast," the promise of warm food stopped the battle. Coats, mittens, and hats soon covered the porch in a wet pile. His father grunted when he bent to pick up the hats and coats, and he worked silently shaking out clumpy snow.

To thaw the tension, Wade asked about the family hop farm. "Dad, have you talked to Brooke? Did Yakima see any of this snow?"

"Your sister said the moisture didn't make it over the mountains, but the cold air did. I just hope we don't lose any apricots with this winter blast." His father's jaw clenched as he stared over the snowy landscape, then his gaze cut to him. "Do you still plan to come to the farm and supervise the planting of your new hop variety?"

"I already said I would. It should take three or four days, tops. Give me the time window for the crew and I'll be there," he promised, yet again.

"Brooke will send you the schedule this week." His father huffed, turned away, and left Wade on the porch to deal with the last of the mess.

He didn't know how his oldest sister tolerated Dad, but for a reason he'd never comprehend, Brooke and Dean seemed to love the never-ending work. His sister and her husband had missed last night's party to keep an eye on things in Yakima. They loved that life, put in countless hours on the hop farm, and deserved to run the business—no matter who their father had mentally slated for the job.

Wade wandered in just as the meal made it to the table. After stalling in the kitchen to pour a cup of coffee, he took a seat between Amanda and Linnea, far away from his dad.

The men shoveled food as talk wove among the women—covering the details of last night's party and the wedding to come this summer. As the conversation moved to catering, Linnea leaned in and asked how the taproom was coming along.

He tilted his head, coaxing her into the kitchen to refill their coffee. After they poured, he turned his back to the crowd at the long table and whispered, "Seth's crew finished demolition two weeks ago. We had inspections on the electric system last week, and now we can finally start construction."

Linnea sighed and shifted her feet. "Are you sure you don't need my help before the taproom is finished?"

He gave her a nod. "Actually, Sis, I was going to ask if you wanted to start working for me a bit sooner."

"Seriously! When can I start at the brewery?"

On her squeal, the private exchange leaped across the room to everyone seated at the table. Wade grimaced, spotting the twitch of muscle in his father's neck as he tried to control his temper. Dad knew this was coming, just not so soon. And he clearly hated to lose his daughter's help on the hop farm, where Linnea ran the technical side of the harvest with practiced skill.

"When can I start?" she asked again.

"Well, I'll be in Yakima at the end of the month to oversee planting the new hops. Is that too soon?" he asked.

"Couldn't I just stay now? I could go back with you in a few weeks to grab my car and load my stuff. I have enough in my suitcase to get by until then." Linnea's enthusiasm spilled across the room to her cousin.

Amanda clapped her hands. "Mom, Linnea can stay. It will be fine, right?"

Linn glanced between Aunt Sandy and Uncle Bill and held her breath, waiting.

Accustomed to a bustling house, Aunt Sandy grinned, seeming to look forward to the change. "We're ready when you are, sweetheart."

Wade huffed out a relieved breath when is mother laughed and added, "Well, there's nothing like a little spontaneity to shake things up."

***

With snow blanketing the ground, Iris knew most of her Northside customers would stay home until the roads cleared. She wiggled the mouse and her computer lit. With her glasses perched on her nose, Iris tilted her head and studied the numbers, mapping concerning trends.

Different worries dogged her mind and last night layered on another. Apprehension about Wade's taproom she could handle—it was almost routine. Scheduled to open this summer, Mosquito's taproom would lure extra traffic to Ashwood. Fortunately, Wade didn't intend to serve food. If she was lucky, a few hungry new customers would drift her way and replace the beer drinkers she was bound to lose to his business.

A persistent decrease in sales remained unexplained. Struggling to find an answer to this dip, she reviewed her records again—the economy had improved, the population of Ashwood had increased, and tourism continued to bring in a steady stream of hikers and rafters. She huffed, frustrated. Given time, Iris would puzzle it out, but the dilemma gnawed at her mind.

Now, a third factor coiled stress well beyond a low hum. Lincoln. Damn it, he was such an unnerving man. Pizza made up a big chunk of her dinner register. Her recipes were solid, but Iris knew there was room for improvement.

Those few moments with Lincoln on the dance floor didn't reveal enough. He seemed like a newcomer to the restaurant business. Maybe he'd be bound, like many others, to burn through cash and wither before ever turning a profit. A girl could hope.

Two of her employees called in, stuck in the snow. Iris knew she could depend on her line cook and floor manager to pick up the slack. She left her office and checked the vacant dining area. The large space looked so drab when it was empty. Killing time, she took liquor bottles from the glass shelves behind the bar and wiped away a thin layer of dust. At least this area could shine.

Cold air whooshed in with her first hungry customer. "Hey, you survived the storm!" Iris hollered across the empty expanse.

"Am I alone?" Kent moaned and took a seat at the bar. The man looked too hungry to leave.

She chuckled while he glanced at the menu. "Don't worry, the sun is out. You won't be alone too long."

Kent decided on a burger and asked her to add a fried egg—this being his breakfast.

As the snow dropped from the evergreen branches, a few more people trickled in. Each time the door pushed open, she glanced up. Problem was, she didn't know if she wanted to see Wade or Lincoln walk through that door.

***

Wade swallowed two aspirin before he dealt with a slew of intrusive emails from his biggest investor. Even that preventative measure didn't keep Coalition Craft Corporation from giving him a headache right between his eyes. After that chore, he needed to hear a supportive voice. He took a moment to call his head brewer, and a smile spread across his face when Erik raved about the latest test batch of their new summer brew. He couldn't wait to have a beer with Erik and Trish at his small original brewery on Mosquito Creek.

He'd never intended to heap so much work on his head brewer or his wife. But he was thankful for their dedication as Mosquito's expansion consumed all his time. Pacing as he talked, his boots wore a path over the wide boards where his brewery in Ashwood was coming together. The late afternoon sun filtered through windows clouded by decades of dirt. Soon, sunlight would pour through washed panes and bounce from bright metal tanks filled with fermenting beer.

He heard the door screech open, and a moment later Linnea's voice echoed through the vacant expanse. "Hey, where are you?"

"Back here, sis!" he yelled.

Linnea rushed in followed by his cousins—Seth and Amanda. His sister stopped then spun slowly in the center of the room, taking in the view. "Wow. This old lumber mill looks so empty now."

"That demo took a while, but it was satisfying. Kent and Rick knocked it out in no time." Seth seemed pleased with the work his employees had accomplished so far.

"It won't be empty long." Wade could already picture the tanks layout in the brewery, but the taproom's design still eluded him, and again, he was thankful Linnea had joined the team a few months early. She was the perfect addition to his brewers—Dillon, Erik, and Trish—but he knew he'd still need to add staff to run the taproom, once it was finished.

Linnea looked eager to start. "I've been collecting pictures of industrial breweries. I'm thinking we could repurpose some of the old equipment. Hey, Seth, do you think your guys could transform that old saw into a table?"

Seth gave her a nod. "Not a problem. Get me those pictures and I'll draw up a design."

"Are you okay with that?" she asked.

Wade grinned, loving her enthusiasm. "The taproom will be in your hands." She beamed and he knew he'd made the right decision. His sister's energy would be needed to handle the mountainous work ahead.

Linnea dashed to the other side of the vast space and ran her hands over a long slab of wood, the surface worn smooth by work and time. "I'm assuming this will become part of the bar?"

Seth gave her a quick answer, "That's the plan, but if this isn't exactly right, there's an entire building near the sawmill full of this ancient stuff for you to check out."

Pacing off the space, Wade fed off his family's energy and pictured the room crammed with beer drinking fans.

Amanda cut off his daydream. "While Seth and his guys busted through the demo, I snapped hundreds of *before* pictures. I can't wait to shoot the *after* shots of this place for your website."

"Thanks, Amanda. I appreciate all the help I can get." Wade knew he couldn't do this without deep family support.

"Speaking of shots, I'm gonna head next door to Whitewater. Natalie's in the darkroom working on some landscapes."

"I'll come with." Seth slapped Wade on the back on his way out the door. "You know where to find me if you have any questions about the construction," he called over his shoulder before he left.

"Thanks for all you've done. Catch you later." Wade knew a simple *thank you* wasn't enough. When his cousin had offered to handle the demolition and construction, Wade had no idea how much time and money Seth's experience would save him. The old lumber mill had quirks only his cousin understood. He'd discovered those oddities while transforming the largest building in the original complex into the shop that held Whitewater Homes. That business sat right next door. The massive workspace he'd designed himself let Seth construct several tiny homes simultaneously, while keeping them out of the wet, Northwest weather.

The way the rest of his family pitched in almost made up for his Dad's complete lack of support. Succeeding with this massive brewery expansion was more important than the money. It'd prove to his father that Wade wasn't a fool for giving up his share of the family hop farm. At least his father hadn't cut Linnea out. She could always go back home if Wade fucked this up.

He knew his worry was showing when his sister trapped him in a bearhug. "Thank you for trusting me with your dream," she said, and it was the precise thing he'd needed to hear.

"I hope you still feel the same in a few weeks." His chuckle shook Linnea and she stepped back, gripping his shoulders.

"Don't worry. We're going to have so much fun. Come on, no more sulking, you promised me a grand tour." She took his hand, dragging him toward a series of rooms Seth had constructed. "Offices?" she asked.

"Yeah, and that's the break room. The one after is the spot where we'll store hops and grain." Next, he showed her the locations where the brewing tanks and vessels would be installed. She quizzed him with a thousand questions about the brewing process then begged to see the tiny place he called home.

After locking the brewery, he led her past Whitewater. "Did I tell you Amanda and I decided to fix up Seth's old apartment?" she said as she jumped a puddle made by melting snow.

"That loft above the garage?" Wade recalled that drafty place, where Seth took refuge after his divorce. Seth had definitely improved his life since—first with the home he'd bought overlooking Osprey Lake, and then with his fiancée, Natalie.

"Yup. Amanda's dad is adding insulation before we paint."

"Good. That loft was cold as hell when Seth lived there."

"It shouldn't take too long to make it ours." Linnea went on about her plans. "We're picking out paint, and Amanda's asking Natalie to come over and help us sort through Seth's stuff. He abandoned boxes of junk up there when he moved."

With a nod, Wade made a mental note to give Seth a heads up, figuring his cousin might want to be in on that expedition through his past.

After they climbed the stairs, he held the door to his tiny home open and Linnea stumbled inside, tripping over the dainty silver flats that had caught his feet this morning.

Her eyebrows shot up. "And these shoes belong to?"

Wade folded his arms over his chest. "Nobody. It's not a big deal." He hadn't intended to share anything about last night.

"Not buying it. Is she that tall brunette who was helping you pour drinks?" Humming, Linnea slowly shook her head. "Please tell me you aren't messing around with an employee."

"She's not an employee," he admitted.

"Gotcha! I knew it. You hooked up." She pointed at his chest. "Who is she, anyway?"

Wade couldn't believe he'd fallen for her act. "This information doesn't leak to Amanda..."

"Understood."

"Her name is Iris. She owns the bar on the other end of town. Northside Grill carries my beer, and I have dinner there more often than I should."

"Because you can't get enough of her?" Linnea asked with a leading grin.

"That's not it. I never have time to cook. Until last night, everything was professional, friendly but—"

"... It all changed when you asked her to dance. How romantic." Linnea heaved a sigh, but when she blinked his direction, she put him on the spot. "I hope you called her today."

"Not yet."

"Coward."

He tolerated his sister's disappointment, but knew she was right. "I'll go see her near closing time."

"Good plan, but take a shower first," she teased.

"What?"

"Dude, you stink." Linnea's nose wrinkled and she brushed the air in front of her face.

Wade glanced down at his grimy T-shirt. He was instantly grateful for Linnea's presence in Ashwood and for her uncensored, unsolicited advice.

***

Iris wiped down the long counter, relieved that her place was finally clearing out. A couple of groups still camped at tables near the back, but those regulars looked like they planned to stay a while. Lack of sleep slowed her feet as she moved from table to table, collecting bottles of ketchup to refill. After closing tonight, she planned to read a book while soaking in a warm bath, if she could stay awake that long.

Last night may have made her sore in the best possible way, but the brewer's silence had left her nerves frayed. She didn't expect anything from Wade, but a call, even about her shoes, would have been nice.

A husband and wife got up to leave, but the bunch at the final table didn't look ready to follow. She waved and wished the couple a good night as they pushed outside. Before the door swished shut,

29

a hand halted the momentum. Backlit by outdoor lights, Wade's tall outline filled the entry with broad shoulders that angled to lean hips.

He scanned the place and spotted guys he knew hanging out near the back. Even though he lifted his chin in a quick hello, his determined strides carried him straight to the stool farthest from them. Iris studied him, her gaze lost in his easy gait. The man tempted her to lose another night's sleep just by walking across the room.

Taking a deep breath, she approached him, enjoying the sly smile that tipped the corners of his mouth.

"Iris."

"Wade."

Her cheeks heated, and she recalled his words from last night—he loved the way she blushed. His eyes hopped over her body as if he could see every place she was turning a rich shade of pink.

"Would you like anything?" she asked, her smile teasing. Apparently, last night would not be an isolated incident.

"Anything?" He laughed. "Yes, but for now, just coffee."

"Let me make a fresh pot. I'll have a cup too, if you plan to stay a while."

"Staying as long as you'll have me." His gaze promised more. Iris put extra grounds into the coffee maker looking forward to another sleep-deprived night.

FOUR

Iris woke in the dark, trapped under the weight of a sturdy arm. She seldom let men spend the night. Sharing her private space usually made her nervous, yet she was surprised to find Wade's presence in her home, in her bed, comforting. The urge to push him out the door was not the first thought to raise in her mind.

In fact, the first thing she noticed had actually risen, hard and long, against her hip. Spooning into him, she fitted her spine, ass, and thighs against Wade's chest, abdomen, and legs. When he still didn't move, she squirmed to wake him, but Wade seemed to be made of stone.

Putting her flexibility to work, Iris snaked her arm behind her back and stretched to stroke his rock-hard cock. He hardly moved. Then, without a word, he surprised Iris, grasping her hand beneath his, assisting with the sensual torture.

"Just like that," he said on a groan. When she tightened her hold, a pearl of wet arousal slicked her palm. Hand behind her and fingers laced together, they pulled his steely length. Out and back, his hips pulsed into the long, hard tugs. The heat of his breath ruffled her hair on each firm stroke.

"Now it's your turn," he murmured against her neck. While pressing his cock against her ass, Wade steered their tangled fingers over her hip and led the exploration of her folds. Fingertips working together, they caressed her wet arousal. Her hands trembled and she hissed, as they plunged simultaneously into her heat.

"Yes," she moaned and pressed the sway of her ass against his girth. When he circled her bundle of nerves with his sex-slick fingertips, she begged, "Please, I need you now."

"Are you sure?" he asked, tenderly.

31

Even though the previous night had left her a little sore, she whispered, "I'm sure." Her eyes rolled back when in one smooth movement, he impaled her from behind.

"Keep touching yourself," he commanded as he grasped her hip and drilled.

"So wet, so sweet." A low growl mingled with her keening gasp.

"And so damn good."

Sparks glittered behind her tightly closed eyes as Iris arched her back and held her breath. The climb to release clawed, just beyond her reach. Wade's fingertips pressed into her skin holding her in place while he plunged deeper, harder, stronger. Every nerve focused on that peak.

Her breath went choppy and her body trembled, but she needed more. A sudden bite on her shoulder gave her that lick of pain, and her climax suddenly erupted. She pushed back taking every ounce of pleasure from the mind-altering release. Left incoherent, she trembled while Wade rammed harder, his groin slapping against her ass with each powerful thrust.

On a growl, he pulled his cock from her body, fisted his length, and spilled his seed between them.

Panting, sweaty, and sated, they lay motionless in a tangled heap.

"Sorry about the sheets, I guess we forgot about a condom," he mumbled against her skin. His lips traced the graceful line where her neck and shoulder met.

Iris scrunched her eyebrows together. "I'm on the pill. Remember?"

***

Wade rolled into Whitewater later than intended. In the office, he found Amanda chatting with Linnea, each one slouched at the opposite ends of a worn, leather couch. As he leaned against the threshold, his sister greeted him with a sly smile, her eyebrows raised in silent question. His quick look confirmed her guess—he didn't make it home last night.

"There's fresh coffee and muffins from Goldfinch Bakery." Amanda's cheerful greeting put him a little on edge—he simply wasn't a morning person.

"Thanks." He poured himself a cup but skipped the muffin, having already shared scrambled eggs with Iris. With no time for family chitchat, Wade tilted his head toward the door. "Linn, why don't we head over to my place? I've got my laptop in my tiny home."

His sister nodded and pushed off the couch.

Before they left, Amanda asked, "Hey, do you want to meet later for lunch? We could give that new pizza place a try."

Linn tipped her head and shrugged. "Maybe tomorrow? I'm thinking Wade and I will probably have to work through lunch today."

Her answer concerned Wade. Sure, he appreciated her dedication, but Linnea tended to work too much. She'd need to carve out time for fun.

On their way through Whitewater, the rhythmic shot of an air hammer paused for a moment as they passed by. Wade glanced up just in time to see Rick tracking his sister's progress as she headed toward the door.

Crap. She hadn't even been in Ashwood forty-eight hours and was already turning heads. After the door shut behind them the air-powered hammer resumed its shots, and Wade knew he'd have to keep an eye on that guy.

Inside the tiny home, Linn claimed a spot at the fold-out table where stacks of invoices and barely legible lists covered the entire surface. Wade collapsed in front of his computer and braced for his sister's interrogation. With the way her eyes glittered he knew they wouldn't accomplish anything until her curiosity was satisfied.

A sly grin tilted her lips. "Spill it, brother. I'm guessing you talked to Iris?"

"Yeah, we figured things out." Trying to ignore her, he took another gulp of his coffee. The bitter swill had gone cold, and he was tempted to spit it back in the cup.

Pleased with her new discovery, Linnea leaned in, her chin resting on her hand. "When can I meet her?" she asked.

"Soon. You'll spend plenty of time at Northside Grill. There really isn't anywhere else to hang out in this town." Wade sat back in his chair and realized that once Mosquito Creek's taproom opened, that would change.

His sister's eyes narrowed, clearly unsatisfied with his meager answers.

Wade drummed his fingers on the table. "Can we get to work now?"

"After you answer one more thing." Linnea didn't hold back, "Do you like her?"

A shoulder shrug brushed off her question. "Sure."

"No, I mean like, *like* her."

He glanced out the window, recalling her beauty and their dynamic connection, but something was missing. Even with all they'd shared, she'd kept a part of herself hidden. "I respect Iris. She's smart, and we have similar interests."

"That would be helpful if you planned to hire her," his sister teased.

A smile hitched the corners of his mouth. "Okay smartass, why don't you give me your list of qualifications, and I'll see if Iris measures up?"

"Shut up, Wade," she said while reaching for a wad of paper. With a quick flick of her wrist the crumpled ball targeted his forehead. After it hit, it rolled across the floor.

Wade narrowed his eyes. He'd had enough.

Linnea's hands shot up in surrender. "Fine. I'll leave the subject of Iris alone."

But he didn't believe the innocent look. Behind the wide eyes, he read determination, so typical in the Michaels' clan. She'd eventually get the information she wanted all on her own.

When his sister didn't press for more, he spun the computer her direction. "Here, take a look. I've got a brewer's conference in Las Vegas next week. I'll be honest, I'm not ready for my meeting with Coalition Craft."

Linnea's spine straightened, bracing for the challenge. "Okay, that meeting will be my first priority," she said while examining the chaos on his calendar. Her eyes widened, and she gave him a sympathetic sigh. "Wade, what were you thinking? I'd need a map to navigate this color-coded system."

"That mess seemed like a great idea at the time."

"I'll simplify it right away." Her fingers clicked, making changes, and he felt like he could breathe. Wade didn't care if she revamped the whole thing, so long as he didn't have to look at it again.

Switching gears, he pointed out another date that would keep them both busy. "Dad's all over me to get the new hop variety in the ground. Will three days in Yakima give you enough time to visit friends and pack all your crap?" he asked while jotting a few notes for the trip back to the family hop farm.

Linnea sighed. "You know as well as I do, I won't have time for friends. Dad will put me on a tractor."

"I'm sorry. Maybe I could ask Dillon to come along and free up your time."

"Don't bother—it wouldn't change anything."

He gave in with a nod, hissed a slow breath, and pressed on. "After the Yakima planting, the beer festival season takes off. At the same time we'll be juggling the last of the build, opening the taproom, and producing the new summer beer. At least Erik's got that under control at Old Mosquito." With a low groan, he pushed both hands over his thighs, wiping away a layer of sweat.

His sister sighed. "Oh, Wade, this is crazy. You should have called me sooner."

"I regret that I didn't." He raked his hands through his lengthening hair. "I haven't even had time to get this unruly mop trimmed."

"Leave it. The long hair makes you look like the bad boy of brewing." Her warm laugh lifted his mood a little.

He usually didn't care if his hair grew long, but the Vegas meeting with the Coalition executives had him second-guessing everything from his appearance to the launch of his summer beer.

"Can I have access to your email?" his sister asked while he was still brooding. "Don't worry, I won't delete anything."

"Perfect. While you work on that, do you mind if I head to the brewhouse?" he asked. "I need to touch base with the guys."

Linnea waved him out the door, her eyes never leaving the screen. "Get out of here and do what needs doing."

Feeling better than he had in weeks, Wade whistled as he headed toward the sounds of pounding hammers and screaming saws. His optimistic tune repeated, as he imagined the new home of Mosquito Creek Brewery.

This bonus time – courtesy of his sister – had him wondering if he could fit in another night with Iris. Was it too soon? Shit, he'd always hated the awkward second-guessing phase.

Pulling out his phone, he sent Iris a text. *Want to get together for dinner tonight?*

Her reply buzzed immediately. *Sorry, but I don't have time. Rain check?*

Wade chuckled. *Sure – the offer is evergreen.*

See you – she replied, and he relaxed, wondering if he'd found a woman who hated the awkward shit as much as he did.

Linnea found him later that afternoon as he cut open boxes filled with bathroom faucets.

"What are you doing?" she asked.

"Checking the shipment against the invoice."

Linnea huffed, held out her hand for the clipboard, and lifted an eyebrow.

Used to doing everything himself, he stared her down, ready for the usual battle. Still, this was precisely why she had come to Ashwood. "I should let you do this, huh?"

She nodded. "That's why I'm here."

He glanced from the pile of boxes to his sister. "I'll let you take this on if you promise two things."

Linn snatched the clipboard from his outstretched hand before he changed his mind. "Two rules? I can handle that," she agreed. "Fire away."

"I'll always be in charge of the brewery."

"No problem. And?"

"If a load is too heavy, get one of the guys to help you lift it."

"Deal." Linnea glanced across the room. Wade followed her gaze and found Rick. Yeah, those two might become a problem.

FIVE

Linnea shot Wade a few more questions as she drove him to the airport. He was impressed. She'd quickly grasped the details of his chaotic life and could handle the brewery expansion for a few days on her own. Still, this badly timed trip had him stressed.

"I hope our sales projection for Coalition Craft wasn't a complete waste of time," he complained. "How can I know how the summer beer will be received before I've even released it to beta tasters?"

"It's delicious. Erik, Trish, and Dillon love it as much as I do."

He nodded, fighting the doubt that clouded his judgement when he launched a new beer.

Linnea exited the freeway and headed toward Portland International Airport. She angled into the passenger drop-off, left the truck running, and gave his arm an encouraging squeeze. "Try to have a little fun, and call me after you've settled in."

"Thanks, Sis. You'll never know how much I needed you here." His simple appreciation brought a tear to his sister's eye, and he pulled her in for a hug. He understood that hit of emotion too well. On the farm Linnea worked tirelessly, but their father made every chore an obligation. Praise from Dad was rare.

The work at his brewery was no less daunting, but he wanted her to make Mosquito Creek taproom her own. As Linnea slipped out of the hug, Wade wanted more for his sister than a job in Ashwood. He hoped she'd find a niche in the small community, to really belong.

Wade merged with an anonymous sea of people pulling suitcases. Some wore tailored business suits, others tropical shirts, all seemed eager to go anywhere but here. He dreaded leaving and feared Vegas would be nothing but an epic waste of time.

The wheels touched down on the tarmac ahead of schedule. He peered through the small airliner window and found Vegas shimmering in the scorching sun. A short cab ride took him past ostentatious splendor toward the posh hotel where the massive brewing conference was scheduled.

Coalition Craft Corporation had offered him a spot in their bank of rooms high in a luxurious tower. Instead of staying on Coalition's dime, he'd sprung for his own room in the casino. His need for independence landed Wade in a cheaper spot on a lower floor.

After checking in, he surrendered his suitcase then found a quiet spot just off the lobby and pulled out his cell. He swallowed his pride, surrendered his freedom, and gave Craft Coalition a call. Immediately, an overly cheerful voice chimed, "It's a lovely day at Coalition Craft Corporation. How may I help you?"

A stiff cough cleared his throat. "Uh, I'm Wade Michaels. Mosquito Creek Brewing. I was asked to call this number when I arrived."

"Yes, Mr. Michaels, one moment please."

Placed on hold, bluesy music entertained him until a bombastic voice burst over the phone. "Wade, glad you're on site. Phil Davis here, product development. So hey, stop by the CCC booth. Grab your shit from that blonde behind the counter, and don't lose your key to the hospitality suite. We've got free booze flowing and it's open twenty-four seven. Get up here and have a drink, so we can welcome you aboard."

Wade never got a chance to inject a single word. Canned music blared in his ear before the saccharine voice came back on the line. "Mr. Michaels, do you need directions to the Coalition booth on the conference floor?" Wade stood stunned for a long moment. "Mr. Michaels, are you still there?"

"Yeah, I'm here. I can find the booth on my own. Thanks."

"Very well. If you need anything at all for the duration of the conference, don't hesitate to ask. I'm here to make sure your stay is both enjoyable and informative." *Click.*

The call ended and Wade groaned. He stuffed his phone in his pocket, wandered back toward the trade show entrance, and immediately spotted the massive Coalition Craft Corporation sign. Just as Phil had promised, there was a blonde behind the counter. As she smiled, Wade wondered if platinum hair and ample curves were job requirements. Seeming to expect him, she passed an embossed folder before he requested it.

The packet contained an entry badge. Conforming, he put it on. Strangely heavy, the identification on the lanyard hung like a noose around his neck.

Winding his way past humble booths on the outer perimeter, he worked his way toward the prized center locations. As he closed in on the big-money exhibitors, the atmosphere shifted from sales floor to all out rock-show. Loud music, light displays, and tanned women wearing tight tank tops lured attendees in to stop, drink, and spend.

Coalition Craft Corporation did not have the largest display, but the facade was immaculate. Built like a movie set, a false brick wall backed a long bar. Oak tables welcomed visitors to stop in and enjoy a cold pint from each represented brewery.

Displayed among the colorful signs of each Coalition brewer, he found an impressive insignia. There, in the midst of established national brands was the name *Mosquito Creek Brewing*. His logo appeared slick, almost too polished, as if the art department had tweaked the colors and sharpened the font.

All at once, the impact hit. He'd dreamed about reaching this pinnacle. It happened so fast he almost missed the climb. Now more than a regional beer, Mosquito would be available across the nation. Lightheaded, he grabbed hold of a large wooden post that held up the corner of Coalition's display. The post shifted when he touched it, made only of cardboard.

He glanced around and laughed. Caught up in the moment, he could not resist a selfie with his insignia. Before anyone noticed, he turned his phone and captured a shot. Checking the screen, he shrugged and chuckled at the awkward image. "Good enough." Phone in his pocket, he approached the counter and chose a beer.

Over twenty beers from various brands under the CCC umbrella were available on tap. He decided on his own India Pale Ale, Mosquito Creek Brewing's Double Deet. The temperature of his IPA was perfect, the quality everything he would expect. It tasted like home. Finding a spot alone, he sat at a heavy oak table and kicked his feet forward, relaxing into the chair.

Drips rolling down his icy glass mesmerized him until a pair of slim legs in four-inch heels appeared directly in front of him. Slow as cold molasses, his eyes traveled. She wore a snug gray skirt and a fitted jacket that pulled in tight at her waist. Her dark hair hung in heavy waves past her shoulders, framing perfect angular features and dark hypnotic eyes.

"May I join you? Wade Michaels, correct?" she asked with a lilting voice that sounded younger than her professional exterior.

"Yes. Absolutely, please have a seat. Can I get you something to drink?" he stammered, forgetting that the beer was comped. "And you are?"

With a warm smile, her rich, gold flecked eyes held him captive as she held out her manicured hand. He carefully wrapped large fingers and shook, surprised by the strength of this petite, fragile woman.

"I'm Ravenna Silvestre. We've exchanged a few emails, and I've been expecting you. It's nice to finally meet you in person."

The professional contact produced a creeping blush across her neck and face. She seemed to glow from within. Wade enjoyed her slight color shift, satisfied that he was not the only one impacted by the tangible spark between them. "Silvestre. I wondered about you from the first moment I saw your name on my contact list. Are you related to Leo?" he asked.

"He's my father. Have you read his book?"

Wade nodded. "And I also took his on-site class years ago in Klamath Falls at Silver Raven Brewery."

"Have you kept in contact?" she asked. Her smile widened as she recognized she was probably looking into the eyes of one of her father's biggest fans.

"You bet. I bounce ideas off Leo all the time. That two-week crash course changed my life." Wade was not exaggerating. Meeting Leo Silvestre initiated a sequence of events that took him from Yakima to Mosquito Creek. He narrowed his eyes. "Wait a second. Silver Raven. Is that a play on your name?" *Ravenna Silvestre.* The thought rang like music in his head.

She dipped her chin, guarding her emotions. Untangling that reaction became Wade's essential goal, now and in the future.

"Yes, it was—and still is, I guess. But of course, you know Coalition now controls Silver Raven." Her lips tightened, but not in a smile. Acknowledging Coalition's power over her life seemed to sting.

"Enough about me and my family," she said with a wave of her hand. "You're now the focus and future of Coalition. I'll be working with you to make sure your transition is smooth."

Leaning back in his chair, Wade put distance between himself and Ravenna as dread constricted. He fought to breathe as the strings attached to Coalition's investment tightened. "What's this smooth transition?" he asked.

Sincerity slipped from her smile, and her words seemed scripted by someone else's hands. "I've been assigned to answer any questions that arise. It will be my pleasure to help you assimilate into our team."

Gritting his teeth, Wade took a moment, then gave her an answer she seemed to expect. "That's exactly who I am—a team player all the way."

***

Ravenna struggled to think of small talk as she led Wade through the electronic glitz on the way to Coalition's party suite. Winners cheered, slot machines rang, and girls in short skirts delivered drinks to bleary-eyed tourists. Every woman they passed on the casino floor noticed the way this man covered ground in his faded, low-slung jeans.

Looming large behind her, she peeked through her lashes at his distorted image in the golden reflection of the elevator doors. With a press of a button, the square car arrived, and she found herself trapped with him in the small, mirrored space. Ravenna went lightheaded surviving on depleted oxygen as they sailed skyward.

Twenty-one floors in an empty elevator? How could that happen in Vegas? And the man refused to relax. That scowl made him even sexier. Damn, he wasn't even her type. His hair was too long, his jeans too faded, and he had that day-growth-beard thing going on.

Finally, the doors flew open on the VIP-only floor. She rushed from the elevator, leading the way, keeping her eyes off his perfect ass.

Once she regained her equilibrium, her business mindset would take over. Ravenna blinked hard and locked this unexpected stab of desire for the wrong kind of man in a bulletproof box.

***

Wade planted his feet and stared ahead, inhaling her alluring, citrus perfume. The entire ride on the elevator had been pure torture. Her dark eyes hypnotized. Her soft curves beckoned. Her rosy lips tempted. That mouth, all he could think about was kissing away every bit of the rich lipstick. Or better, how perfect that lipstick would look on his cock.

Gritting his teeth to the point of pain, he'd be damned if he didn't hear her breathing pick up as they sped from floor to floor. The elevator doors sprung open, and he was pleased when she took the lead.

Hips swaying, her heels snapped, and that snug skirt inched a little higher with each quick stride. Ravenna's round swaying ass did not help the tightness of his jeans. He stared at the ceiling and counted the number of light fixtures they passed on their trek down the hall. At the very least, he had to enter this room full of execs without a raging hard-on.

Sweeping her key card, the door chimed. A travertine tiled entry opened to an expansive room that overlooked the gleaming, Las Vegas strip. Heat bent the atmosphere, adding surreal life to a view of glass, metal, and concrete.

A few guys he recognized lifted chins in quick hellos. Wade had crossed paths with these men in Boise, where his talks with CCC began last October. Ravenna stepped into business mode the moment her high heels crossed the threshold.

"Look who I found downstairs, Wade Michaels, Mosquito Creek Brewing." Her musical voice seemed to draw every eye in the room. *Damn it.*

Jeff's familiar face felt like a lifeline. "Wade. Glad you're here. What can I get you? Beer or something a little harder."

"Hey, Jeff, great to see you again. I'll wander over to the bar later." He glanced past the shifting crowd. "This is quite the view."

"You could have one just like it. A room is still available. What do you say?"

"Nah, that's okay, I've already settled in," Wade lied. He hadn't even had time to stop by his room. Scanning the crowd, he found Ravenna moving effortlessly from one conversation to the next. His eyes tracked her, unable to look away from her delectable curves for more than a few seconds.

"I see you met Ravenna," Jeff said, his words dashed with more than casual interest. "Listen to her. She'll be the most valuable member of your new team."

Wade tempered a stab of undeserved jealousy and asked, "My team? What are you talking about?"

A chuckle shook Jeff's shoulders. "No shop-talk tonight. Have some drinks and get to know everyone. Most of all, let us get to know you." A slap on the back ended the conversation, but caution prickled the hairs at Wade's neck. He could only nod when Jeff said, "Let me introduce you to Phil Davis. He heads up product development."

Jeff tilted his head toward the booze, encouraging Wade to follow. Phil, a stout man with a booming voice, was discussing trends with another brewer, and the direction those trends would take the winter product line. Wade's stomach twisted. Trends meant following the latest fashion. Not taste. Not creativity. Not quality.

When the bartender asked for his order, Wade mumbled, "Whiskey neat." Glass in hand, he mingled the room, kept his mouth shut, and listened.

SIX

Iris spotted Wade's sister loitering just inside Northside Grill. Linnea's hesitant smile went bright and sunny when she found Natalie and Kelsey in the crowd. Her unexpected presence stirred Iris's curiosity, and she realized how little she knew about the man who'd recently shared her bed.

Northside Grill was hopping. Couples danced, all three pool tables were full, and regulars lined the bar. Tucked into a corner, Linnea's small party sat in the dining room tonight. Iris understood the subdued choice when Amanda walked in. Not yet twenty-one, the youngest girl in that gathering looked longingly beyond the chaotic swarm, deeper into the darker recesses of the bar. When her eyes hit Kent, they lingered. But Ashwood's most notorious player didn't notice Amanda's long-distance attention. He polished off his beer then bent to line up a shot at the pool table.

Iris grabbed a few menus from the pile and headed across the dining room. Owning a bar had sharpened her people-reading skills, and those four girls—Linnea, Natalie, Kelsey, and Amanda—all seemed distracted by wildly different things. Wade's sister looked like a bundle of nerves, stiff as the new girl at school. Iris knew Linnea shouldn't be nervous—not with the way all the guys were checking out the curves that had landed in their midst. Maybe if she ordered a glass of wine, she'd relax.

Natalie's warm smile greeted Iris. Always gracious, Seth's fiancée made introductions right away. "Iris, have you met Linnea?"

Blushing, Linnea fluttered her fingers, a timid wave. "Hi, that's me. I'm Amanda's cousin and Wade's sister, just another member of the Michaels' clan."

"Nice to meet you," Iris said as she handed off the menus. "I can't wait to get to know the latest addition to Ashwood. For now, why don't I get you something to drink?"

When Linnea hesitated Natalie filled the momentary silence with, "A cabernet for me, please."

Kels piped in, "I'll take the usual IPA."

Lamenting her limited options, Amanda swept her hair back and sighed, "Just iced tea, I guess."

Iris committed that drink to memory while noticing the swath of dried paint on Amanda's forearm. "Are you working on a home improvement project?" she asked, buying Linnea a little more time.

"Yeah, Linn and I are fixing up Seth's old apartment over the garage." She pulled up her sleeve, revealing a little more light-coral arm. "What do you think of the color?" Amanda asked.

"It's nice."

"Check my hair for the accent shade."

Iris laughed, eyeing a dried splotch in Amanda's auburn hair. "Oh, that's a bright shade of teal."

"You're telling me. Just think of that covering an entire wall. It's blinding." When Amanda shot Linnea a look, Iris knew who'd made the bold choice and figured Wade's quiet sister was a force to be reckoned with. After she chose a nice Chardonnay, Iris gave the girls time to check the menu while she prepped their drinks. By the second round, Linnea was laughing.

Even with the good time going on around her, Amanda kept her eyes on the guys shooting pool. As if he could feel the heated gaze, Kent turned and grinned. Taking all this in from a distance, Iris worried about that obvious connection.

The party broke when Seth stopped by the register to cover the tab before taking Natalie home. His sister, Amanda, didn't stick around long. She sulked away, shoulders curled, without ever making contact with Kent. Iris sighed, hoping she wouldn't need to have a talk with that man.

Kelsey joined the guys at the pool table, and Linnea passed on the invitation to come along. She surprised Iris by heading toward the bar instead of the door. Claiming a seat at the end of the bar, her posture stick straight, the poor girl nearly fell from her stool when a local took a seat two spots down. Iris rolled her eyes when the guy perused Linnea's curves with unashamed interest.

Iris moved in, just in case Linnea needed a lifeline. "What can I get you to drink?"

"Maybe a light beer? In the bottle's fine," she blurted without thinking.

"Coming right up. Hey, we didn't get a chance to talk earlier. Did your move to Ashwood have anything to do with Wade's brewery?" she asked, acknowledging their connection.

Linnea smiled and relaxed. "It did. I'm here to help with the taproom."

Iris twisted the cap, set the bottle on the bar, and settled in to talk for a moment. "And you're sharing a place with Amanda?"

"Yeah. We're fixing up the loft above her parent's garage. It's basic, but I like it."

"It won't take long to make that place your own." Iris poured another drink, taking care of customers as she talked with Linnea about the changes they were making to the apartment.

After a gulp of beer, Linn toyed with the label. "My brother told me you're originally from Kansas. How did you feel about leaving the family farm?"

Iris studied the floor for a moment. Damn, had she really revealed that detail to Wade? She'd have to watch that. Bringing her eyes back, she decided sharing a little about her past wouldn't hurt. "I miss the connection to the land, I guess. The work was unrelenting. It's probably the same whether the crop is wheat or hops."

Linnea nodded, "Too true. The work I didn't mind, but I won't ever miss the isolation."

Iris gave her a weak smile, leaned over the bar, and whispered, "Wait 'til you're gone a few years. You just might miss it."

"How did you go from farming to owning a restaurant?" Linn asked as Iris poured another whiskey for the guy with the roaming eyes.

"Oh, that's a story for another day. A day when I can join you with a cold one, maybe at Mosquito. Mind if I stop by to check out the progress?" she asked as a couple at the end of the counter signaled for a check.

Linnea nodded, seeming to like that idea. "I'll give you a call once my schedule settles down."

"I'll hold you to that." Iris got back to work while keeping Linn in her peripheral vision. Eventually, the light beer surrendered its label to her nervous fingers. While her body moved subtly to the piped in music, Linnea watched the dance floor in the mirror that backed the bar. She moved a little more when a Kenney Chesney song came on. The movement attracted the attention of the guy who'd been admiring those undeniable curves. He scooted over one stool and said, "Hey, beautiful, can I buy you a drink? I must know you from somewhere, cause baby, you look exactly like my next girlfriend."

Hearing that lame pickup line again, Iris bit her lip and chuckled to herself. Her eyebrows rose as someone at the pool tables left the game. The night was about to get interesting.

Linnea plastered on a smile. "Thanks, but I'm about at my limit."

"And she's with me," Rick's claim rumbled. The deep voice from beyond her shoulder stiffened Linnea's spine, and the guy at the seat next to her shrank back.

"Oh, hey, Rick, I should have known the most beautiful girl in the room wasn't available. Why did you leave your fine woman here all alone?"

Linnea's cheeks flamed as Rick stepped closer.

"She was hanging with her friends, but I knew exactly where she was the entire time," Rick said and Iris grinned, admiring his resolve. She sighed to herself, wondering if she'd ever find an instant connection like that. Wade was nice, but he'd never looked at her the way Rick was seizing Linnea with his possessive gaze.

"Join me, Linn?" Rick offered his hand and Linnea took it, following him to the dancefloor.

After a second, slower song, he led Linnea to a table, a quiet spot near the back of Northside Grill. Iris kept refilling their glasses, catching bits of their conversation as she tidied the bar. Hours later, the slosh of a mop broke the insulated trance. Rick pivoted in his seat and chuckled. "Damn. We've outlasted everyone."

Linnea's gasp carried through the empty bar. "Have I talked your ear off?" she asked.

"Not at all. This was great. But I guess we better leave so Iris can go home." Rick seemed to realize he hadn't ordered anything. Before leaving, he shot Iris a thank you wave, tossed a wad of cash on the table, then followed Linnea out the door.

When his hand grazed the small of Linn's back, Iris smiled. She knew he'd probably pull Linnea close for a kiss. And if she shivered, he'd put his arm around her to keep her warm.

A small sigh turned Iris back to her task at the register, counting out cash. As she tallied quarters, dimes, nickels, and pennies Iris wondered if the friends with benefits thing she had going with Wade was enough.

SEVEN

Each day he listened. Each night he escaped to his Vegas hotel room and took detailed notes. Coalition planned to push an immense amount of his Double Deet IPA to a nationwide market. To control competition within the Coalition brands, they also had the final say on his new releases. The established product lines had first priority over the launch of new seasonal beers. And the festival schedule—an area where he had built a faithful following—would fall under the scrutiny of marketing.

Wade struggled to find a way to ease the tight fist crushing Mosquito Creek Brewing. Focus was essential, yet he also dealt with a giant distraction wrapped in a petite package. At every turn, in Coalition meetings and on the casino floor, Ravenna Silvestre was there. During the day she'd appear, wearing one of those snug skirts that drove him wild. She'd pull her dark hair into a conservative twist, baring her sleek, pale neck. Such a tempting target.

Evenings were worse. When Ravenna came to dinner looking like a goddess in a pale gold cocktail dress, the vision left him mute. The opulent surroundings looked dull compared to the way she shined.

He'd made it to the final day of the conference and was more than ready to say goodbye to Ravenna. Expecting to see her in polished business attire, the clothes she chose shocked him to his core. Beads of perspiration adhered his shirt to his neck. For a long suffocating moment, he couldn't breathe.

Ravenna rushed up to him, her eyes glowing as she smiled. She wore a snug tank with the Mosquito Creek logo splashed across her chest. His knees went weak gaping at the tantalizing sight.

"What do you think?" she asked, then nipped her full bottom lip. "I tried to keep all the elements in place you've worked so hard to establish."

He fought a groan and looked her over from bottom to top. Without her usual heels, he towered over her in her little black sneakers. Sleek jeans molded to her curves like paint on canvas. The Mosquito Creek tank dipped low, revealing a touch of cleavage that drew his eyes to her lush breasts. Her dark silky hair was tied in a ponytail that bounced when she moved. Everything about her screamed temptation, but he knew he shouldn't touch.

With her head tilted up, Ravenna's wide eyes sought his approval. Her grin lit her from within. "We adjusted the scale of the logo a bit and went with a more flattering cut for the top," she said.

He nodded, wondering if his smile appeared as tight as his jeans felt.

"Do you like it? I was hoping to add this line for your grand opening!" Her bounce put her on tiptoes, so earnest in those damned little sneakers. "Do you think this swag will sell in the new taproom?"

Charmed by her enthusiasm, he stepped forward and invaded her space. He reached for the strap of her tank top and touched it, but not her silky skin. His thumb toyed with the fabric and her lips parted. With a tilt of her head, Ravenna chased that attention, bringing his fingers to a strand of her ebony hair. He'd never felt anything so soft. In a quiet voice meant only for her, he said, "It's perfect. I can't wait to see *more*."

She blushed and looked away. "Yes, I can give you more."

***

Early the next morning, Wade escaped the casino, the hotel, and that petite siren. He figured the packed airport terminal was the best place to hide. Bitter coffee cleared his head as he watched planes leave Sin City. In a few short hours, he would be back in Ashwood. But he wasn't ready. He needed a few days alone to figure out how to handle Coalition and clear his head. An impulsive idea hit. Four hours later, he sped north out of Las Vegas in his slick new truck.

The desert landscape helped him breathe. Shimmering with heat, his road vanished like a needle between mountains on the horizon. He'd covered forty-five miles before he felt relaxed enough to give his sister a call. "Linn, it's me."

"Hey, you forgot to send me your itinerary. I hope you're not in Portland already."

Tapping the steering wheel, Wade swallowed his guilt. He was days, not hours from home. She'd be in charge of the brewery longer than he intended. "About that, I'm not at the airport. I decided to drive back."

Silence stretched before she finally said, "Drive? Wade, is everything okay?"

"Yeah. Or it will be. Do you mind keeping an eye on the brewery, just for a few more days?"

"Not a problem." Her steady reassurance eased his ragged nerves. "Take all the time you need. Don't worry. Your team has everything handled."

Linnea understood. She always had, even when they were kids. Wade remembered the way she used to visit him when he hid in his fort, sometimes sneaking him cookies she'd baked. On warm summer nights, when Mom let Wade spend the night in that fort, Linn would wave at him from her bedroom window. As in the past, he needed time and space to think. Linn got that. She never worried too much, and would be watching for him to roll into Ashwood. When he did, he'd have a plan in place.

Wade stopped for the night in what looked like a ghost town. He felt lucky to find a clean, one-story motel, decorated in a western theme. After he checked in, he glanced down the narrow street and spotted a bar one block away. He walked the cracked sidewalk, hoping to find a decent burger. The steps led to swinging wagon-wheel doors, and the creaky wooden floors reminded him of Northside Grill. He took a few pictures and sent the images to Iris before his burger and fries arrived.

As he ate, he glanced at the emails and missed calls. Ravenna's name appeared on every list. He swiped the screen and ignored her messages, but had a difficult time erasing the memory of her in that Mosquito Creek tank top. His fingers twitched recalling the sensation of her smooth warm skin.

A college baseball game on a dirty screen kept him company while he finished his second whiskey. After the meal, he roamed the vacant streets. Each step confirmed his initial ghost town impression.

A small pawnshop with a radio blaring inside seemed like a good distraction. Barred windows were just as welcoming as the faded *open* sign. He pushed through the door and set off an irritating buzzer. The sound stopped and a nasal voice echoed from the back, "Is that you?"

"Ah, no," Wade answered, but he didn't know who he was talking to. Eventually, a gray head ducked around the corner. She looked comfortable in her khakis, suit jacket, and John Deere baseball hat.

"Your open sign was hanging in the window," he said offering a reason for his presence.

"Of course it was, cause we're open. You here to buy, sell, or pawn?"

Given the choices, he answered, "Buy, I guess." The words became a commitment he hadn't intended. Now he had to find something to buy. Cases of electronics, tools, and guns held his attention for a moment. The wall of guitars halted his steps. A familiar tingle moved his hands to a Telecaster and he played a few runs without an amp, producing an unsatisfying sound. A Martin acoustic had a fair price, but the Taylor was a fucking steal. This side trip took an expensive turn as he paid for the guitar and left the pawnshop.

Buzzing streetlights illuminated his path back to the motel. Perched on the corner of his bed, he picked familiar songs on strings that wouldn't hold a tune. Still, he played, pouring out his hopes, fears, and frustrations across the mother-of-pearl fretboard.

He hadn't picked up a guitar for a long time. Finding it again set things right, and he played a little longer and a little louder than he should. An angry fist pounded the thin wall that separated his room from the unit next door. The banging put a stop to Wade's music. He grinned, feeling better as he rubbed the painful dents made by the strings.

Well past midnight, he still couldn't sleep and sent a text to Iris. She called him back immediately.

"Did I wake you?" he asked.

"Nope. You know my hours. Where'd you send that picture from earlier today? That place looked like a set from an old John Wayne movie."

"I'm somewhere in Nevada. And you're right, I keep expecting to see somebody on horseback. What's going on in Ashwood?" he asked and his chest tightened, missing home.

"I met your sister. Seems she was invited on a girls' night out with Nate, Kels, and Amanda. She's great."

"Better than great. I should have begged her to come to work for me sooner. Linn knows my weaknesses and takes care of things I dread. Somehow, she does it all without making me feel like a damn fool."

"You're lucky. Family can help in the best way possible or know precisely which button to push to piss you off." Iris's laugh sprang into his ear. He could tell, she had experience with both.

Wade leaned back onto the hard motel bed as he laughed. "That sums up my relationship with my Dad. It seems like we take turns pissing each other off. We're so much alike that it irritates the hell out of both of us."

"I get that, my brother and I never really connected. Mom feels like she failed us, but it's too late to fix that now." Before he had a chance to ask about her family, Iris pushed the conversation back to a safe topic. "Where will you stop next?"

"Home, I think. It should take me about twelve hours. Could I come directly to your place? It might be late . . ."

"Find me at Northside."

"All right, I'll hunt you down." As he made plans, a thread of guilt twisted into a knot. After the week he'd spent staring at Ravenna, Wade didn't know if prowling back into Iris' bed felt right.

***

Ravenna tried to call and attempted to email. Sending a text got the same result. Nothing. Each call to Mosquito was answered by the same woman, Linnea. The voice was new, but for a recent hire, she seemed surprisingly seasoned.

As pleasant as she was, Linnea's stalling tactics were growing tiresome. Ravenna came up with a plan to bring this ploy to a decisive halt. After scanning Ashwood on the internet, she fashioned an idea.

An email to Whitewater Homes received a quick efficient reply from a woman named Natalie Journey. The modern temporary accommodations in a rental tiny home had two location options. Natalie let her choose between Osprey Lake, about thirty miles outside of Ashwood, or a spot next door to Whitewater, which was closer to town.

The tiny home was so cute, Ravenna responded with an email the same day.

Thank you for your help with my stay. I'd prefer the in-town location and will arrive next week. Please send an invoice and I'll pay the deposit. Again, I appreciate your help and look forward to meeting you in person.

Ravenna was satisfied with the progress she'd made with no help from Wade Michaels. Smiling, she clicked a link and stared at his bio on her computer screen. "Just you wait, I'll do my job whether you like it or not. Wade, you might be big and powerful, but I'm small and mighty.

***

Before dawn, a deserted road led Wade through barren valleys flanked by low mountains. When he landed on familiar Oregon highways, his thoughts untangled. Wade recalled all he endured to launch his brewery. Battling his father, buying his home, perfecting his craft—each obstacle prepared him for this conflict with Coalition Craft. The inky dark and the sound of the seams in the pavement deepened his calm.

***

Linnea shut down the computer at nine that evening. Her half-finished sandwich from the Stop and Shop lay dry and unappetizing on a paper plate. She tossed it in the trash and tidied her desk. Satisfied, she hoped all the boxes she'd ticked from the to-do list would free her brother from distractions when he finally arrived.

A sharp knock on the office door jolted Linnea from her chair with a yelp. Rick eased the door open, looking potent in his local volunteer fire department uniform. His apologetic grin flip-flopped her stomach.

"Sorry, Linn, I didn't mean to scare you. I spotted Whitewater's lights on after an aid-call and wondered if we forgot to shut things down."

"That's okay. I was about to take off for the night anyway. An aid-call? Is everything all right?"

"Yes, it was just a call from one of our regulars, a little old lady that lives alone. Between the fire department and the sheriff, she finds a way to have us visit a couple of times a month. Everyone knows it isn't anything serious, but I guess someday it could be. We rush over there just the same. Half the time she apologizes and offers everyone a cup of coffee."

"That's terrible. Maybe she needs a roommate or a hobby?"

"You'd think so, but honestly, I think she likes having younger guys around." He shrugged and chuckled, a little less nervous than the last time they talked. He'd kept his distance since that night Northside Grill. After that kiss, she'd half-expected a call, but he couldn't do that if he never asked for her number.

"Well, that's creative." She laughed and blurted, "Are there women out there who make up emergencies just to meet hot guys in uniform?"

Rick burst out laughing. "Not all women are so easily deceived. These clothes can't hide a fat guy's plumber's crack."

When she recognized what she'd said, Linn laughed right along with him. With all his muscles, Rick definitely didn't need a uniform to get a second look.

His heavy leather boots shuffled side to side, but he didn't budge from the office doorway. "If you're still working, I can stick around. I don't like you here all alone."

Linnea shook her head. "That's okay. I was about to call it a night."

"Let me help you lock up."

A task that could have been romantic was completed far too efficiently as Rick helped Linnea flick off the lights and lock the doors. As she tipped her head to thank him, she couldn't keep her eyes off his lips. When he just stood there, Linnea realized the steamy kiss at Northside Grill meant little to him. He may never ask her out, but she hoped to keep him as a friend. With the office secured, she hurried to her car, anxious to escape so Rick wouldn't see how badly she wanted another kiss.

She tore open her door and put the metal and glass between them. That shield gave her something to lean on and the courage to speak. "Thanks for checking on me. Next time I work late, maybe I can bring an extra sandwich and entice you to join me?" Her eyes begged him to accept and save her already wounded pride.

He answered with a nod, reached over the door, and tucked a strand of hair behind her ear. "Linnea, that sounds terrific."

EIGHT

At a little past one the Grill was closed. Wade knew nobody would recognize his new truck, but he parked behind Northside Grill to keep small town gossip from blazing like fire in tinder-dry grass. When he sent Iris a text, she invited him inside. Taking the same door he always used to roll in kegs, he turned toward the column of light streaming from her office.

The sound of his footsteps lifted her eyes from the computer, and he stopped just inside the door's threshold. She gazed at him through glasses he'd never seen before. The sexy-librarian persona sent a shot of lust south. And the way she wore her hair, clipped up in wavy disarray, left her neck on tempting display. Her white blouse dipped low, giving him a peek of her lace-trimmed bra.

Wade shut the door.

Her body turned rosy as his eyes came to rest on that gap in her blouse. The cool breeze of the air conditioner moved the filmy fabric against her sensitive skin. Maybe the air had pebbled her nipples against her silky bra, or perhaps it was his molten gaze. He did not care, either way.

"Don't move," he commanded when she began to swivel her chair. She froze in place as he walked toward her. Kneeling on the floor between her knees, his palms parted her thighs. The movement pushed her skirt a few inches up her soft warm flesh. Patiently, he teased each button of her blouse apart and pushed the delicate garment halfway down her back, trapping her elbows behind her in the soft material. Iris' lips parted—she looked exposed, ensnared, and aroused.

Wade pulled the chair toward him and leaned in to lick the swell of each breast. "Did you wear this for me? This skirt, this sexy bra?"

Iris nodded. "Yes."

He pinched her nipples through the lace, rolling the hard pearls between his finger and thumb. A gasp slipped from her soft lips—exactly the sound he longed to hear.

"Slide forward," he instructed, and she moved without hesitation, spreading her knees against his torso. Gliding his hands over the inside of her smooth thighs he growled as his fingers teased her wet heat over the edges of her matching thong.

"You have a thing for sexy lingerie?"

"Yes."

"Under the conservative clothes you wear to work?"

"Always."

Stroking the edge of the decadent silk, he smiled. "Imagining this every time I see you will kill me." His hands teased beneath the flimsy fabric, and Iris closed her eyes, absorbing the pleasure.

"Eyes open, Iris. I need to see you come." Her gaze locked with his as two fingers met her swollen, wet flesh. His hand tangled with the silky fabric of her thong. Hungry for more, she moved forward to the edge of the chair. His thumb pressed against her clit as he slipped a finger inside and studied her response.

A sharp intake of air trapped in her throat as he eased his touch into her slick space. When her body tightened around his fingers, he swirled his thumb and reached again to tease the peak of her breast. She arched her back—sensual, sleek, and feline.

Wade was hard as steel but pushed back his insistent need. Her hips pulsed forward, seeking more of his unrelenting touch. Iris moaned. Her channel clenched around his fingers as the leading edge of her pleasure began to climb. Pulsing his thumb, he tightened his grasp on her peaked breast to enhance her release.

"Come for me," he said, and she came apart at his command.

Her eyes widened, never moving from his as her sensitive flesh responded to his perfectly timed attention.

"Beautiful," he whispered while placing soft bites on the rise of her breasts. Each mound jutted forward, an erotic display with her arms still ensnared in her blouse. Once she recovered, she seemed to realize that other than loosening a few buttons, not one stitch of her clothing had been removed. Giving him complete control of her pleasure left Iris vulnerable and free.

Wade stood, pulling her sinuous body against his. He took his time kissing her thoroughly, tasting her bottom lip, nipping her vulnerable open mouth until she moaned. Button by button, he arranged her clothes back in place. Powerful hands smoothed her skirt over her lean hips, but it took Iris an extra minute to put her mind back in order.

In a hurry to have her home, he asked, "What can I do to get you out of here quicker?"

Glancing around, she smiled and recognized that yes, she was still in her office. "I can be out of here in twenty."

"Why don't I sneak over to your place? I've been on the road all day and could use a shower," he added with a heated smile. "On second thought, if you want, I can wait for you to join me."

"Go make yourself at home. I won't be long. And yeah, let's take that shower together." She tipped her face to his and stole one more kiss. Flushed and satisfied, Iris looked even sexier when she slid those glasses back in place. Back at work, Iris kneaded her lip as her slim fingers flew over the keyboard.

Wade groaned. "I'd better leave, before I put that desk to use."

On a blink, she looked to him, seeming to recognize the power she wielded over him with just a single glance.

"Iris...baby, when you come home, *wear the glasses.*"

Using her finger and thumb, she lowered the rims and peeked over the top. "Yes, sir."

***

Natalie woke early. She'd corresponded with her new summer renter and decided to move her tiny house into town without Seth's help. Work on the Mosquito Brewing project brought him home exhausted each evening and had him out the door at dawn. Instead of adding this to his long list of tasks, Natalie gave Kels a call and asked her to help guide the home through the short tricky section near the lake.

"I've gone through the checklist. The house is ready to move," she said as she climbed into the cab of her diesel pickup.

Walking a few yards ahead, Kelsey navigated her through the tight spots along the gravel drive. Once they were through, Natalie stopped to let Kels hop into the passenger seat. With gentle pressure to the accelerator, Natalie rolled her Ford F-350 forward gently, tiny-home in tow. "Thanks for doing this, I know you're super-busy."

"Hey, no problem. I love this little house. Do you ever miss living at the beach?" Kelsey asked as she settled.

"The beach?" Natalie thought back to last fall. "I miss Faye, and I wouldn't trade the experience. Those solitary months on the coast focused my love for Seth."

"After that kind of freedom, I don't think I could give it up," Kelsey said with a hint of longing in her voice.

"You should take this house to the beach sometime, for a long escape," Natalie offered.

Kelsey's brows furrowed. "You'd trust me with this?"

"Sure. I'm serious, Kels. Venture's great, but you need a break from the unrelenting pace."

"Maybe I will, after the guiding season slows down this fall. I enjoyed everything about Driftwood Shores and would love to reconnect with Faye again." Kelsey's sigh gave too much away for Natalie to ignore.

"Faye? Don't you really want to reconnect with that surfer, Mark." They both giggled.

"Well, of course there his that. He was hot. Have I ever told you that our paths cross every few months? I don't know how I'll find time for Mark if he shows up to surf the Northwest beaches this summer. These trips with Venture are sucking all my time."

"I'm surprised he came back." Natalie shrugged. "He seemed ready to blow away with the wind to chase the biggest waves."

"I'm just happy when the winds blow him my direction." Kelsey turned her head, stared out the window, and avoided Natalie's searching gaze. After a few miles she asked, "Nate, why are we moving your home?"

"I'm renting it to a woman who's working in Ashwood for a few months."

"And where are we taking this beast?"

Natalie cranked the wheel to navigate the tiny home onto the main highway. "The only place equipped to handle it. Whitewater. We'll park it next to Wade's. I'm sure he won't mind a new neighbor."

***

Wade surprised Iris with breakfast. He took over her kitchen, made coffee, and perfect bacon and cheese omelettes. The slow-paced morning felt right. Over the sudsy sink, he grabbed another dirty dish. "It looks like I'm going to be on the road again, this time to Yakima to oversee the planting of a new hop variety. Linn's going with. I have a lot to tackle before we go."

"No worries. After last night, I need time to recover," she teased. "And as you can tell, I'm capable of taking care of myself." Iris passed him a towel so Wade could dry his hands.

"I'd like to think you enjoy it when I take care of you." When Iris didn't answer, Wade lassoed her with the kitchen towel and tugged her lithe body to his. While nipping the side of her neck, he teased the top of her pants and Iris shivered. She was independent, but she never struggled when caged in his arms.

The phone buzzed in his pocket. For a moment he ignored it, until a second call followed thirty seconds later. Wade plundered her neck with a goodbye kiss. "I need to leave," he said against the smooth column.

"So do I," she admitted and stepped from his embrace.

***

Wade rolled to a stop in front of Whitewater's office. He couldn't wait until his own was finished next door. Once he had room for his desk, he'd spread out and double his productivity. Still behind the wheel, he spotted Linnea inside Whitewater. She sat huddled over her laptop and Wade wondered who had inherited a greater portion of their father's addiction to work. So far, his sister had him beat.

Just as he climbed out of the cab, Seth pulled to a stop beside him. "Hey, I didn't realize you were back in Ashwood," his cousin said. "When did you get the new truck?"

"Picked it up in Vegas and decided to drive back."

"Wow. Did you plan that or just get an amazing deal?" Seth circled envying the slick detailing on the new model.

"I knew what I wanted, but you know me—I needed time and space to get my head together," he admitted and shrugged.

Seth opened the passenger side door, took a look at the interior, and grinned when he inhaled the new-car smell. After slamming the door, he said on a turn, "I get that. How were the meetings?"

"Eye-opening. I don't regret the expansion, but after learning what those execs have planned, I need to dig in and fight. If I don't, CCC will dictate how often I can even take a shit."

Seth shook his head. "Damn, sounds bad."

"It's not great." Wade gripped Seth's shoulder. "Thanks for having my back. Coalition doesn't have the first damn clue about your ownership of the mill where Mosquito will open soon. If you don't mind, I'd like to keep it that way."

"Not a problem. The less they know about the strength of our family the better." Seth led the way inside.

As soon as she spotted Wade, Linnea jumped up, grabbed his neck, and gave him a brief, desperate hug. "I've never been so happy to see you walk through that door."

"Sorry Sis, I know you've had a rough week. Now that I've had a few days to think, I'm ready to tackle anything."

"I hope so, because the moment you left Vegas the execs from Coalition started blowing up our phones."

"Let me grab a cup of coffee before we tackle the mess." Wade poured a cup as she brought him up to date. Every department had questions—product development, marketing, distribution—the list went on and on.

Ready to get started, Linnea tapped her pen on her yellow pad and said, "Ravenna Silvestre should be your first priority. I think she has influence in Coalition, and her messages outnumber the rest."

"Ravenna," he mumbled. A pulse of awareness shot straight to his groin. He counted himself lucky. At least there were several states separating him from that tempting woman.

Linnea led the way out of Whitewater to Mosquito Creek Brewing next door. Her steps seemed to be drawn to the guy working on the customer bathrooms. While keeping his eye on the interaction between his sister and Rick, Wade admired the quality of his work. "I'm speechless. I can't believe how much you've accomplished."

"She kept us on track," Rick said with a grin.

"I know what a taskmaster she can be," Wade teased and grinned, preparing for Linnea's comeback. But she hadn't heard a word and neither had Rick. The pair seemed to be trapped in their own little world.

Eventually Rick emerged from Linnea's pheromone haze. "How was Vegas?" he asked.

"The best part of the trip was seeing the strip in my rear-view mirror." His chuckle came out as a half-groan.

"Yeah, Linn told me you bought a truck. Hey, I do my best thinking on the road, too."

She'd told Rick that? A glance between his sister and Rick revealed the depth of their connection. It bugged him that Linn hadn't said a word.

Clearing his throat, Rick grabbed his tools. "I better get back to work. See you later for lunch," he said, confirming plans that Wade knew didn't include him.

"I can't wait." Linn skipped away. Wade finally caught up on their way to his tiny home on the far edge of the Whitewater property.

He had intended to grill his sister about what happened while he was on the road, when a large distraction swept everything else from his mind. A bigger home had been parked right next to his. Staring at it, he asked, "Is Natalie having repair work done?"

"Not that I know of. I thought she kept her place at the lake?" The door swung open. Natalie stood smiling with cleaning supplies in one hand and her broom in the other.

"Hi Wade! Welcome back. I had hoped to run into you. I wanted to let you know that you'll have a neighbor for the next few months."

"Is Ben planning a visit?" Wade asked.

"No, my brother's in North Carolina this summer. Last week, I got an email from a woman looking for a temporary place to stay in Ashwood. I don't know much about her, but she has an interesting name. She must be Italian."

His stomach pitched. *No, it could not be possible.*

Natalie blew an escaped curl of auburn hair away from her face. "Her name is Ravenna Silvestre, isn't that beautiful?"

In pained unison, a simultaneous groan rose from Linnea and Wade.

A bottle of Windex escaped Natalie's fingers and fell to the ground. "What? Do you know her? I hope she isn't an old girlfriend trying to stalk you."

"Worse," Linnea said. "She works for Coalition Craft Corporation. That woman has been dogging Wade, trying to micro-manage every aspect of Mosquito's expansion."

Unhinged by the news, Wade's body responded with a volatile wave of desire and panic. "When?" he muttered as he shifted his feet to battle the girth in his groin.

"Day after tomorrow." Natalie's shoulders lifted. "I am *so sorry*. It's too late to stop her. The lease is signed, and she already paid the deposit."

"It's okay." Stretching to his full six-foot-three, Wade readied himself to do battle with Coalition and to face this beautiful nemesis head on.

***

"I made it to Portland." Ravenna absorbed strength from her father the moment he answered his phone. Their routine was the same each time her job took her to a new city. A childhood spent in his brewery at her father's side had laid the foundation for her love of craft-brewing. He understood the demands of her job, and she valued his input. After catching up on the latest family gossip, she said, "I have a question if you have time."

"I always have time for you, sweet girl."

Ravenna closed her eyes and gathered her thoughts. "Papa, do you remember a brewer named Wade Michaels?"

"Mosquito Creek Brewing? Sure, I know him. He took my brewing crash course. We've kept in touch. Solid man. Great instincts. I was surprised to hear he signed with CCC."

"I agree. He's established, and there's little room for Coalition to leave their indelible mark. The man just doesn't fit Coalition's usual profile." Ravenna didn't try to hide her worry.

"Does he have something else Coalition wants?" her papa asked, his concern clear.

She recognized their parallel thoughts. "That's what I've been wondering. If you hear anything unusual in your circle of friends, would you please let me know."

Leo continued cautiously, "Keep your eyes open, and be careful. But Ravenna, don't risk your career. Wade's capable of looking out for himself."

"Don't worry. I won't risk too much for *him*. So far, he's not my greatest fan." She dreaded the job with Mosquito Creek Brewing before it had even begun.

From three hundred miles away, her father offered his support. "Remember, Wade chose to sign with Coalition Craft, and everyone on the board, including a washed-up old relic like me, knows you're the best person to help with his expansion. In the end, Wade Michaels has to live with his decision, even if he loses a bit of his independence."

Ravenna sighed. "You're right. I'm sure everything will be fine."

"I'll see you soon, for your birthday. I Love you."

"Love you, too," she said and ended the call.

***

Needing to talk, Wade joined Seth on his deck overlooking Osprey Lake. The men had handled after dinner clean-up before settling outside. Natalie didn't follow, saying it was too cold, but Wade knew his cousin's fiancée was giving them space to talk. From the door, she turned and apologized again. "Sorry about the mess I made with Ravenna."

With a grin, Wade shook his head. "Don't worry about it. This girl is tenacious. At least I can keep an eye on what she's planning, especially with her living a mere fifteen feet away."

Laughter eased the tension and Natalie left to curl up with a book.

As the sun set, Wade swallowed another sip of whiskey. The gold liquor burned, clearing his mind with its potent smoky taste. Seth lit the outdoor heat lamp to fight the chill.

"So tell me, what's this girl like?"

"Ravenna's exquisite. Shit, that's what makes this so fucking complicated." Wade sunk forward, elbows to knees, recalling the power this woman had over him. He spun his nearly empty whiskey glass between his hands.

Seth brought up the obvious. "What about Iris?"

"You know I'm seeing her?" Wade asked, his head bent low.

"Small town, no secrets, you know the drill." he sympathized.

"We have a lot in common. Iris is smart, she's sexy—"

"But?"

"When Ravenna was far away, I couldn't stop thinking about her. Now that she'll be close enough to touch, I'm obsessed."

"Shit." They sat in silence sharing drinks and cigars, instead of a solution. Some things just couldn't be fixed. Eventually, the propane tank firing the outdoor heater hissed and went out, and the chill chased them inside.

NINE

Nerves were on edge. Everyone paced the planks at Whitewater and waited for Ravenna to show. The Michaels' family had united first thing in the morning to support Wade. In the brewery, Seth, Natalie, Amanda, and Linnea huddled together talking. Aware of the cause for the underlying tension, Rick, Kent, and Carlos hovered in the shop nearby, tools silent.

Wade patrolled. "This is ridiculous, everyone needs to get to work."

"He's right, we all look like fools sitting around waiting for the sky to fall," Linnea agreed.

"I'm starved," Natalie admitted. "Why don't I grab us lunch at the Stop and Shop."

"We'll go with you." Linnea slipped on her jacket while Amanda took sandwich orders from the crew.

Once everyone cleared out, Wade paced in a circle alone, wondering what the hell to do. He had prepared for an early battle, but the little warrior was nowhere in sight.

His phone buzzed with a text. An apology from Ravenna hit him in the gut. *Sorry for bothering you. I don't have anyone else in the area on my contact list. I hit a chunk of metal with my rental car. It's making a terrible noise. I'm about thirty minutes outside of Ashwood. Could you send a tow?*

Wade sprinted for the door while calling Ravenna back. She didn't pick up right away, and each ring increased his apprehension. "Why isn't she answering?" he said as he launched into his truck.

A pent-up exhale deflated his chest the moment she picked up. "Wade, sorry for this inconvenience. Do you know a tow company in the area?"

"Are you okay?" he asked already speeding down the highway.

"I'm fine, but my car isn't." Her stress bubbled through the phone on a nervous giggle.

"Where are you?" He pressed the accelerator closing the distance between them.

"On Highway 141, I passed a rafting business a few miles back. They might be open. I could walk that direction."

Over the engine's growl, he said, "Stay where you are. I'll be there in twenty."

***

Ravenna found unexpected comfort in knowing Wade was coming to her rescue. A tow this far from everything would have taken hours. Reclined in the seat of her broken sedan, she let the stress of the day fade away by increments.

She inspected the rugged surroundings while her car's interior warmed comfortably in the sun. Tall trees framed an imposing glacier-covered mountain in the distance. Everything seemed wild, and she decided on a four-wheel drive for a replacement vehicle.

To pass the time, she checked her emails. Her eyes rolled when she found that three different managers were already demanding updates. She typed careful messages, promising to keep them informed. The intense scrutiny from so many was disturbing. There was definitely something different about this deal with Wade Michaels.

A shiny truck appeared on the horizon, but it couldn't possibly be him, not yet. She had calculated the distance from Ashwood to her disabled car. If this was Wade, he must have hauled serious ass.

Their eyes met. A heart-stopping grin stretched across Wade's face. Ravenna sighed, and knew she was in deep trouble. He looked so good. Disheveled waves of sandy-blond hair rested on his shoulders. It looked like he'd recently worried the strands with his hands—a distracting habit she'd noticed in Vegas. She imagined her fingers tangled in that thick hair, but she shot down her desire with one thought—*I have a boyfriend. Steven.*

After circling his truck in a wide arc, he sheltered her vehicle from passing traffic by angling his rig behind her rental. Out with a quick jump, he jogged her direction.

Faded jeans stretched across his trim hips. The sight filled the glass in her rear-view mirror. Pulled by curious temptation, her eyes strayed to admire an impressive bulge. A flush spread over her face, and Ravenna averted her eyes to study the center of the steering wheel instead.

A tap on the glass turned her head. His fingers rattled the handle of the locked door and he waited while she fumbled to locate the switch. With the door finally open, he bent in half. "Pop the trunk and I'll get your luggage. Take everything out of the car."

Her voice stuck in her throat and she nodded, pushing the release on the trunk. Eyes on the mirror again, she was rewarded with a view of his taut butt. Fumbling for her purse, she tucked in her charger and slid her sunglasses case inside. Last, she snagged the small leather tote holding her laptop from the passenger seat.

While watching him load the luggage into the bed of his truck, she made a plan for the climb into the lifted cab. Sometimes being petite really sucked. Ravenna looked up and found his eyes surveying her frame, his smile tipped with a hint of concern. Clearly, he could tell she'd need a boost.

"Are we leaving the car here?" she asked while staring into his steel-gray eyes.

"Does it run?"

Her nose wrinkled. "Yeah, but it sounds terrible."

Wade nodded. "I already talked to a friend of mine. He lives about a half mile down the road. I'll drive the rental if you'd like to follow in my truck. We can park the car at his place until we can arrange for a tow."

"Sure, no problem." Ravenna handed him the keys and circled to the driver's side of Wade's pickup. He opened the door and guided her into the cab. Balancing her heels on the running board, Ravenna shivered when his hands met her waist, and her breath held until he let go.

A roll of low laughter broke the tension. "I guess we need to move the seat. I hope you can reach the gas and brake pedal."

"I'm not that short!" She joined his contagious laughter and waited while he used the mechanism on the side of the seat to ease her forward. Their fingers tangled when she reached down to fine tune the adjustment. A sizzle of awareness passed between them, but neither pulled away. Wade's eyes darkened, locking on hers.

Her voice shook. "I think I can reach the pedals now."

Wade encased her small hand in his as he lifted her fingers to the steering wheel. A bite of her lip suppressed her nervous giggle.

"Follow me. It's not too far," he instructed. She nodded as he closed the door and watched him while he jogged to the disabled sedan. The rental didn't sound too bad when he first turned the key, giving her false hope. When a metal on metal scrape shrieked, she prayed the sedan would make it more than a few hundred feet.

After a quick check in the rear-view mirror to make sure she was ready, Wade crept along the shoulder of the road in her broken car. Ravenna pressed the truck's accelerator and couldn't stop her smile. The animal growl of the engine felt familiar. Her dad had taught her to drive in an old pickup, and she missed this commanding perspective, sitting high above the road.

In less than a mile, he eased the car into a gravel drive. Flicking the signal, she followed close and parked behind Wade. An elderly man appeared from the small home and gave her a polite nod. She returned his kindness with a wave and a grin and opened the door, ready to climb from the high perch. Before she descended, the man shook hands with Wade, and her rescuer hustled back. Hips scooting, she hopped her butt across the bench seat to the passenger side.

Wade stood at the door, but he didn't climb in. His eyes crinkled at the edges and he mumbled, "I'm not gonna fit." He adjusted the seat to make room for his much longer legs. While she waited, her heartbeat climbed. Her mouth went dry when he joined her inside and slammed the door, trapping sizzling tension.

Eyes focused on the road, he ignored the electric connection and rambled, "That's all taken care of. Frank will give me a call when the tow shows. You were right, whatever debris you hit did a number on that car."

When Ravenna couldn't think of anything to say, she tried to find safety in their shared love of brewing. "This isn't how I hoped our day would go. I still look forward to seeing your progress at Mosquito Creek Brewing." His jaw tightened and she flinched, knowing she'd destroyed the rapport.

Knuckles white on the steering wheel, his irritation snapped. "We'll get to that soon enough."

She shrank in the seat and stared out her window, convinced that he'd never see her as anything but an adversary.

Wade's eyes narrowed on the road as he asked, "What would you like to see first, my brewery or the place you've rented?"

She glanced across the cab at his scowl and prepared for conflict. "Well, why don't we drop off my luggage first? Unfortunately, without a car, I'll need a ride to the brewery."

"Oh, you won't have any trouble getting to Mosquito. Natalie parked your home on the same property that houses Mosquito Creek."

Her eyes widened as she discovered the depth of his information. So much for the element of surprise. In a small town, apparently stealth was impossible. She huffed a short chuckle. "I thought I was staying near a place called Whitewater Homes."

"Oh, you are. Whitewater belongs to my cousin Seth. The woman you corresponded with is Natalie, his fiancée. Whitewater and Mosquito Creek Brewing sit side by side."

"How convenient," she added with a roll of her eyes.

***

Wade relished her silence. When she huffed, he grinned, knowing he'd successfully rattled Ravenna's nerves. He pulled off the road at the south end of the old lumber mill property and pointed his rig toward a towering rusty beehive burner. Leaning forward in her seat, Ravenna craned her neck to get a better view. "Wow. I haven't seen a burner like that in years. Most have rusted and collapsed. Please tell me you're using that logging relic in your marketing."

While the tower of metal distracted Ravenna, he studied her beautiful profile. Her plump lips opened slightly in awe as she stared skyward. Brightened by genuine interest, her deep brown eyes seemed to absorb every architectural detail, tempting Wade to trust a woman he barely knew. "I checked into repurposing the burner," he said. "But it's too expensive to bring up to code. It would be cheaper to build a replica, but that's—"

"Imitation," she finished his thought, then brought her gaze to him on a blink.

The fact that the genuine article meant something to her pleased him. He eased past each building and let her absorb her surroundings. "We're using reclaimed wood, milling it on site. Mosquito's here in the center, and that massive shop at the end is Whitewater. We'll take a look around, after you've moved in."

"Great." She hissed out a long sigh, and Wade sensed her unbalance. If she felt trapped in his domain, he wasn't going to do a thing to ease her nerves. After rounding Whitewater's shop, he rolled to a stop and turned to find her eyes shifting between the two side-by-side houses.

Cutting the engine, he let the slow tick, tick, tick of the cooling motor magnify the silence. Finally, he said, "The larger home on the right is yours."

"And the other, with the porch?"

"That's mine." He smirked as her mouth dropped open. *Perfect, she's just as disturbed as I am.*

"B-but, I thought you lived out of town," she stammered, wide-eyed.

"My house is an hour north, and I go home when I find the time. With the project flying, this made more sense. More often than not, I'm right here."

He barely heard her whisper, "How convenient," then Wade's mind drifted to Iris. Even if her place was an easy escape from his tempting new neighbor, using Iris to avoid this woman seemed wrong. He had to find a way to make this work.

Ravenna rushed to escape the cab, her fingers fumbling to find the handle. Wade hopped out, circled the truck, and pulled her suitcase from the back. He'd just made it to her passenger-side door when Natalie and Seth appeared. After quick introductions, he explained why she needed a ride.

Friendly as always, Natalie greeted Ravenna with a quick hug, and seemed determined to make sure the new arrival in Ashwood felt at home. "Wade, could you bring her suitcases inside. I'll give Ravenna a tour and see if she has any questions."

He could only nod as he watched Ravenna follow Natalie inside. The distance between the homes seemed to shrink as Wade carried her heavy suitcases up the stairs. Inside, the space was smaller still. Trapped this close to Ravenna, he choked out, "Would you like these in the bedroom?"

Through long lashes, her dark eyes peeked his way, dancing. Shit, she was enjoying this way too much. "That's okay. Just leave them here," she said, her voice sugar-sweet. "I'll take my time and find the perfect place for all my things later."

Wade dropped the suitcases, rushed to escape, and stumbled into Seth where he waited outside. His cousin's rolling laughter mocked Wade's misery.

TEN

Ravenna noted the family resemblance before Wade introduced her to his sister. Linnea seemed friendlier than her brother, but the way she stood by his side was still intimidating. She couldn't tell if they were intentionally overwhelming, or if it was just the way they towered above her. Being petite was such a pain in the butt, sometimes.

Taking the lead, Wade robotically pointed out features of the brewery. Ravenna tried to tease useful information from him, but he insisted on answering her questions with clipped efficiency. Instead of pressing him further, she poured on the charm. "I'm impressed by your progress. You've made my job easy, maybe even irrelevant."

"Easy?" Wade pulled his hand through his hair as he seemed to brace for a jabbing critique, and she sensed that someone in his past had withheld even the tiniest morsels of praise.

"Yes. You've made so many solid decisions, I'm having trouble finding any room for improvement." Even though her comments were sincere, she could tell she hadn't earned his trust. She hoped Linnea's confidence would be easier to win. As soon as his sister took over the taproom portion of the tour, Ravenna sensed a promising shift. Bright and informative, Linnea asked as many questions as she answered. With each compliment about their outstanding progress, Ravenna watched his sister's quiet solidarity dissolve.

Ignoring Wade's booted steps, she focused her attention on the pleasant half of the pair. "Linnea, your instincts are great. How many taprooms have you visited?"

"Since taking this job, only three."

Ravenna nodded. "Well, I think we'd better start with a visit to Portland. How would you feel about touring taprooms with me for a day or two?"

A smile crept across Linnea's face. "That sounds fantastic. I've been so buried in work, I've lost sight of the fun."

Wade's steps stopped not far behind. "Fun my ass," echoed in the hollow room. On a quick turn, Linnea speared her brother with a sharp look.

Pasting on a pleasant grin, Ravenna asked, "What was that, Wade?"

"Nothing," he said, and his eyes dropped to his boots.

Seeing a hint of regret, Ravenna took a chance, and asked, "I know you've probably visited more breweries than I have, but you're welcome to come with us to Portland."

"No need. I trust Linnea's judgment," he grumbled.

Ravenna wouldn't' let his indifference destroy the progress she'd made with Linnea. "Then, since it's just us girls, I think an overnight trip would be best. Coalition can treat us to a mini-vacation. Linn, when would you like to go?"

Linnea bit her lip, fighting to hide her excitement from her brother's glare. "We've already got a trip to Yakima scheduled. How about after we get back?"

"Perfect. I'll take care of everything."

"Ooh, I can't wait." A sincere smile lifted Linnea's cheeks and Ravenna felt satisfied by the progress she'd made. Still, the day had been difficult, and she couldn't fight an exhausted yawn.

"I'm sorry, but would either of you mind if I call it a day?" She rolled her weary shoulders. "I'm still on Chicago time."

Linn tipped her head toward the Whitewater office. "We'll see you tomorrow, and thanks for the great feedback on the taproom."

Wade plunged his hands in his pocket and pulled out a set of keys. "There's a pickup parked outside. Use it. Linn will be around if you have any questions." The keys dangled between them, hanging from his stiff fingers. After all her effort, his icy brush-off caused Ravenna pain.

Stepping toward him, she accepted this small kindness. "Thank you, Wade." Her voice, barely more than a whisper, pulled him one step closer. "I really appreciate the rescue today." When she took hold of the keys, their hands touched. The energy that had always zipped between them snapped back in place.

Heat infused her as she tipped her head and found that his eyes had softened. "I liked being there for you," he said, released the keys and walked away.

***

Ravenna explored her tiny home and found well-stocked cupboards that saved her from a grocery run. "Thank you, Natalie," she said aloud and opened the refrigerator to discover even more.

A helpful list lay face-up on the counter written on happy pink paper. The Wi-Fi password, instructions for the sound system, and the number for a new pizza place that delivered were listed above Natalie's cell. Her favorite person in Ashwood had finished the cheerful note with an invite to get together for coffee.

"I think I may love that girl." Ravenna sighed, knowing that she'd need all the friends she could find in this small town.

A fresh pasta dish came together with ease. She sautéed chicken while listening to music. Cooking usually steadied her mind, but thoughts of the man next door invaded. She squashed them with a plan to call Steven following dinner and opened a bottle of wine. After dinner she poured herself a second glass, and sent Steven a text, letting him know she'd like to talk when he had a moment.

Her boyfriend preferred a text *request*, not a call, when she wanted to talk. If he found himself too busy, usually with work for Coalition, he replied with an efficient message. This way she would not sit around wasting her time while waiting for his call.

Steven's inflexible quirk pushed against her desire for spontaneity. Early in their relationship, she had brought it up. The short argument had ended in his favor. He assured her that his method allowed him to give her his undivided attention. She'd wanted to yell, *bullshit,* but kept *that* opinion to herself.

After hitting send, she took another swallow of her deep earthy wine and climbed the steep stairs to her loft. Stretched out on the soft comforter, she found a new book to pass the time. Steven's ringtone extinguished the wine's languid effects.

"Hello," she answered, trying to sound alert.

"How was your flight yesterday? Have you settled in?"

"My flight was good, but I had a problem with my rental. Some metal road debris tore into the bottom of the chassis and damaged the car."

"How did you handle that? Aren't you in some puny hole of a town?"

"No. Ashwood is, well, friendly." She put her arm behind her head and squirmed but couldn't get comfortable.

"Did our company deliver another car?"

"Not yet. Wade Michaels lent me a pickup from the Mosquito fleet."

"Are you sure that puts you in the best position? You don't want yourself beholden to this man. Remember, he works for *us.*"

She rolled her eyes, thankful Steven couldn't see her. "I guess that's one way to think about it. Still, I'm here to find common ground and support his success."

"Fine. Build trust. That's your approach and it works well *for you.*"

"It won't be this way for long. I've already arranged for a new car." She brought her wine to her lips, but the next sip didn't taste as satisfying.

"I know you just arrived, but have you had time to survey the property?"

"The brewery? Yes, it's gorgeous—"

"Last fall, when I set this deal up with Mosquito, work hadn't started. How does it look?" he asked carefully.

Excitement sped her words. "The old lumber mill couldn't be more perfect. The taproom location has so much raw potential, lofted beams, tons of natural light, and antique equipment."

"*No*. I mean, how far has he progressed?" Irritation bled into Steven's tone. "What about the quality of the materials? Does Wade Michaels seem strapped for cash?"

The hair prickled at the back of Ravenna's neck, even though Steven's questions were legitimate where Coalition was concerned. Unclenching her jaw, she answered without embellishment, "The quality is above average. He has plenty of raw material to repurpose on-site. I haven't had time to meet with his brewers, but the men working construction seem professional."

"Ravenna, have you seen any sign of his family?"

She lost her composure and blurted the first name that came to mind. "Who? Do you mean his cousin Seth?"

"Who the hell is Seth?" Steven's irritation rose another notch. "Just how inbred is this puny town?"

An overwhelming urge to hurl the phone across the room seized her, but she closed her eyes instead. "He's just Wade's cousin, nobody important. He was around when I arrived."

Steven's interrogation had brought on the sharp edge of a painful headache. She kept her eyes closed and tried to relax. Self-preservation prompted her to move the conversation in another direction. "When do you leave for your next trip? Was it Florida?" she asked, paying little attention to his answer.

"No, Tennessee. We need to strengthen Coalition's presence in the South. I'm looking at a couple of brewers near Nashville."

"That would be an easy market to brand." Ravenna half-listened as he filled her in on the top three brewers he planned to approach. Yet, her mind puzzled about Steven's persistent interest in the

83

Michaels' family. The arrangement wasn't unusual. Many breweries were family run.

"Are you still there?" His question broke her train of thought.

"Yes, I'm here. Sorry Steven, it's been a long day. Jet lag. What was that again?"

"Your birthday, we planned to spend it in Portland or at the beach. I wonder where you'd prefer to stay?"

"Probably the coast."

"I'll take care of everything. Trust me. Let me surprise you."

She sighed and relaxed, remembering why she enjoyed dating Steven. He was dependable, attentive, and always in control.

***

Wade passed Northside Grill for the third time and struggled to find the right answer. Iris was smart, honest, and incredibly sexy. She fit, but he could not stop obsessing about Ravenna. Pursuing Iris while he battled this magnetic draw to another woman seemed unfair. On the other hand, tossing away an opportunity with someone he had so much in common with would be stupid. What kind of idiot would choose lust over a chance at a solid relationship?

Not this idiot. Ravenna has a boyfriend, she's leaving after her job is done, and I can't trust a woman who works for Coalition.

On a wide spot in the road, he cranked the wheel, determined to pursue a woman he could trust. When he rushed through the side door a few of her employees glanced his way. Wade moved with clear intention through the break room, office, and kitchen trying to locate the sexy owner of Northside Grill. Her staff had to know he'd been seeing Iris. Hell, the whole town probably knew, but until the two of them acknowledged the relationship in public, they wouldn't be official.

Wade stopped moving when he found Iris behind the bar, half-hidden from customer view. Her hips swayed slowly side-to-side to the music. A few people hung all over each other on the dance floor, yet their moves had nothing on the way her body merged with the sensual rhythm.

Propped against the frame of the door, he watched until she sensed his presence. Under the force of his heated gaze, Iris inched toward him. By the time she reached his side, half the customers at Northside Grill stared their direction.

"I didn't expect to see you tonight," she whispered.

"I'm here."

"That's good."

His eyes dipped to her mouth and back up. He wanted to kiss her, but here, on her turf, that was her call. Conversations died out around them, and an audience of sorts held a collective breath. Iris placed one hand on the side of his face and pulled his mouth to hers until their lips touched.

He wrapped his hand around her hip holding her close. The heat of her body sizzled through her clothes, transmitting desire against his palm. "What color did you choose today?" he asked against her lips.

She smiled at his obsession with her lingerie and answered, "White."

Her eyes sparkled, and he knew she wasn't wearing practical cotton. No, this was her secret. The lace would be sheer and the cut risqué. Wade held that vivid fantasy in place until he stripped her clothes that night.

ELEVEN

With a grunt, Wade heaved Linnea's luggage into the bed of his truck. He didn't need to ask, just the weight confirmed she'd packed about a dozen books. She turned to him and sighed, "Do I really need to go? I'd be happy to stay here and keep an eye on things at the brewery."

"Sis, get in the damn truck. Mom and Dad are expecting you." Seeing Rick hover around Linnea lately added another reason for his sister to go with him to Yakima. He kicked himself for ignoring the growing connection between Linn and Rick. But the brewery expansion, avoiding Ravenna, and spending nights with Iris had distracted Wade from talking to that guy.

When she glanced toward Whitewater, he considered tossing Linnea in back with her suitcase until she finally gave in with a shrug and said, "Fine."

She ignored his presence for the first thirty miles of their eastbound drive. Eyes on the horizon, she gazed over the landscape as it transitioned from tall pines to rolling wheat fields. Eventually, Wade grew tired of the silent standoff and asked, "When did you plan to tell me that you and Rick were dating?"

Her lips tightened and she shot a mute glare his way but continued the silent treatment. "Come on, just admit it. He never leaves when you're working late. You eat lunch together most days, and he can't go more than an hour without wandering into the office to talk to you."

"It's not like that." She hunkered down in her seat and sighed. "Lately, it seems like Rick's decided we're better off being *just friends*."

Her air-quotes made him chuckle. "Good, I like that even better." When Linnea's chin trembled, Wade realized he'd said the wrong thing. *Shit.* The tears brimming her eyes sent him scrambling. "Are you kidding? Rick prowls around you like a grizzly bear. It's a lot more than *just friends*. I've known the guy a while. If he's taking things slow, that means you're different. You're special."

One side of her mouth inched up. "You really think so?"

"I know so."

She glanced out her passenger side window. "Rick's just so distant sometimes."

Now that she'd mentioned it, Wade realized how little he knew about the guy. He volunteered at the fire department and worked his ass off building tiny homes for Seth, but when Rick's parents left Ashwood a few years back, he'd stayed. The muscle-bound guy seemed all right, but that didn't mean he was good enough for Linnea.

"Hey, if you need me to beat some sense into him, I will." Wade teased, hoping to erase the last of her tears. "But I might not live through it."

She shook her head and her smile reappeared. "Don't risk your neck. I know you're right, Rick's just taking things slow. I guess I'm just a little disappointed—this morning, I thought Rick would come out to the truck and say goodbye."

With a long, slow sigh, Linnea flicked on the radio. A smile finally met her eyes when she found a station playing *Banana Pancakes*. She sang along with Jack Johnson as Wade drummed the steering wheel.

After the song ended, he turned down the volume and asked, "Can you do me a favor?"

Linnea nodded. "Sure."

"I'd like to keep the Iris thing between you and me for now."

Her laughter erased his apprehension. "Don't worry. I *never* intended to say anything about her to Mom and Dad. Still, they may have heard something from Uncle Bill and Aunt Sandy."

"I know, but if Iris doesn't come up—"

"Gotcha. Same goes for me. Don't leak anything about Rick to Dad." Her smile vanished on a pout. "Not that it probably matters much—I've been slotted to the friend category."

Wade glanced across the cab. "Would you mind if I grabbed a beer with him? Maybe shoot some pool?"

"I guess. But don't scare him away. Remember, you *are* just like Dad."

Her eyes danced as he chuckled. "Now that was just vicious."

***

Linnea burst through the door. "Mom, we're home!"

Wade followed the sound of his mother's voice and found her in the kitchen. She already had his sister trapped in a hug. "Why did I let you move away? I've missed you so much." She held Linn at arm's length for a careful study. "You've grown up over these past few weeks."

"Same old me," Linnea said, uncomfortable with her mother's inspection.

Deciding to save her, Wade dropped the duffels on the floor and asked, "Hey, Mom, where's my hug?" While he had his mother wrapped up, he asked, "Mind if I raid the refrigerator?"

"Go ahead but be quick. Dad needs you in the hop yard."

"I'm on it."

As he made a sandwich Linnea whispered, "Are you ready to face Dad?"

"Once I'm planting those hops, he won't have a reason to complain."

"You better get out there," she warned, and he decided to eat his sandwich on the way to the field.

Along with the crew, Wade dug holes for gnarled hop rhizomes, planting them far below metal cables stretched high on poles. The heavy vines would climb to the top and bear hops by late summer. It

88

had taken three years to perfect this new variety. He and his father held the patent for Rusk, a hop they'd named for a glacier on Mount Adams. Wade knew this mango-citrus variety would set him apart from the herd of craft brewers crowding the Northwest market. Rusk's spring planting would more than triple last year's yield, enough for a new IPA.

That night, the cool evening air followed Wade and his father into the mudroom where they kicked off coats and work boots. His oldest sister, Brooke, rushed to meet him, and hugged his neck. "Oh, it's been so long. I've really missed you."

"Missed you, too." When he let her go, Brooke dashed off to meet her husband, Dean. He'd been working hard alongside Wade the entire day, making sure the new hop would succeed.

Brooke and Dean nearly filled the family table. The only sibling missing was Sylvia, who lived in a dorm a couple hundred miles to the east. Over dinner, their conversation moved to all the work they needed to accomplish over the next few days.

The family meal, like so many others, ended with conflict. Talk of hops turned to questions about beer and culminated with Dad digging for information about Mosquito Creek Brewing. His father targeted each judgmental word with hawk-like precision, ambushing his son.

"Listen to me, Wade. I don't see why you need to concern yourself with the product when you control the keys to production. Your true gift lies in hop development. Those patents will ensure a lifetime of income, unaffected by the whims of whatever beer happens to be in fashion."

"You know beer isn't a whim for me. When will you let it go?" His father always started these arguments logically, but Wade knew what was coming. He braced for more while the rest of the family escaped. On a glance, he apologized to his sister as Brooke and Dean snuck out of the dining room. Linnea grabbed a few plates, clearing the table, sneaking away. Mom stayed on, supporting Wade for as long as she could. She finally sighed and gave up, leaving to slice cake for Brooke and Dean to take home. Wade sighed, knowing the argument had destroyed any hope of a quiet evening spent with his sisters.

Still, his father wouldn't relent, and Wade refused to bend to family tradition. He never believed that only an oldest son should inherit the hop farm. "I'm always here when you need me. And I'll help Brooke when she asks. Don't you see? I have access to the best testing ground. You never have to hear second-hand if our hops produce great beer."

"What will you do if Dean and Brooke ever decide to shut you out!"

"Don't pit me against her. My sisters and I have always watched out for each other, and we always will."

The same argument produced the same result. Wade escaped to the land to walk off his anger, while Dad retreated to his office, feeling betrayed. Still, no matter how much they disagreed, by morning the work went on.

***

Ravenna watched from inside the taproom, knowing one of the Michaels was about to show up at the brewery. She had tried to stay busy while Wade and Linnea visited Yakima, but deep loneliness had set in. At least it wouldn't be long before Papa visited for her birthday.

In the shadows of the unfinished brewery, Ravenna stood, coffee in hand, when a small sedan she didn't recognize pulled into the parking lot. Linnea got out and Ravenna sighed. She'd forgotten the siblings would be returning separately. She smiled, trying to be happy to see the friendlier half of the Michaels pair. Such a fool, she knew it was wrong to yearn for a man who didn't miss her at all.

Determined to make the best of the situation, Ravenna started for the door. She stopped short when one of the men from the construction crew met Linnea at her car. She'd noted the golden-haired guy was a shameless flirt, but she didn't think Kent had his eyes on Linnea.

Of course, the snug skirt Linnea chose to wear showed off her amazing curves. And Kent couldn't keep his eyes off the long legs Ravenna envied. Barely able to hear their conversation through the open window, she smiled when Rick's truck rolled in. This could get interesting.

Aware of his new audience, Kent shamelessly perused Linnea's form. "How was Yakima?" he asked.

She blushed under the careful inspection. "We got the hops planted, so I guess it was good."

"Looks good from where I'm standing." He leaned against his rig with his muscled arms flexed over his chest and gave her that *damn woman—you look fine* smile.

A door slammed behind Linnea. She startled but ignored it, keeping her eyes on Kent as she chatted casually about the details of her trip.

Ravenna bit her lip. She knew it was wrong to eavesdrop but couldn't force her feet to move away from her lookout at the window.

Glancing beyond Linnea's shoulder, Kent's eyes flicked to Rick, brows raised in a clever challenge. His grin tipped as Linnea shifted her nervous feet. It was almost like she could feel Rick's eyes heating her ass with his gaze.

Ravenna sighed, recalling how warm she felt when Wade looked at her that way. She blinked slowly to erase the memory, squashing the potent response to the forbidden attraction. Wanting Wade was wrong for a million different reasons, the greatest being Steven. Her lips moved without a sound. "Remember, you have a boyfriend."

Outside in the lot, Rick stepped forward and Kent hitched his chin. "Hey, Rick. Look who's back," he said and Linnea squirmed. Yet, a small, sly grin gave Linn's reaction away—she was loving this attention.

"I saw," Rick said in a voice so low, Ravenna could barely hear him from her hiding place. Inching closer to Linnea, his hand met the small of her back, and Linn leaned into the touch.

Kent's head tipped back as he laughed, then he spun on his heels, heading Ravenna's direction. She swallowed a squeak, and with no other alternative, was forced to come outside. Too bad, Linnea seemed to be having such a nice time torturing Rick.

When Kent made it to the door, Ravanna pushed through and held it open. He gave her that knee-melting smile as he passed. She raised a hand in a friendly wave, and called, "Welcome back, Linnea. Isn't Wade with you?"

"Uh, no. He'll be here in a day or two."

"Another stop at Old Mosquito? What's he working on up there?" she asked as she closed the distance between them, trying a bit too hard to cover up the fact that she'd been snooping.

Linnea hesitated. "Um, he's probably just brewing more Double Deet. We're all doing our best to keep Coalition happy."

"That's great." Ravenna didn't need Linnea's reassurances. As far as she was concerned, Mosquito Creek Brewing had nothing to worry about. Still, the weekend alone had given her time to research Coalition's keen interest in Wade's brewery. She had more than a few concerns. If she understood Wade's operation beyond Ashwood, she might be able to warn him.

"I didn't know he could still brew at his original location up on Mosquito Creek. Do you think he'd mind if I took a look at it sometime?" Ravenna danced around the question, trying to keep her interest light.

"Let me check with him." Linnea's smile wavered when Rick tipped a silent greeting to Ravenna then followed Kent inside. When Linn's shoulders caved, Ravenna knew she'd need to find a way to make up for the accidental interruption. Even though the pair were perfect together, they still seemed to need a nudge.

"Should we go over our Portland plans?" Linn asked as soon as Whitewater's doors closed behind Rick.

"Sounds like a great idea." She couldn't wait to escape for a few days and take a mini vacation to Portland on Coalition's dime.

**

Ravenna tried to enjoy the Portland escape, but she couldn't keep her mind on work. She hadn't counted on the fact that Wade's sister would be constantly checking in with her brother. Yet, Wade still refused to communicate with Ravenna at all.

She kept this fact to herself as Linnea tasted another one of their competitor's craft beers. They'd chosen a popular local taproom with an industrial theme to go over a few ideas for Mosquito Creek's decor. Linnea's gaze swept over the busy taproom. "This place is stunning, but I intend to use all that old lumber mill equipment to give our taproom a historic Northwest spin."

Ravenna nodded, "Great idea. Not only will it save time and money, you'll have an authentic look no one will be able to duplicate." As she took another sip of beer, she watched Linnea, but still couldn't figure out why Wade had avoided all her attempts to communicate. It seemed like dodging her had become a cat-and-mouse game.

Linnea played with a drip running down her glass. "With the way the taproom is coming together, I'm relieved that I don't have to worry about serving food."

"If you at least serve apps, your customers might drink more beer."

Linnea nodded. "True, but Wade doesn't want to compete with Iris. Northside Grill has been key to Mosquito's growth."

Ravenna held her smile in place, fighting her response when Iris' name was mentioned.

"Did I tell you that we've decided to rent the taproom for weddings and gatherings?" Linnea continued, completely unaware of Ravenna's inner battle. "Wade wants to keep the price low to help the community. He's already talked to the fire department about their Holiday Party."

"I like it. Events will help you during the rainy months when tourism dries up." With the way they supported the community, Ravenna realized how much she admired this brother and sister team. Her stomach pitched, missing Wade deeply, but she blamed the ache on too much beer and too little food. "I think we've seen plenty. If you're as hungry as I am, maybe we should skip the next taproom and look for a spot that serves more than popcorn and chips."

"I'm starved. Let me check some reviews." Linnea pulled out her phone, chatting as she searched for a place to eat nearby. "I appreciate everything you're doing for Wade. Do you always do this much for every brewer who comes on board with Coalition?"

"I wish I could do so much more. Mosquito's different. Wade's already mastered the things I do for most new brewers." Hesitating for a moment, she wondered if she'd found an ally in Linnea. "I'll be honest, I'm puzzled by many aspects of his partnership with Coalition."

Linnea's gaze slid from her phone. Now that she had her attention, Ravenna took a long breath ready to reveal more. "Coalition usually finds a brewer with one or two great beers and brings that product to a bigger market. Those brewers usually lack experience with scaling up or marketing, but Wade's already an expert in both."

"Wade only needs someone he trusts to share the workload."

"Exactly," Ravenna continued, "and he has family support. His cousin is obviously involved in more than construction. I don't need to see a contract to know Seth's made a large investment in Mosquito Creek."

Linnea bristled. "Well, I don't understand why family support makes a difference to Coalition."

"Usually, it doesn't." Ravenna shifted forward in her seat. "Coalition's used to calling the shots on everything from the design of the labels to the ingredients in the beer. Cost and image. That's the message I typically deliver."

Linn's brows scrunched. "But we're different?"

"Yes. Coalition is giving Wade too much freedom. And what bothers me, is I don't know *why*."

"You have me worried." Linnea nibbled her bottom lip. "By telling me this, are you crossing some sort of line?"

A slight nod dipped Ravenna's chin. "My job often puts me in difficult situations. I'm used to brewers pushing back when we ask them to make adjustments. But I'm always honest, and I'm being honest with you. In Mosquito's case, the execs aren't asking for changes to the label or cutting costs on ingredients. They're seeking information. They're asking me to find out where Wade's money is coming from." Ravenna waited for Linnea to absorb the weight of her concern.

"Does Wade know?"

"Probably not. The problem is, he's avoiding me. As far as I know, your brother hasn't stayed a single night in his tiny house since I moved in next door."

A hiss pushed through Linn's teeth. "Seriously? Damn. I'll talk to him."

"If we work together, I know we can figure this out."

Linnea's shoulders fell. "Will it even make any difference? The Coalition contracts are already in place."

"I don't know if it's too late or not. But Coalition isn't being honest with me. And I refuse to be used by my company. I have my integrity to consider."

"Please, be careful."

Ravenna grinned and shook her head. "Careful? Not my style. I won't be manipulated by Coalition, and I'll be damned if I let them *use me* to manipulate someone else."

***

Wade stepped behind Northside's bar, poured his sister a Coke, and added a slice of lime. Linn tapped her fingernails on the worn wooden surface, impatiently waiting for him to join her on the customer side.

"What happened in Portland?" he asked and looked around. "And where's Ravenna? I'm surprised she's not with you."

His sister's eyes flared. "Ravenna? Why do you care? She told me you've been avoiding her."

His jaw clenched, yet Linn's bold honesty concerned him. "Just tell me what happened in Portland."

She blinked slowly, seeming to gather her thoughts. "Ravenna shared some things with me, at a risk to her own career."

"Damn, this sounds serious."

"It could be, but we can't know for sure. Ravenna's not certain about the details, but I trust her intuition." Wade listened as Linn shared everything she learned and some things she guessed. After hearing it all, Wade agreed, Coalition Craft Corporation couldn't be trusted.

"Do you trust Ravenna?" he asked.

"Yes, but I think Coalition is using *her* to manipulate *you*."

He leaned forward, his brows furrowed. "Why the hell did she come to you instead of me?"

"Come on, Wade. You're avoiding her. And do you *really* want to talk about the reason *why* at *Northside Grill*?"

He glanced around the room, but he didn't see Iris. "How does Ravenna feel about working with me?"

"Does it really matter? You're both adults and need to focus on the brewery expansion. If it helps, her boyfriend, Steven, will be visiting soon."

His lips pressed hard against his teeth. "I'll suck it up if she will."

TWELVE

Two hours of worried discussion accomplished nothing. Trapped with him in the makeshift Mosquito office, Ravenna fought to keep her eyes on business while she watched the enticing brewer pace the floor. He stopped and groaned. "We can look at this from every angle, but until CCC makes a move, we won't know exactly what they're after."

Wade raked his hands through his overlong hair. The movement stretched his thin T-shirt over flexed pecs, and Ravenna forced her eyes to stay locked on his face. "You're right. Unfortunately, it may tip them off if we do anything different," she said.

Looking up from her notes, Linnea giggled. "Wade, why don't you just be your same old stubborn self."

"It's not stubborn if I'm always right," he said with a grin.

Struck by a thought, Ravenna added, "Your sister has a point. If you go along with every request, the execs might not continue to dig."

"I could try to be more of an ass."

"Why not?" Linnea agreed.

Ravenna grinned. "I like this idea. If you push Coalition while I keep looking for clues, they just might reveal their hand."

Wade kneaded the back of his neck. "Ravenna, I don't want you to risk your career. This has already crossed a line for you. In fact, if you want to drop everything and return to Chicago, I'd understand."

The softness in his eyes throttled her heart as he revealed that he actually cared. She couldn't leave him to deal with this on his own. "So long as I do my job and try to help Mosquito succeed, I have nothing to worry about."

When Wade tilted his head and studied her, she squirmed. "Help me succeed?" he said. "You know, right now you remind me of Leo.

But you're a hell of a lot prettier than your dad." He laughed aloud and the infectious sound eased her nerves.

She giggled and blushed, enjoying both compliments. "Thanks ... to both."

His eyes skated over the nearly finished brewery. "Without your father's help, I wouldn't have any of this."

"As difficult as this is, I still envy you." Ravenna's gaze drifted toward the window. "I hated the day Papa sold out to Coalition Craft. Silver Raven was humble, but that brewery was my second home."

Linnea sympathized, "I understand. I may not love the hop farm the way Dad and Brooke do—but knowing it will always be there grounds me."

Ravenna swiped a tear from her cheek and felt safe enough to open up to Linn and Wade. "Papa left brewing to focus everything on Mama's fight with breast cancer. After her long recovery, they bought a rundown collection of fishing cabins on a lake in Southern Oregon. To spend more time with her, he renovated the cabins and built a little restaurant and store."

Wade's gaze settled on her. "I know he doesn't regret what he gave up. Leo told me he's satisfied with his home brewery."

The fact that Wade knew those details surprised her. *Papa must really trust this man.* "My father may not be tempted to reopen Silver Raven, but I still hang on to that dream."

"I never knew what Silver Raven meant to you." Wade glanced at the gleaming new tanks, shining like sentinels.

With a sigh, she added, "Did you know that old brewery looks exactly the same as the day Papa locked the doors?"

"You mean he didn't sell the equipment?"

"No, only his recipes and label shifted to Chicago."

He avoided her eyes, maybe to escape his fear of losing everything to Coalition. "I'm so sorry, Ravenna," he said more to the floor than to her.

"It's okay. We still own the property, and I like knowing it's all there. Maybe I'll turn it into a craft brewing museum someday." She wrapped her arms around her middle. His hands twitched, he took a step forward and stopped. With the way she was feeling, Ravenna would have accepted his hug.

Relief washed over Wade's face when Linnea moved to fold affection around Ravenna. "Thanks, Linn. I guess I needed a hug." She sniffed away unshed tears and enjoyed the warmth.

"Ah, I'm getting in on this." Wade chuckled and wrapped both women in his arms.

A few seconds later, from the center of tangled limbs, Ravenna giggled. "I'm sorry, but you two are smothering me!"

***

Linnea was the first to look at the door. "It's late and I haven't spent enough time with Amanda. If we're finished here, I think I'll go home and maybe catch a movie with my cousin."

Reaching out, Ravenna squeezed Linn's hand. The simple touch conveyed a friendship that Wade never anticipated between these two women. "It's been a long day. See you tomorrow."

Ravenna headed toward her tiny home and Wade followed his sister out, locking Mosquito's makeshift office as they left. "Let me walk you to your car," he said to Linnea, wanting a minute with her alone. At her driver's side door, she turned and smiled, and he realized how lucky he was to have a sister who loved without limits. "What you did probably saved my business," he said. "Ravenna would never have opened up to me on her own."

Linn tilted her head, and he knew she intended to let him off easy. "I don't know, she might have, eventually."

"No. I could have lost everything. Thank you. I love you, Sis."

"Love you, too. Everything will be fine, you'll see." His sister had inherited that glass-half-full attitude from Mom. He knew he suffered the flip-side but was tired of blaming that on Dad.

"See you tomorrow." After squeezing his shoulder, she got in her car, and left him standing in the gravel lot.

Walking alone toward his tiny home, he couldn't recall the last time he'd been inside the small space. He shuttered, imagining the mold that must be growing in the fridge. When he rounded Whitewater's shop, he found his home dark, except for the automatic porch light that lit each evening. Ravenna's home glowed next door, light pouring from every window.

Movement caught his eye, and he stopped to watch the gorgeous woman framed by her kitchen window. Pulsing bass matched the rhythm of her body as she danced through her meal prep. Her dark hair glistened, tied in a sleek knot at the nape of her neck. Every so often, her lips joined the lyrics of her song. With a shake of his head, he tore himself away from her enchanting pull.

After climbing the steps of his home, he swung his door open and found a place that seemed too tidy. Linnea's note on the kitchen counter solved the puzzle. *Elves didn't tackle the whirlwind known as Wade, your little sister did. I tossed and replaced the food that had turned into a disgusting science experiment. Welcome home – love you. Linn.*

He pulled his phone from his pocket and thanked his sister with a quick text, adding that he loved her too.

Opening the cupboards and refrigerator brought a grin to his face. His sister had stocked all his favorites. How had she known he'd be back? The freezer held steaks, ice cream, and a sleeve of pre-made burger patties ready to go on the grill. He pulled out the makings for burgers and got to work.

Stepping outside, he glanced toward Ravenna's tiny home. She sat at her small dining table, turning the pages of her book while nibbling a salad. As she read, her hand drifted up to twirl a loose strand of hair between her fingers. Lovely.

His stomach growled. While the grill heated, he went back inside to clean lettuce and slice sharp cheddar. Each task helped him focus on something other than the beautiful woman who was only a few yards away.

Digging into a cupboard, he found his favorite Jalapeno chips. In a few moments, he stood out on his deck, drink in hand, flipping a burger on the grill.

***

Ravenna tried not to watch when the lights clicked on next door. She tried not to stare as Wade moved around his kitchen. Her eyes didn't want to linger. The man stood under the dim lights on the deck, flipping a burger, drinking a beer, looking delicious in faded jeans that hugged his taut butt.

Trapped in exquisite torture, she re-read the same page of her book. She couldn't recall a single detail until he moved indoors to eat. Focused on the pages, she regretted the steamy romance novel when the vivid fiction assumed the role of a living man.

Next door, her paperback-fantasy moved outside into the cool night air. The porch had a small outdoor heater tucked into a hidden space overhead. When the red glow turned on, Ravenna moaned.

Once he sat, he glanced her way. Drawn by the hypnotic power of that single look, she moved from her seat, shrugged into a jacket, and refilled her wineglass.

***

Wade's pulse accelerated. The sound of her door, hidden from his view, left her movements to his imagination. A moment later, a fairy-like woman appeared in the moonlight. The night felt alive now that she moved through it.

"Mind if I join you?" she asked while her feet climbed the steps. "I love sitting outside at night, but it's too spooky alone this far out of town."

The thought of her here on her own punched Wade with a hit of regret. How could he have abandoned her on this remote property, isolated in the woods on the edge of town? He shook himself from dark irrational thoughts of wild animals surrounding this nymph in the woods.

From her spot in the Adirondack chair, she sighed. "The heat lamp, oh my God, it's so warm. I could get addicted to this."

"Come over anytime." He hoped she'd come often, even though she probably shouldn't. Noting the glass of velvety liquid in her hand, he asked, "Is that your family's wine?

"Yes, it's the last of it. I'll have to make a Portland run to find more." She took a sip. "Mmm, it reminds me of my grandparent's place in California."

She passed the glass without asking if he would like a taste. Their fingers met and Wade wanted to touch her everywhere. He settled for placing his mouth on the edge of the glass—the spot left wet by her lush lips.

***

Ravenna watched when he closed his eyes and when the wine hit his tongue. He seemed to use all his senses to enjoy the experience.

"Delicious."

The low rumble of his words vibrated her entire body. She fantasized that it was his sexy, *I'm taking you again,* voice. When his eyes shut, his long lashes lay over his tanned cheeks, giving Ravenna a moment to study the way his throat moved slowly as he drank the wine. She inhaled a long slow breath to keep from sighing.

Beneath the fabric of his T-shirt, his pecs rose with each breath. She slid her gaze south to glance at the taught stretch of his jeans over the apex of his thighs. Good Lord, she knew she shouldn't let her eyes linger, but temptation won out.

He took another sip before returning the glass to her slim fingers. Wade noticed as she shamelessly enjoyed the view. Their eyes linked, her face heated, and Wade's smile took on a sinful slant. A long moment passed before he asked, "How did your dad make the move from vintner to brewer?" His voice washed over her, as mellow as the wine.

Ravenna gazed, unfocused, into the dark night. "Ah, that would be the story of how my parents met. If you give Papa a few drinks, he will spin the tale in rich detail. I'll give you the high points, but next time you see him, bring it up. He loves to re-live the moment in the telling."

"I'd like to see Leo again."

"You will. Papa's planning a visit." When a happy tear trailed down her cheek, Wade reached over and stroked her hand. She tilted her head, pleased that she didn't have to hide her potent love for her family around Wade.

"My grandparents on my mom's side owned a small vineyard in the Willamette Valley, not large or terribly successful, but the climate was terrific, and the grapes perfection."

"Papa came up the coast from California. Our family had sent him on a scouting trip for future grape purchases. He stumbled across my grandparents' place. My mom gave him a tour of the winery, vineyard, and as fate would have it, the hop yard."

"Oh, this is good. And I'm sure Leo loves to tell the tale—"

"With his own special flourish," she said while embellishing the air with a magician's sleight of hand.

His chuckle seemed to respond to her spell. "Did Leo ever go back to California?"

"Not until my mother went with him to visit his family, with her sister along as chaperone."

"From the time they met, until they were married, how long?"

"Only ninety days."

Wade's whistle made her laugh. "Oh, Leo had it bad."

"So did my mama. They'd be lost without each other."

***

With a mouth stained burgundy by her rich, red wine, Ravenna took another sip. The taste of that vintage still lingered on his tongue, and Wade longed to deepen that flavor by licking it off her tempting lips. Wade took a relaxed breath, settled into his chair, and cleansed his mind with a sip of whiskey. The liquor scorched away the remnants of the wine with a satisfying burn.

"Not drinking beer?" she asked noting the preference.

"I've been trying to find the perfect whiskey to barrel-age a winter stout."

"Oh, that sounds like enjoyable research."

"It is. Who knows, I may try my hand at distilling someday."

She stretched her arm toward him to request a sample, looking relaxed, flushed and deliciously warm. Wade didn't know if her glow came from the overhead lamp, the wine, or his presence. He just enjoyed the beauty as he placed the heavy whiskey glass in her grasp. Delicate fingers took the weight and he wondered how those fingers would feel wrapped around his cock. Eyes shut for a moment, he let the vivid fantasy expand.

Pulling the whiskey tentatively to her lips, she inhaled the scent before taking it into her mouth. She sipped slowly, giving the gold liquid time to linger on her tongue. A sharp gasp, cough, and an embarrassed smile followed her swallow. Her eyes watered as she passed the drink back into his hand.

"I guess I'm not as tough as I thought." Amusement danced between them as he took another taste from the spot just touched by Ravenna's lips.

They sat in comfortable silence as cold filtered around them. Even the red coils of the lamp could not keep the crisp evening air at bay. Ravenna pulled her arms around her body and said, "This chill has won out."

She stood before he could offer a blanket, but he knew that was for the best.

"I think I'll snuggle in for the night," she said as she took a step toward the top of the stairs.

"Good night, Ravenna. And thank you for today, for everything." He was suddenly aware of the high risks Ravenna was willing to take. In addition to his thanks she deserved an apology. "I'm sorry—" he began.

Hand in the air, she shrugged away his worry. "It's okay. If the circumstances were reversed, I'm sure you'd make a similar choice for me." A shiver shook her body and Ravenna took the stairs quickly, as if the cold were chasing her home. Before disappearing, she peeked over her shoulder and called, "Welcome back to the neighborhood."

He stayed on the porch and tracked her movements as she shut the curtains and turned off the lights. Her home was dark, yet he remained under the glow of the lamp wondering if he was really capable of taking a similar risk.

Ravenna put his future ahead of her own, at a cost she could not possibly determine. And she did this for a man who had shown her little respect. No, they were not similar. His choices were selfish, yet this beautiful woman defined integrity and strength.

Thinking on this, Wade flicked off the heat lamp and retreated to his home. The quiet seemed too loud, and his guitar beckoned to fill the silence. He grabbed the neck and rescued the instrument from its spot in the corner. Pulling out new strings, he spent the next half hour restringing the most recent addition to his guitar collection.

The Taylor resonated with rich tones, even as he adjusted the tuning. Its neck fit smooth and warm against his palm. He fumbled with a few bar chords before his fingers recalled the quick changes with muscle memory. Smiling, he flew through some freeing riffs.

Without effort, he discovered a song waiting to leap from the guitar. A simple melody followed, then the first fumbling attempts at lyrics. By two in the morning, he'd wrung his creativity dry. Wade stood, satisfied, and leaned the guitar back in its place in the far corner of his temporary home.

THIRTEEN

We could use another keg of Sweet Venom. Iris's text tipped Wade's smile. At Northside Grill, his favorite test market, the new summer wheat he'd been working on at Old Mosquito was moving at a record pace. Friends and neighbors doled out honest opinions—this new summer beer was fantastic. The blackberry flavor was subtle and clean, and the lower alcohol content gave thirsty drinkers more to love.

When he placed a call to Iris, she didn't pick up. Instead of sending a text, he climbed into his truck—loaded with two kegs—and opted to help with the lunch rush.

Arriving at Northside, he brought the kegs of Sweet Venom to the walk-in fridge. The air outside had warmed enough that the chill of the cooler felt good. Iris found him before he left the large refrigerator and snaked her arms under his shirt. He enjoyed the contrast of the cold room to her warm skin.

She buried her face in his shirt and inhaled. "You smell delicious."

"It's the scent of the cedar being installed on-site," he whispered against her neck. His index finger tipped her chin and he turned her face to his and snagged a kiss.

Since returning from Yakima, he'd spent a couple of nights each week at her house. The bit of separation seemed right. Iris was cautious and preferred this slower pace.

"How are plans coming along for your trip to California?" she asked on a shiver.

"Linn has it handled. Are we still on for this weekend?"

"Mm-hm. I can't wait to see Old Mosquito, that mysterious place off the grid." She shivered again, and Wade dragged her out of the privacy they'd found in the walk-in cooler.

He chuckled and tucked her against his side. "Hey. I lived up there for years. It's not that remote. I have power and water, you know."

"And a backup generator that could run a small city."

"That's true. But with generators, size matters," he said with an almost straight face. Iris playfully attempted to push him away, but he held her that much tighter.

***

When Wade bailed early for the weekend, Ravenna found herself moping around the brewery, alone again. She hollered at the empty room, "Enough brooding! I need to go out." After looking through her closet, she chose a cheerful spring dress and left to join most of the town at the farmers' market.

Pulling into the overflow lot, Ravenna spotted bright banners beckoning her to organic gardeners, bakers, and artisans selling a stunning array of local goods. Cool morning air filled her lungs, yet the clear day promised to warm by noon. Spotting a few people she recognized from local shops, she returned their smiles when they nodded hello.

A familiar cinnamon scent pulled her to the baked goods hidden beneath a vintage glass case. She recognized the baker she visited twice each week to buy her decadent apple fritters. "Hey, Maggie, how are you?"

"I'm great, and I'm so glad you found us. What do you think of opening day?" Maggie asked.

"I love it. It feels like home." Ravenna hissed a breath to deal with her watery smile and realized she still hadn't got her bout of self-pity under control. Sugar might fix that.

Maggie's eyes softened. "Are you homesick? Where are you from?" she asked.

"I grew up near Klamath Falls in southern Oregon."

"Ah, so our small-town charm appeals to you."

"It does." With a nod, Ravenna salivated at the goodies in the case. "I love your fritters, but I'm in the mood for something different. Any suggestions?"

"The apricot-oatmeal bar is terrific. I had one for breakfast. If you want something more decadent, the double-chocolate cookie will start an addiction."

"One of each. And my next stop will be the coffee cart." Ravenna was digging into her bag when a familiar voice behind her asked the baker to put the order on her tab.

Ravenna grinned on a quick turn. "Natalie, so good to see you. Since you got the treats, I'll buy the coffee, and we can split these if you like."

"Perfect." They wandered to the coffee cart, ordered, then grabbed a table to talk. "What do you think of our market?" Natalie asked as they sat.

"I love it. It's a cure for homesickness," she said as she split the double chocolate in two.

"When I first moved to Ashwood, Maggie had to bake extra batches of these addictive things," Natalie said before she took a bite of the gooey chocolate cookie.

"I can understand why. It's decadent." Ravenna licked her fingers, savoring the taste.

"I'm glad I ran into you. Seth and I are having a get-together at our place next Friday. Will you come?"

"I'd love to. Text me your address and let me know later what I can bring."

As they ate, their conversation drifted to Natalie's wedding plans until Seth wandered over to nuzzle his fiancée's neck. "Hey, sweetness," he murmured against her nape.

Natalie leaned into his hip. "Want to sit for a bit?"

"I'm grabbing a coffee," he said, "and then I'm back to the tiny house."

"You brought a home here?" Ravenna asked.

Seth nodded. "We did. This tradition started last fall when we finished Natalie's home and she brought it here during a test drive."

"It always draws a crowd," Natalie added.

She gazed up at Seth, as he picked up the thought, "Now, when my crew and I finish a home, we always bring it over. The community stops for a tour and my sister Amanda takes pictures—"

"And she hands them off to me for the website." As Natalie finished Ravenna smiled, enjoying the easy way the pair finished each other's thoughts.

Seth unfolded from his chair. "Gotta head back, sweetness. Love you," he said while stealing a thorough kiss from Natalie that forced Ravenna to look away. A funny sensation pressed against her ribs when she realized her boyfriend Steven never kissed her like *that*.

"I'll be over in a few," Natalie said and watched him go, a little dazed.

Ravenna waited for her new friend to recover. "The two of you ... it's rare."

"Oh, I know. And to think I was foolish enough to nearly leave this town and Seth behind." She shivered away the thought.

"If you hadn't returned, he would have hunted you down. That man loves you."

"Thank God. But part of me wishes we could just skip the wedding planning and get to the happily-ever-after part." Natalie rolled her eyes. "The decorations, dresses, flowers—It's not my thing."

"Do you need help? I've been a bridesmaid in more weddings than I can count. I come from a big Catholic family," she explained.

Natalie leaned in, speaking a bit softer. "I shouldn't complain, but Kelsey, my maid of honor, is busier by the minute with her new business. This wedding stuff is new territory for me, and my mom lives in Arizona. I'll admit, I'm a little lost."

Ravenna grabbed Natalie's hand and wouldn't let go until she got the answer she wanted. "Let me help, please. I'd love a distraction from the brewery."

"All right, but you may regret it!" Natalie showed Ravenna the pictures she'd pinned, and they added a few more. Once they'd marked their calendars with another time to meet, Natalie begged her to follow her over and check out the new, tiny house.

"After I've had a chance to look around."

Ravenna wandered each row of stalls and bought a hand-woven basket, filling it with art and potted herbs to make her temporary place feel a bit more like home.

***

The guests at Seth and Natalie's party had already parked two rows deep. Ravenna's nerves kicked up a notch when she spotted Wade's truck. Kent and Amanda pulled in as she walked to the door. A bit jumpy, she waited for them before going inside. In one hand, she balanced a pasta salad made with Grandmother Silvestre's secret Italian dressing. Across her other shoulder, a canvas bag held two bottles of wine from her family vintner. Kent reached for the large bowl, and Amanda held the door as the three walked into the massive home that overlooked Osprey Lake.

Scanning the crowd, Ravenna pasted on a welcoming smile. Most people she recognized, several she knew well, but only a few would consider her their friend. Natalie's personal touches appeared everywhere—cozy blankets folded on leather furniture and sunflower canisters along the kitchen counter. Outdoors, huge pots of flowers overflowed with pink, yellow, and purple blooms. Most of the men huddled near two grills which were set out on an expansive deck, overlooking a sparkling lake in the valley below.

When Natalie spotted Ravenna from across the room, she rushed to her and took her arm. The long-time residents warmed to Ravenna once Linnea and Rick pulled her into their circle. Wade smiled and tipped his head, but kept his distance, his arm at Iris's waist.

Loneliness pitted her stomach, until Ravenna joined Natalie in the kitchen. She brought out the wine she'd brought, opened one of the bottles, and shared it with Linnea, Kelsey, and Natalie. From the very first sip they all vowed to find more in Portland. As she sipped the rich, red liquid, Ravenna noted Wade's movements. When their eyes locked, he didn't smile, and he never left Iris's side.

***

Wade found his cousin on the deck. "Great party, do you need me to take a turn at the grill?"

Seth shook his head and flipped another burger. "Nah, Erik beat you to it. He's grabbing more patties before taking over."

"Let me know," Wade said, then plunged his hand into the cooler for another bottle of beer. After he passed one to Iris, they moved to the railing to take in the stunning view. Across the deck, he spotted Linnea chatting with Ravenna. She glanced his way and smiled.

"Who's the woman with Linn?" Iris asked as she balanced her bottle on the rail. Her eyes came to his and stuck. "She seems to know you."

Wade spun, putting his back toward Ravenna, shielding the two women from one another. Sweat trickled down his spine. "She works for Coalition overseeing the expansion."

Iris's eyes went wide. "Oh, so that's Ravenna. Why haven't you brought her by Northside?" A simple question, he knew, but he struggled to find an answer. Her brows lifted while waiting for Wade to come up with something. He swallowed hard and shoved his hands in his pockets. "Work is work. And well, you're not."

Iris studied him and her smile thinned. "Okay," she said with a nod

Seth spun toward him and asked, "Wade, can you do me a favor and refill the coolers?" The request could not have come at a better time.

Wade spent the rest of the night convincing himself that Iris was perfect—a woman he could eventually learn to love. Yet everything about Ravenna drew him in. With each minute that passed, guilt for action he never intended to take burrowed under his skin.

FOURTEEN

When Steven's flight touched the tarmac, Ravenna used his arrival to halt her ridiculous obsession with Wade. She was tempted to rush and find him, but as always, he insisted she wait in her car. The efficiency irritated her. Romantic reunions at the gate were gone, but she longed for something wonderful. Just once, she wanted to be caught in a public *I missed you so much* embrace at the airport.

Steven didn't agree. Ravenna bent his rules and waited outside her Jeep at the curb. After receiving his text, she paced the sidewalk, expecting to see him pop through the doors at any moment.

In crisp pants and wearing a light lamb's wool sweater, Steven stood out against the rough-edged bearded men populating the Northwest. His sleek shoes were ill-prepared to take on the terrain waiting for him in Ashwood.

Ravenna approached as he searched for her with a hawk-like gaze. The bright smile on her face went unnoticed, but this wasn't unusual. She was so petite that her small frame was easy to miss in a sea of tall people.

He finally spotted Ravenna outside on the curb. His dark brows wrinkled into a frown. She'd broken her promise to stay behind the wheel and wait.

"Steven!" She leaped into his arms, shocking him with a swift kiss. He accepted her with a brief one-armed hug, yet his grip stayed on his rolling suitcase.

"Let me get rid of this," he said as he tossed his small bag into the back and took the keys from her hand. "I'll drive."

Once both hands were free, Steven delivered the kiss she'd waited for, a complete study of her lips that softened her knees and warmed her center. A slight grin tipped the corners of his mouth when she sighed. Escorting her to the passenger side of her Jeep, he held open the door and waited for her to climb in and buckle. A quick nod showed his approval.

Behind the wheel, he took charge of the space. He adjusted the mirrors and found suitable music on his playlist before he pulled from the curb. She was capable of accomplishing all these things herself, but control suited him, and she enjoyed giving him the reigns. He always took care of everything when they were in the same zip code, which seemed to be happening less frequently.

"I've made dinner reservations and booked a room for tonight," he said.

She smiled at his first lavish surprise. "I wish you would have told me; I would have packed a suitcase with something special inside."

"Don't worry. I've chosen a full-service resort. The shops will have everything you need," he said without apology. "After we check in, we'll have time to explore the property or soak in the spring-fed hot tub in our room."

As he laid out his lavish plans, she relaxed. "Thank you, Steven, everything sounds perfect."

***

The imposing lobby, of black iron, cedar, and glass, took her breath away. While he checked in, Steven asked her to buy what she needed and to charge it to the room. Ravenna lost herself in the posh shops near the lobby. The simple black bikini she bought would only be necessary if they visited the pool. Along with a few basics, she chose a burgundy silk shift dress to wear to dinner and delicate lingerie.

Dinner was perfection. The lodge featured a mix of seafood, wild game, and organic Northwest cuisine. The meal progressed slowly from a crab appetizer to a creamy chocolate dessert. As they caught up on the details of their lives, she remembered why their relationship worked. Steven's intensity was consistent and passionate. He was an exciting man to be with, in and out of bed.

After dinner, champagne and strawberries waited for them in their room. On the private deck, dim lights illuminated an exquisite hot tub that overlooked a river bordered by dark evergreen trees.

Steven waited for her in the hot tub, sipping a glass of champagne. He held her hand to guide her into the bubbling water. "You must have bought that bikini downstairs. It looks beautiful. I can't wait to peel it off," he said, his eyes molten with desire.

"Oh, that's hot." Her breath hissed as she sank into the liquid heat.

"It's about to get so much hotter." Steven perused her slim body, his lips tilting up at the corners, pleased with the view. Ravenna trembled, anticipating his next move. He poured her a glass of champagne and placed it close by, then reached for a strawberry and held it while she took a bite.

When the juicy red fruit stained her lips Steven tilted toward her and licked away the sweet taste with the tip of his tongue. Patient as always, he reclined to his elbows and watched her nipples pearl against her wet bikini. "I bet you're already throbbing and ready for me," he said on a low growl.

Steven's hand wrapped around her neck and caught the thin string that held her bikini in place. He gave it a slow tug. Two triangles of fabric fell away from her breasts. Her dusky nipples ached as the cool night air circulated around them. She longed to sink into the water, but his gaze held her in place.

Gliding his fingers from her neck to her nipples, she tingled under his touch. She glanced down to savor the erotic view of his tanned skin caressing her pale flesh. Leaning forward, his other hand hooked around her body and snagged the other string to remove the top. He lifted the fabric and arranged it next to the bowl of strawberries.

In the same movement, Steven selected another berry, bit off half and used the juicy flesh of the fruit to tease her nipples with wet sticky strokes. He lapped up the sweet temptation. Each lash pulled a purr from Ravenna. Her small hands trembled as she reached to skim her fingers over the hard planes of his chest.

Steven cupped her ass, sending water sloshing when he pulled her to his lap, her slim thighs straddling his torso. She tilted her head back in an open invitation to nip, bite, and suck the graceful line of her neck.

He moved with purpose, traced his hands over her hips, and released the string-ties of the bikini bottoms. As with the top, he gathered the scrap of fabric and placed it on the edge of the hot tub then plucked another berry from the bowl.

"Stand up, baby. I need to taste you," he commanded.

Ravenna slid from the warmth of the water into the cool night air. A shiver hit her body, but the warm steam curling from the water soothed the chill. Again, Steven took a bite from the tip of the strawberry. With the exposed slick fruit, he drew the pulp across her bare skin.

His eyes glowed with feral desire as he teased every inch of her sex with the flesh of the ripe fruit. Possessed by potent need, Steven pressed his mouth against her wet juncture, tasting a mixture of strawberry and sweet arousal.

"You're perfection," he growled and explored the wet contours with his lips and tongue. As she pulsed forward for more, he stroked the collection of nerves at the apex of her sex. His fingers explored her body, diving inside as she bucked. Deprived for so long, she exploded into an all-consuming climax. Waves of ebbing pleasure weakened her body, leaving her breathing in ragged gasps, clinging to the edge of the hot tub.

"That was beautiful. I'm taking you in bed," he said as he stood in the water. His erection jutted forward, dripping with wet heat and his impending release.

Steven eased her back onto the smooth sheets, tracing the drips of water rolling off her body with his tongue. Ravenna stroked his chest, gliding manicured nails over his contours. Using the tip of his cock, he teased her wet folds, dipping in a fraction as she gasped. The fire in his eyes matched his craving.

"I want your mouth," he growled. She rolled to the floor, landing on her knees. He moved forward and fisted her hair in one hand while guiding his cock to her lips. She mapped the contours with her tongue, taking his girth as far as her throat would allow. Her fingers trembled when she cupped his tightening balls. Steven stroked the base of his length in cadence with the movements of her stretched lips.

"Fuck, that's intense. Swallow it baby, I need to go a little deeper." He firmed his hand across the back of her neck. "Right there. That's it."

His pace picked up. Her mind released, and he stole the last remaining thread of control. Heat hit the back of her throat as Steven exploded. Her name left his lips with a satisfied growl that had Ravenna squeezing her thighs, seeking a small measure of satisfaction. Scooping her up, he placed her back on the bed. Steven only left her alone for a moment to find the champagne. He poured her a tall glass to wash his taste from her mouth.

She curled next to him but couldn't sleep. Even the sound of the wind in the trees didn't soothe her.

When Ravenna woke the next morning, it took a moment to remember where she was. The sound of the shower, the view of tall evergreens, and the Egyptian cotton sheets helped to reorient her memory.

Steven came out of the bathroom wrapped in a towel. A few seconds later, he answered a knock on the door. He had ordered her favorite breakfast, eggs benedict. He sipped black coffee, checked his email on his phone, and glanced her way to watch her eat. She envied how powerful he looked in the morning. Self-assured. Arrogant. As if he knew his day would proceed according to his plan because he willed it so.

***

Steven gripped the wheel and groaned, watching the odometer as another mile ticked by on the winding highway. "Shit, what was Wade Michaels thinking when he chose this location? Ashwood will cut into our profits with the added transportation costs alone."

"I wondered the same thing when I first arrived." Ravenna nodded and dug for a little more information. "Do you have any idea why Coalition agreed to this location?"

With his eyes locked on the horizon, his irritated words slipped. "Even you must have figured out our agreement with Wade has a different focus. This brewer came up with capital from unexpected sources. Unfortunately, Coalition now has less leverage." Brows furrowed, he shot a warning glance her way.

She absorbed the insult with a smile and said, "I understand."

Rounding another tight turn, he hissed, "Who the fuck even bothers to drive up here?"

She bristled, defending Wade. "The town draws hikers and climbers year-round, and Whitewater rafting pulls in more tourists every year."

He drew in a slow breath, seeming to consider all angles. "Any hotels or resorts?"

"No, but there are a few places with quaint rustic cabins. Ashwood is so popular they're book solid for the summer. That's the reason I'm staying in a tiny house."

Apparently losing interest, Steven shook his head and shrugged. "Well, I do look forward to seeing where my girl has been spending her nights."

Usually, his attention warmed her. But his uncanny ability to switch from business to pleasure left her feeling cold.

FIFTEEN

Wade arrived at the brewery early to check on batches in the tanks. Once he was finished, he paced the hollow taproom alone. It was yet to open, but the brewery ran at full capacity keeping up with demand for his Double Deet IPA. The lofty goals fixed by Coalition left little room for error.

Now that he and Erik were using the facility at Old Mosquito to produce his wildly popular Sweet Venom, the risk amplified. His summer wheat was selling *that* fast.

Linnea arrived later with Amanda. Wade noted the sunburn on his sister's nose and knew she'd gone on another weekend hike with Rick. After talking to his sister, he ducked his head into the office next door. "Hey, Amanda, have you seen Ravenna this morning?" He'd searched the brewery and found no sign of the petite woman.

"No, but I know she picked her boyfriend up at the airport this weekend. Maybe they're still in her house." Her sly smile and lifted brow grated his nerves. The thought of Ravenna trapped with Steven rattled him, but he smothered the jealousy. He had zero claim and he reminded himself of that fact several times a day.

"Thanks, Amanda. I guess she's bound to show, eventually." His rushed steps didn't escape Amanda quite fast enough.

"Maybe. But I saw pictures of Steven. They might hide in her house for days." His cousin whistled as Wade turned away, hiding a grimace.

When he'd first met Steven the previous fall, Wade thought the man was a certified ass. His position in Coalitions finance department meant that all new potential brewers had to get past the arrogant man. What Ravenna saw in Steven he'd never understand. The association alone gave him a reason to question her judgment.

Giving up the search, he escaped to the quiet corridor that took him behind his brewery. Outside, Wade leaned against the ancient wood siding and struggled to breathe. Body bent in half, he gripped his thighs and tried to cleanse Ravenna from his mind. Each day Iris revealed more of herself. He admired everything about her—she was smart, sexy, and brave. Yet, he wondered if there would *always* be something missing between them. And sleeping with Iris while he had another woman on his mind was ripping him apart. Maybe once this project was over, and Ravenna left, he'd be free.

Familiar laughter pulled him from his thoughts and drew him inside. Wade watched from a distance as Ravenna introduced his sister to her boyfriend. Steven's slicked back hair and crisp clothes pissed him off. He'd love nothing more than to bruise his clean-shaven jaw with his fist.

Ravenna turned first, attuned to Wade's presence. Their eyes locked and she blushed. The heat of her gaze tightened his jeans. He should have spun away, but her smile ensnared him, and in a moment, he found himself standing in the office.

Steven attempted to seize control. "Wade, there you are. Why don't you tell me how the brewery is coming along? I've looked forward to your personal update."

Wade grinned, leaned against the doorframe, and hooked a thumb in his pocket. His laid-back attitude had always pissed this guy off. He enjoyed the sneer that stretched over Steven's face, knowing he had the power to put it there. "Before coffee? Relax, you just got here."

"I hope you're not unprepared. You should always be ready for the unexpected."

"Nah. I've never been one to hurry the good things. I'll give you time to settle before showing you Mosquito." He dismissed Steven with an easy one-shoulder shrug.

The executive cleared his throat, preparing to make a demand. Wade turned his back to the intruder and faced his sister. "I have shit to do and will be back later. Call if anything *important* comes up." Ignoring the pretentious prick, Wade walked out.

"No problem, see you later." Linnea's overly sunny tone chimed from behind him. His sister knew to give him space. On those rare occasions when his anger erupted, his family preferred to be far from the target.

Lacking good judgment, Steven followed him out of the office and into the brewery, his expensive leather shoes clicking across the hardwood floor. "Leave if you like, but I'm taking a look around *now*. I don't need a road map to figure out if this brewery is ready to run."

"Be my guest." Wade's arm painted a wide arc in the air as he kept moving. Before leaving, he added a loud final shot, laced with jealousy, for all to hear. "Ravenna, why don't you keep an eye on him? I'm guessing you know how to handle Steven."

Wade accelerated the pace of his steps. Anger sizzling, he had to get away from Ravenna before his fury brought her any more pain.

Her calm voice echoed in the brewery. "I know my way around and would be happy to answer any of Steven's questions."

A backward glance discovered Ravenna's small hand hooked on the bastard's arm. Steven grinned, watching Wade's reaction as he bent to kiss her temple. Seeing the move as a clear challenge, Wade gritted his teeth. He knew Steven was only using Ravenna. And it was obvious—the prick didn't give two shits about Mosquito Creek Brewing.

**

Sweet Venom's orders increased. Wade kept his most experienced crew cranking out the summer beer at Old Mosquito. At the same time, he worked in the Ashwood location, trying to complete the task of two men. He outlasted Linnea when she gave up long after dark and went home. Exhausted but wired, he was more than ready to spend the evening in Iris's arms.

Parking next to her green VW, he entered through the kitchen. Most of the after-dinner crowd had gone home, but a few younger guys remained at the pool tables. He found her behind the bar, and she welcomed him with a smile. Rising onto her tiptoes, she planted a kiss on his lips. "Long day?"

"Very. The festival season is about to launch. My time will be stretched to new limits." He begged for her patience and apologized for the neglect that was coming.

"Hey, I get it. Summer is busier for me, too. There's always more tourists, and the locals want more beer, thank God."

"Have you still been slower than usual?"

"Yeah. I took a hit when that new pizza place had their grand opening. My regulars are back, but I think I figured out the other problem." Her brows lifted.

"Do you want to sit? I'd like to help or listen, whatever you need." Wade knew this problem had plagued her for weeks.

"Yeah. Let me wrap this guy's tab and I'll join you. Pick a table away from the customers."

"No problem." He poured a Sweet Venom for himself and made the hot tea she preferred.

She took the seat across from his, "Tea, thank you, you read my mind." A happy hum resonated from her body and her stress eased a bit as she sipped.

Toying with the rim of the cup, she leaned in. "Last week I was running low on produce, and the delivery was still a few days off—so, I decided to run down by the river, and stopped by the outlet to pick up a few supplies."

"Okay, and ...?"

"Well, while I was there, I stopped at Rolling Columbia Grill."

He nodded. "Yup. To check out the competition. I do that too."

"I noticed that several of my regulars were there. I sat at the bar so I wouldn't run into them in the dining room."

"Wow, isn't that sort of strange? That seems too far to go for a meal similar to what you serve at Northside."

"My thoughts exactly. After I left, I sat in my car to think. Those same customers walked out the front door and went right across the street."

"Where?"

Iris whispered, "The pot shop." His eyes shot wide and they shared a little smile. "Now, I don't have *any* problem with that. Hey, it's the new economy. However, if the city council insists on keeping the marijuana industry out of town, we'll all feel it. You, me, the grocery store. Everyone."

He nodded. "You're right. If the locals drive out of town to buy their quarter-ounce, they'll finish their shopping out of town too."

"Exactly. And once they run all their errands, they'll go straight home to *chill out*."

Wade leaned back in his chair and nodded. It made perfect sense. "Are you sure?"

"Yeah, it felt sneaky, but I hung out for a while and saw more than a few people from Ashwood visit the shop. If our locals want to buy pot, we should have that business here, not send them to the next town to get it."

"I wish I could jump right in and help you with this, but I'm not on the town council. They don't bring in new members 'til the next election in November."

"That's okay. I'm not ready to tackle this, not yet. But soon, I may need your help, if you're willing."

"Absolutely. I'll run this by Seth, but he may have a different take on things. With all the equipment they run, he has a no drug policy at Whitewater."

She nodded and took another sip of her tea. He finished his beer in silence, thinking on what Iris had found. It just made sense. His business could suffer if everyone left town to buy weed. He didn't need this complication. Not now. And definitely not with Steven breathing down his neck.

***

Ravenna spotted her brewer the moment he walked into Northside Grill. Her stomach clenched when he didn't notice her at all. As he met Iris with a kiss, her breath caught in her throat, yet a wave of relief washed over her when he sat with his back facing her. Steven finished checking his emails, and she tried her best to hold his attention. The last thing she needed was another pissing contest between these men. Her boyfriend, dangerous when challenged, used money as a weapon. If pushed, Steven could make Wade's life miserable.

Steven glanced up. "I've found another festival perfectly positioned for you to scout with that asshole, Wade."

She hid her flinch and asked, "Where is that?"

"Yakima."

"Are you sure? His hometown market is already locked in."

"Yes, but it would give *you* an opportunity to meet the family. With you there, Wade will want to show off his impressive hop farm. Wouldn't you like to know a bit more about that part of the business?"

Her brows furrowed. "Steven, my grandparents grew hops. They may not have been as successful as the Michaels, but I'm pretty comfortable with my knowledge of the industry."

"All the more reason to encourage the visit. You speak their language." Steven's steely gaze meant that he would not relent.

An agreeable smile pressed across her lips. "When is this event?"

"Not until August, at the beginning of hop harvest."

"Well that's perfect. Wade already has that event on his calendar."

The moment he heard her words, a flare of excitement flashed in his eyes. Noting this reaction, she pushed for a little more. "Maybe I could lend a hand on the Michaels' family farm? What do you think, Steven? I'm sure everyone helps during harvest. His family does own one of the largest hop yards in Washington."

"Actually, in the world," Steven muttered, correcting her apparent oversight. His keen interest practically electrified the air, but she knew Coalition had never had any interest in the hop industry.

She needled him a bit more. "That's a few months away. I just assumed I wouldn't be around. Won't my job with Mosquito Creek Brewing be done by August?"

Steven shook his head. "You need to stay in Ashwood through October."

"Are you sure? This team's handling the expansion beautifully."

"If Coalition needs you here, then this is where you will be."

Her jaw dropped, but she didn't answer. And the expression on his face kept her silent.

"I hope you've finished eating," Steven said and stood. He pulled a stack of cash from his pocket and extracted more than enough to cover the tab from his money clip. "Come on, we've already spent too much time in this shithole bar."

By taking his hand, Ravenna was able to get him out the door without Wade or Steven seeing each other at all.

***

Her seat across from Wade put Iris in a prime location to study the tension swirling between the beautiful couple from Chicago. As soon as their argument resolved, the dark-haired guy stood and tossed a stack of cash on the table, then Ravenna directed her boyfriend out the door.

After they were gone, Iris gazed at the rugged man across from her as he talked. She enjoyed having Wade in her life *and* in her bed.

But if Ravenna stayed in town too long, Iris doubted she would have the power to keep him there.

SIXTEEN

All week, Wade looked forward to the season's first brewing festival, to getting on the road, to put miles between himself and one of the biggest assholes he'd ever tolerated. Just when he thought he could breathe, Steven invited himself along.

Wade took joy from one measly reward—the cultured turd was too refined to stay on-site with the crew. Instead, Steven had booked a room at a nearby bed and breakfast, an opulent place with white down comforters, vases filled with flowers, and breakfasts served with cups of watery tea.

With Ravenna haunting his thoughts, Wade led the convoy to Sacramento. Seeing his small fleet behind him on the road put his head in the game. He was anxious to see what the wider public thought of Sweet Venom, his new summer beer. Even if it pit him against the other brands in the Coalition stable, he'd take the heat. A little competition didn't matter if the beer was good.

Opening day progressed from beginning to end with flawless ease. The smell of hops, fried food, and sunscreen dissipated as the last fan polished off their final beer. Even though he was exhausted, Wade whistled a tune while he cleaned the taps, still feeling the buzz of the Friday night kickoff. Sweet Venom had created a stir. Competitors from across the festival had rushed to his tent to take a taste before his supply ran out. His only worry was whether he brought enough kegs of the blackberry summer wheat to last the second day.

"Why don't we call it a night?" Wade said to his head brewer, Erik.

"Hey, honey, you about done?" Erik asked Trish, who was busy yanking open another box of T-shirts.

She glanced from her task. "Wade, don't worry about us. I'm almost done restocking the last of the merch." Once she finished,

Wade knew the couple would head to their getaway in the back of their trailer. The pair was comfortable with the cramped sleeping quarters—it was part of the festival routine.

"Gotcha, I'll see you in the morning." Wade wandered away with a wave, looking for old friends among familiar faces. He didn't get far before Ravenna and Steven caught up with him.

"I need to have a word," Steven insisted, and the beautiful woman tucked next to his side cringed. Seeing this, Wade rolled his shoulders to deal with a man who set his teeth on edge.

Steven's gaze tracked beyond Wade's shoulder where the Mosquito Creek banner snapped in the breeze. He hitched his chin and said, "Looks like Sweet Venom found a few fans. I know you must be proud of your achievement, but we need to temper your success. Coalition doesn't want the established brands to be outshined by your new beer."

"Is that so?" Wade's flat expression masked his anger.

Steven's stare targeted Wade like a laser. "We brought you on as our IPA guy, and you need to push Double Deet. Coalition can't have our brewers competing for the same market share."

Ravenna stepped from under Stevens arm, shock clear on her face. "Why haven't I heard anything about this?"

"Darling, you know Mosquito's *unique*. With such a stable following, Wade can afford to take a hit for his fellow brewers."

The chilly response sent a recognizable shiver down Ravenna's spine, and it took her a moment to regain control.

Every cell in Wade's body wanted to separate Ravenna from that snake, but he had to remind himself that she worked for Coalition. Masking his rage, Wade chose his words carefully. "Obviously, I'm going to need this in writing. Until I do, I'll proceed with Sweet Venom as planned."

"Oh, you'll see something in writing soon. And I suggest you read every word carefully. We wouldn't want you to suffer the consequences of violating your contract." Steven spun, gripping Ravenna by the shoulder.

"It's time to go," he said and gave her a tug. When Ravenna's feet planted, Steven's hand tightened on her shoulder drawing his woman to his side. "We're leaving. Now."

Ravenna nodded and whispered, "Fine."

Wade knew she was being used against him, but until she detached herself from that bastard, there was not a damn thing he could do. His lips formed the word, "Ravenna," but his voice remained silent.

Seeing his concern, her eyes widened, begging him to stop. Wade waited, hoping for a sign. She gave him a small smile, and he stood powerless watching her leave with the man's rigid arm propelling her steps.

They disappeared into the night, and Wade couldn't speak. After pacing the vacant festival grounds for an hour, he finally calmed down enough to make a call. "Seth, I need a favor."

"Anything."

"I've hit a snag in Sacramento. Natalie's lawyer, the woman in Seattle, could you set up a meeting?" Wade figured his best option was finding a way out of this suffocating contract. At least then Ravenna couldn't be used against him like a fucking pawn.

"You bet. When?"

"Early next week?"

"Consider it done."

Relief washed over him. This wasn't the first time the Michaels' family stepped in to help and it wouldn't be the last.

***

On the second day of the festival Ravenna hid in her room. She simply couldn't face Wade. Safely trapped, she wept the moment her boyfriend left for his meetings with the local brewers. His schedule gave her time to have a good cry.

Steven's dominance embarrassed her, yet for some foolish reason, it lured her with a promised to meet her every need. At least her place by his side gave her a vantage point to learn Coalition's plans.

Needing a distraction, she opened her laptop and lost herself in a friend's future instead of her own. She gave Natalie a call, and they narrowed down choices for flowers and favors. The lace and organza wedding details put a smile on her face as she exchanged ideas, giggled, and planned.

Later that evening, she returned to the festival with her business persona firmly in place. Pasted to Steven's side, Ravenna set aside her personal wishes and did all she could to help Wade Michaels.

***

The mysterious text, an invitation to Natalie's house, confused Ravenna until Amanda opened the door. A shouted "Happy Birthday," brought tears to her eyes. She didn't think anyone in Ashwood had remembered. Not only had they not forgotten, she was overwhelmed by streamers, a delicious dinner, and a frosted cake with a single candle burning on top.

Linnea placed the cake on the table and said, "Make a wish." Ravenna's gaze shot to the ceiling while she thought for a moment before blowing out the candle. She wished for the impossible, to find a way to remain friends with everyone she'd met in Ashwood. But her job took her all over the nation, and she knew how difficult it was to stay in touch. Knowing this, she decided to enjoy the moment and watched Natalie slice the cake.

The first bite melted on her tongue, rich vanilla and strawberry cream filling. Ravenna moaned. "Oh, Lord, this is delicious. I'll definitely miss Goldfinch Bakery when I move on."

"Where to after Ashwood?" Linnea asked.

"Probably Nashville. Coalition wants a greater presence in the South. I'll miss you all so much."

Reaching across the table, Linnea squeezed Ravenna's hand. "We'll miss you too."

From a small pile of gifts, Natalie passed her a beautifully decorated bag filled with handmade lotions and soaps. "I noticed you wear a citrus perfume. Amanda and I had these made especially for you."

Opening a bottle, she sniffed the lovely aroma and smoothed the creamy lotion on her hands. "This is perfect. It smells just like the lemon orchards that grow near Ravenna, Italy."

"Here, open this one next." Linnea passed her a box. After ripping away the gilt paper, Ravenna found a delicate silk scarf. Linn smiled when Ravenna put it on. "That's just perfect, I knew those rich hues would match your eyes.

She gave the long scarf another twirl around her neck and sighed. "Thank you so much, it's gorgeous."

One small box waited on the sideboard. "This is from Wade," Linnea said with a grin. "He asked me to bring it over and give it to you."

"Wade?" Ravenna's mouth dropped slightly as she accepted the unexpected gift. "What is it?"

Linn shrugged. "He didn't tell me. Open it and see."

Shaking a little, her fingernail slipped under the gold medallion sticker that held the square box closed. Removing the lid, she peeled back the glossy tissue and gazed at the delicate cuff bracelet tucked inside. "Oh, my. It's beautiful," she whispered.

Ravenna held her breath, took the bracelet from the box, and slipped the slim loop past her hand. She lifted her wrist and admired the intricate silver raven carved into cobalt enamel. With tears swimming, she had a hard time seeing her friends when she blinked up from the gift. Her words caught in her throat, but judging from the silence, her friends were just as stunned.

***

Finding time to visit Danielle Evert was chaotic, but he knew the trip to Seattle was essential. Even though his own lawyer had already examined the contract, Wade hoped a second look might find a path of escape from Coalition Craft. She welcomed him into her stylish office. His runaway nerves had him wiping away the sweat on his shirt before he shook her hand.

"Nice to meet you," she said as he sat.

"Thank you for seeing me on such short notice, Ms. Evert."

"Please, call me Danielle. I have to tell you—I'm a big fan of Mosquito Creek. I've even managed to find some of your new Sweet Venom. It's fantastic."

"Glad you liked it. Would you like to come to the grand opening of the taproom?" he asked. When she nodded, he fished in his wallet for a card and jotted down the details.

She accepted it with a smile. "I'll put the date on my calendar. Now, let's take a look at this contract."

With a few keystrokes, she opened his documents and sat back with a sigh. "I went over the contract, and as your lawyer noted, it's reasonably typical. However, a few sections stood out." She explained that each year Coalition had the option to renegotiate what was asked of his brewery. This clause gave them leverage. If he couldn't meet production demands, other brewers could produce his award-winning product. This clause allowed Coalition to maximize profits of their most popular lines.

"Because of this, each year it could become more difficult to extricate yourself from this agreement. In theory, you may slowly lose control as their demands increase."

"Time has become my enemy. I feared that I would need to move quickly."

"The buyout is determined by their investment and a percentage of future earnings calculated on a diminishing scale. One interesting point ... there seems to be a more attractive option when an asset is substituted for some of Coalition's cash investment."

"Are they talking about the taproom?"

"Not likely. The brewery and taproom are already included in the initial investment. Technically, they are part owners of both."

"Damn. What about my original location, north of Ashwood?"

"They overlooked that property, probably because most brewers transfer equipment to hold down costs. I'm sure they thought it would be useless after you moved to the new location."

"So could that be an asset they are willing to bargain with?"

"Also not likely. It's not worth enough and the location is remote. I was wondering—did your father invest in the brewery?"

"No, and he never will. He would like me to return to Yakima and run the hop farm."

"That asset *is* large enough to tempt them into this loophole."

Wade dragged his hand through his hair. "That hop farm has been family-owned for five generations. No one from Coalition who did ten minutes of research would be foolish enough to think that was an option."

He slumped in his chair as the discussion shifted to the amount of money needed to escape the contract. The staggering number left him nauseated. Armed with knowledge but not much hope, Wade thanked Danielle for her help and her time.

Once he was back on the road, he replayed the details of the conversation. Coalition seemed to be on the hunt for one thing—a physical asset. It didn't make sense. Everything he owned was already tied to Mosquito Creek Brewing.

SEVENTEEN

Ravenna rushed outside and flew toward her father's approaching car. Once it stopped, Wade watched this beautiful woman fall into her papa's embrace. He took a moment to drink in the emotion of their exchange, then turned away, trying not to intrude.

Across the shop, standing in the shadows, he spotted Steven watching the same interaction with poorly veiled disdain. Leo still held a spot on the board of Coalition Craft Corporation. And while that position was more figure than function, everyone respected Leo's standing in the brewing industry. Steven's glare oozed with so much contempt, Wade wondered if the man was counting the days until the old guard would dissolve from Coalition's board.

***

"Papa, I've missed you so much." She held on tightly to the solid man who grounded her world.

"Ravenna, what's wrong?" he asked pulling away to look at her from an arm's length.

"Nothing." She closed her eyes and inhaled slowly. "Having you here fixes everything."

Leo wouldn't let go but waited until she met his steady gaze. "Remember my dear, you are small, but you are mighty." This declaration over her was her father's constant mantra. She loved to hear it spoken with his conviction.

When her smile returned, he swept his hand toward the brewery. "Show me the place I've heard so much about from you and Wade." Taking his hand, Ravenna led him through the open door of the taproom and into the brewery beyond.

"Have you been talking to Wade?" Her voice shook with surprise.

"Of course," he admitted, then spotted the tall Michaels man. "Wade, it's been too long, my friend, far too long."

Wade's lengthy strides carried him straight to Leo. Towering several inches over the compact Italian, Wade still shrank like a nervous gangly youth in his friend's solid hug. Ravenna laughed witnessing her father's joy.

"Let me look at you," Leo stepped away. "Ah, I see it . . . this brewery has put wisdom in those eyes."

"Yes, it has, sir, and some mileage." The brewery rang with their laughter.

"You know better than to call me sir. I'm simply Leo. Oh, and thank you for lending me your tiny home while I visit."

Ravenna's eyes flicked between them, wondering just how often these two men talked.

"Happy to have you here. And you'll be right next door to Ravenna."

"That's perfect. Now, let me take a look." His eyes skirted the room, surveying the entire scene. "You've done it, Wade. This is far more spectacular than anything I was able to piece together. Congratulations!" Leo slapped him on the back, proud of Wade's stunning accomplishment.

"Ravenna, I see your hand in the details as well. Beautifully done." His gaze passed from Ravenna to Wade and back to his daughter. Ravenna averted her eyes. Her father knew her too well. Unable to mask the way she felt about this brewer, she prepared herself for a conversation about Wade during her father's stay.

Snapping a staccato beat across the wooden floors, Steven's strides brought him to Ravenna's side. The pressure of his hand against the center of her back pulled her from her father.

"Leonardo Silvestre, nice to see you again." He held out his hand and Leo took it, shaking it with three quick snaps.

"Steven, interesting to see you here. Grand openings aren't your usual haunts."

"Ravenna and I spent her birthday together. I decided to extend my stay and enjoy the celebration," Steven said with fluid polish.

"That reminds me, dear. Mama sent a few packages for your birthday, but one needs to find its way to your kitchen."

"Not tiramisu?" Ravenna leaped with joy when he nodded. Her mouth was already watering, anticipating the taste of her birthday treat. When Steven followed, she wondered which of the men appreciated the escape from each other's presence more.

***

"Why don't we start with a tour of this brewery? My daughter can find us later."

Wade followed Leo as his mentor asked questions about the latest technology. His friend agreed, these updates made brewing far more efficient and removed some of the guesswork. Leo also shared his honest concern. He believed the automation removed some of the artistry.

As the tour continued, Erik and Trish joined them. Leo congratulated them on their work and their ability to tolerate the young brewer. Their loud laughter pulled in Dillon, Wade's close friend from Yakima. Having met Leo in the past, Dillon was greeted with a solid back-slapping hug.

At first, the new hires hung back. Annie disappeared to continue her work with Linnea. Their newest employee, Vince, lingered. Wade was happy to see how eager Vince was to learn from this legend in the brewing world.

The tour ended with a beer tasting that finished with these two old friends needing a ride to Northside Grill.

Iris anticipated the large group. She set aside a section of her restaurant just for Wade and his guests. More than twenty sat together, and Iris joined them, finding her spot next to Wade.

Easy conversation shared with well-prepared food entertained the crowd. Even Steven relaxed and stretched his arm over the back of Ravenna's chair, enjoying the celebration.

***

On the morning of Mosquito Creek taproom's grand-opening, Sheriff Jerrod Holden called in his deputies to assist with traffic snarling the two-lane highway south of town. Ravenna and Linnea had prepared for the swollen numbers. Massive white tents stood outside the brewery to handle the overflow.

To handle the catering, Iris didn't mind closing Northside Grill to focus on this lucrative job. The one-day closure wouldn't cut into her profits. She expected a terrific month between this event and the influx coming to see Wade's new brewery. Whether that uptick would last was a lingering question.

Before the doors opened, Wade stood surrounded by his experienced staff and the two new employees. Vince, a lucky find with experience, had been hired to work on the brewing side. Annie, a local, helped Linnea run the taproom.

Wade hollered across the hollow room, "Seth, can you gather your crew? I'm going to take a stab at a speech before we unleash the throngs."

"A speech? This should be fun." Seth laughed. "Give me a second to find everyone." He came back with Natalie, Carlos, Kent, and Rick. Linnea put an arm around Rick and held Ravenna with the other. Erik and Trish hung with Duncan and Leo. Annie and Vince stayed behind the bar with Iris. Stephen crept far enough into the shadows that Wade could pretend he wasn't there.

"Mosquito Creek Brewing." Wade paused, inhaled a slow breath, and blew it out to tamp down his emotions. "When I started this hobby in the back of a shop, I never anticipated this. All I can say is thank you. Linnea, you uprooted your life to help your crazy brother. Iris, you promoted my early efforts and put up with my absence these past few months. Seth, you stepped in when the rest of the Michaels clan thought I was a damned fool. And Leo, you were there at the beginning, encouraging me to follow this crazy dream."

Wade's gaze settled on Ravenna. "Thank you for helping me get there in one piece." He swallowed hard and savored the warmth of her smile.

"For the work that lays ahead, I thank you all, in advance." Wade coughed and couldn't speak, and his small band of friends, family, and coworkers applauded. His smile burst wide and he yelled over the applause, "We've got thirsty people outside. Let 'em in!"

Kent and Rick each took one side of the heavy wooden doors and rolled them open across the suspended rails. Summer sunlight spilled inside, illuminating gold tones on the freshly varnished oak surfaces. Bright silver tanks filled with fermenting beer reflected the gilded light.

A sea of people electrified the atmosphere as they flowed inside. Some stopped to listen to Foundry as their drums and lead guitar turned the opening into a party.

Overwhelmed, Wade scanned the room and absorbed the moment. He spotted Linnea pouring pints. Rick joined her to help and snuck a playful touch when he thought nobody was looking.

Near the brewery, Leo already drew a crowd. His mentor's presence added credibility to the expansion. Wade never realized until now how much he depended on his friend. More than that, Leo guided him when his father refused to support his dream.

Still, the day wasn't perfect. He sensed Ravenna's struggle to balance her commitment to Coalition and Mosquito Creek

Brewing. At least Steven wasn't crowding him—Wade chose to enjoy that small victory.

***

During a rare lull Ravenna found her father. "I'm so thrilled. The opening's a complete success."

"I'm proud of you and Wade. You two make a great team."

"I feel lucky to know him." Emotion pushed against her ribcage, more than she'd ever felt on any other Coalition job. She couldn't admit it, but Wade seemed more like a partner than an assignment. "If only Coalition weren't tangled up in the reason we met. When Wade and I talked, we discovered how many times our paths had nearly crossed."

Her father pulled her away from the throngs toward the tall metal tanks. "Perhaps you were meant to guide him through this."

Leo understood the challenges she faced, but Ravenna still held her fear close; fear of losing her job, fear of never seeing Wade again when this was over. Her fingers worried the intricate raven bracelet wrapped around her wrist. The cool metal gave her a little comfort. Wade knew her, understood how much her past meant, and just maybe he understood her dreams.

Her Papa turned, grasped her shoulders, and gave her a gentle smile. "By now, I'm sure you've learned to trust Wade, but you should also trust yourself. You must remember, we cannot control those things that bring us together, but we can control if those things tear us apart." Trapped in his hug, Ravenna wondered how much her father sensed her growing feelings for Wade. She'd tried so hard to keep boundaries in place. Apparently, those who knew her best saw past her masquerade.

"I need a moment," she said as a group of beer enthusiasts headed their direction.

"Take all the time you need," he said and led the throng away from his daughter's hiding place.

***

Amanda tore open another box of tank tops. They could barely keep up as growlers, mugs, and bandanas flew off the shelves. Linnea wrapped a glass in tissue paper and placed it with three others in a Mosquito Creek Brewing bag.

Linnea looked up from her task and brushed a curl of hair away from her face. "I've run out of tape for the register. There's a stash in the cabinet in the Whitewater office."

Amanda nodded. "No worries. I'll find it and be right back." With throngs crowding Mosquito's front entrance, she dashed out the back door. Her ears buzzed with the instant change of volume from din to quiet, escaping the insanity.

She cut behind the mill complex and jogged to the rear entrance of Whitewater Homes. Other than security lights, the vacant shop was dim. Sunlight streamed from the front through the large office windows casting long bands of light her direction.

Movement in the office slowed her steps. She wondered if someone sent on the same errand had just beat her here. A dark-haired man sat in front of the desktop computer. He leaned forward, and his fingers moved rapidly across the keyboard.

She stopped. Wait, she knew him. What was Steven doing in her office?

The double-monitors screens were filled with numbers. Amanda grabbed her phone and snapped shots of Steven as he studied financial documents. When he inserted a thumb-drive into the computer, she took another photo.

Fingers flying, Amanda hurried to send alerting messages. Her first text found Seth, and she sent a second to Kent. *Emergency in Whitewater office. Hurry.*

***

The guitars blazed as Foundry covered Mr. Brightside, and the zone in front of the stage surged with a compact sea of bodies. Kent and Seth weren't standing far from the stage. Both abandoned the party, eyes catching as they moved in tandem toward Whitewater's office. Natalie followed a few steps behind.

"What's going on?" she asked as she caught up to the jogging men.

"No clue. I got a text from Amanda. I'm guessing you got the same?" Kent asked Seth, in a full run now.

"Someone's in my office," Seth said when he crossed to the front door.

"I'll block the way out." Kent rushed, eyes wild, hurrying to help Amanda.

***

Steven cringed when two large men bolted past the office windows. A woman he barely recognized followed a few steps behind.

"Fuck." Steven snagged the thumb-drive, shoved it in his pocket, and lunged for the door. He laughed at the stupid girl who attempted to block his escape. "Get out of my way."

"Not moving, asshole." Amanda grasped the frame of the door. "You don't scare me city boy—not after growing up with three brothers, all much bigger than you." He grinned, at least the girl had guts.

"Have a seat, Steven." Seth's anger filled the office.

Kent circled to the other door and pulled Amanda to his side. She inched away. In her current state of mind, she did not intend to be coddled.

With a smooth chuckle, Steven took a seat in front of the computers. Everyone stepped forward and the room seemed to shrink.

"He has a thumb drive in his front pocket," Amanda told her brother. Steven's eyes narrowed and she smirked. "Thought you could get away with it, didn't you?"

"Ah, your grit has me hard."

Kent growled and Seth cracked his knuckles. "Before I call the sheriff, do you want to tell me what the hell you were doing?"

His eyes sharpened but Steven's voice remained calm. "The authorities. Really, Sherlock? Do you think Wade needs bad press to celebrate his big grand opening?"

His arrogance kindled angry fire in Seth's gaze. Kent took a step forward, fists clenched. "Let me take care of him, myself."

Steven laced his fingers behind his head and tilted the chair. His smile broadened, baring perfect white teeth. "These enlightening financial records brought something to my attention. Seth, your substantial investment in Mosquito Creek Brewing entitles me to information held within your computers."

"What the fuck?"

"Full disclosure of investors has always been a requirement of Coalition. Hiding key financial information places Wade in an unfortunate position. A breach of contract, where you, Seth, now find yourself entangled." Steven stood. "If you will excuse me, now that I've got what I need, I think I will rejoin the party."

"You're not moving a fucking inch," Kent said, his neck muscles twitching.

Seth turned and calmly asked, "Natalie, could you find Sheriff Holden and ask Danielle Evert to join us?"

"I'll just be a minute."

Steven's eyes narrowed. "Wade has press here representing outlets from Seattle to San Francisco. Do you *really* intend to ruin his grand opening with flashing lights and small-town cops putting me in a police car?"

"Give me the thumb-drive." Seth held his hand, palm up, a few inches in front of Steven's nose.

***

Natalie cut through the crowd and spotted Danielle. Dressed in jeans and a T-shirt, her lawyer appeared so different that Natalie nearly missed her in the sea of people near the stage. But the sheriff was nowhere in sight, probably dealing with the snarled traffic in front of the brewery.

Danielle's smile widened as Natalie approached. "What a success. You must be thrilled with the turnout."

"I'm afraid something has come up. Would you mind following me?" she asked, pulling her lawyer away from the noise of the drums and rhythm guitar.

With a nod, the pair scurried between a maze of cars and pick-up trucks as Natalie fed information. In those moments, Danielle transformed herself from party-goer to legal advisor. Exposed without the armor of professional clothing, she stood tall, mustered authority, and walked into the midst of the conflict.

EIGHTEEN

Her father lingered with four brewing fanatics while three more stood ready to take their place. Ravenna bowed away, knowing Papa would be occupied for quite a while. The rich sound of a familiar laugh drew her toward the recesses of the brewhouse. She found Wade surrounded by brewing fans. When Wade shifted his feet and glanced her way for a rescue, she knew he was growing uncomfortable with their compliments.

"Here she is! The young lady who needed rescuing when her car broke down alongside the road. Were your pretty little ears burning?" She recognized Frank when he gave Wade's arm a friendly punch. "This brewer has been saying great things about you." When she realized she'd been the topic of conversation, Ravenna blushed.

"Thank you again for your help," she said, as heat faded from her face.

"Always happy to rescue a young lady." The man rubbed the gray scruff on his chin and turned back to Wade. "You picked a fine line-up when you built your team. We know you could have saved money by taking this operation to the city. I, for one, appreciate your loyalty to our little town."

"I wouldn't have wanted it any other way." A slap on the back pushed Wade forward. The sinewy farmer was stronger than he looked.

"Well, I'm still thirsty. And I think it's my turn to buy the next round." Frank led his friends away from Wade and Ravenna, leaving them standing in the midst of a mechanized hum.

Wade settled his arm comfortably around her shoulders and tucked her petite body to his side. She eased naturally into the hard plane of his chest as the rise and fall of her breathing countered his. After a long moment, Wade bent his head to her ear and whispered,

"No matter what happens between Coalition and me, it was all worth it. You were meant to be here—to be part of my life."

His honesty brought her eyes to his. She was about to agree when a glint of silver on her wrist caught his eye. Wade reached to stroke the metal dangling from her arm, and said, "You wore the bracelet."

"I love it," she said as his fingers caressed the sensitive skin on the inside of her wrist. Lifting her hand, he pressed his lips to the center of her palm.

Unsteadied by the intimate attention, she pivoted, bringing her hand to rest on the center of his chest. He gripped her waist, tucking her close. The loud celebrating throngs in the taproom faded entirely. They became one man and one woman wrapped in the warmth of each other's touch. She met his eyes with a wish, "If only we had met years ago when you studied at my father's brewery."

"We came so damn close. Everything might have been so different."

His fingers tightened around her waist. Control snapped, and he succumbed to the irresistible lure of her lips. Encased in his embrace, she turned to meet a kiss that merged their divergent worlds into one.

Moaning softly, she opened to him, relishing the warmth of his tongue on her mouth. She accepted more from this kiss than pleasure. The desperation she tasted marked her soul. As his patient attention enticed, she shifted her body, begging for more. A mingled moan passed between them before Wade gripped her waist a bit tighter and forced himself to pull away.

The sudden loss of contact sent a shiver down her body. Still trapped in his arms, Ravenna's trembling hand drifted to her lips. She whispered past her fingers, "I'm so sorry. We shouldn't have—"

Tears pooled in her eyes while she tallied the cost of their actions. She wriggled from his arms and ran from the brewery, taking the nearest door that put her behind the massive structure. Ravenna stopped outside to breathe under a canopy of trees, but out in the open, she felt exposed.

Searching for safety, she ran to her tiny home and slammed the door, holding it shut with her inadequate weight. The solid wood couldn't shut out her mistake.

Eyes closed, her fingertips traced her mouth and relived Wade's intimate kiss. Heat had simmered between them since they met in Vegas. Why did he choose this moment to pour fuel on that fire? He had not acted alone—she had fanned those smoldering coals. Maybe they both wanted this to happen.

***

Wade escaped to a storage room at the farthest corner of the brewery. The smell of grain and hops was a meager replacement for the visceral sensation of Ravenna's kiss. Every bone in his body ached to find her. She'd called that kiss a mistake. Fuck that—it was as inevitable as the pull of the tides. So many times their paths had nearly crossed, as fate toyed with them in a reckless game.

Over the years, he'd visited Leo many times. And he was aware that his friend had a daughter, yet he and Ravenna had never met. The clues had littered the Silvestre family home—small shoes in the entry and a petite jacket hanging on a peg near the door. Her picture on the mantle had depicted a grown woman, but her belongings were so small, so delicate, it seemed she was a nymph.

Perhaps she really was enchanted. With only one touch of her lips, his world had shifted. Ravenna's kiss was transformational. Yet her sudden reversal was a stunning blow. *I'm so sorry, Wade. We shouldn't have.*

Yes, we should. That bewitching woman had carved channels in his soul and no one else could ever fill the space. Determined to find her, Wade spun toward the door and collided with his sister. The impact whooshed the air from his chest and he couldn't speak.

Linnea stomped her foot. "What are you doing back here?" Her face glistened with sweat. "Good Lord! I need help and I can't find half of our family. First you disappeared and then Amanda. I've been covering a taproom that is absolutely slammed!"

Wade shook himself and recalled why this day was so important. His entire future rested on the successful opening of Mosquito Creek Brewing.

"I'm sorry Sis, lead the way," he said to Linnea and followed her back. Rounding the corner, the din of the band washed over him. The clamor of conversation put his focus back where it belonged. He picked up his pace and aimed for his spot behind the bar.

***

Seth paced his office and listened to Danielle. Her eyes apologized when she said, "Unfortunately, Steven's correct. As a representative of Coalition, he's entitled to the investment details. However, this breach of contract violation is an empty threat." Her glare focused on Steven and dared the arrogant ass to press her further.

She tried to soften the bad news with her even tone. "Seth, you are within your rights to call the sheriff. He may have been trespassing, but it appears that nothing was destroyed."

A collective hiss passed from person to person as each one coped with the disappointing news.

Steven chuckled, satisfied, and rose from the chair ready to make his escape. "I'd like my thumb-drive back."

Taking his time, Seth shoved Steven aside with his shoulder then copied the files that had been hijacked. After pulling the drive from his computer, he placed the small device on the surface of his desk. He was unwilling to hand it to a man who was no better than a thief.

Seth stood in place, a human wall that Steven was forced to step around. With a grunt, he snatched the device on his way out.

"You'll be hearing from me and my lawyer," Steven snarled as he left.

When the door slammed, everyone heaved a collective breath.

"None of what happened here today leaves this room," Seth directed. "Wade worked too damn hard to have this day tainted by that miserable snake and the corporation he slithered from."

Danielle agreed, "I know I'm an outsider here, but Seth is right. Now is not the time to expose Steven. Wade has more than enough to worry about today."

Amanda lurched forward, her hands in a fist. "I think we should keep Steven, Ravenna, and Leo away from Wade."

Shocked by the implication, Natalie gasped. "Certainly, you don't think Leo and Ravenna have anything to do with this?"

Kent flung his hands in the air. "Come on. This is theft. I don't know about Leo, but Ravenna's been hanging around and she has all the passwords. That woman knows our computer system inside and out. It's clear to me, Steven had her help."

"That's ridiculous! She's helping Wade to figure —" Seth's cough cut Natalie's words short. She shook her head, her voice quivering, "I just don't believe it. Ravenna's a close friend."

"But she's not *family*." Amanda punctuated her opinion with a pointed glare.

Seth stepped between his sister and the woman he loved. "Amanda, that's enough."

Pivoting to face Seth, Kent defended Amanda, "What about Steven? We should at least keep an eye on him."

The growl of an engine turned their attention. Everyone stared as Ravenna's four-wheel drive tore out of the gravel lot, rocks flying in its wake. Steven sat behind the wheel with no sight of Ravenna on the passenger side.

Kent's open hand pounded against the window casement, shaking the glass. "That son of a bitch left as soon as he found what he was looking for."

Amanda collapsed onto the worn leather couch. "Are we seriously going to pretend like this didn't happen—like it doesn't even matter?" Kent fell to her side and put his arm around her. On a sigh, she closed her eyes and leaned into his chest.

"It'll be okay, princess." He stroked her arm and tucked her a little but closer to his side.

"I just feel so violated. We trust everyone in Ashwood. Why did that awful man have to destroy our trust?" Amanda laced her fingers with Kent's, and he stroked the back of her hand with his thumb.

He brought his eyes up. "If you all don't mind, Amanda and I will hang out here for a while."

"Natalie, I'm sorry for freaking out," Amanda apologized and then her eyes went wide. "Oh my, I almost forgot. Linn sent me here to find tape for the cash register. She's probably pulling her hair out by now."

"I'll take care of it." Natalie located the tape in the storage closet. Danielle and Seth followed her out, leaving Amanda and Kent curled together on the couch.

***

Ravenna couldn't believe he was gone. Steven had shocked her, storming into the tiny house to swiftly pack his luggage. At first, she'd thought he'd seen *that* kiss—the kiss that had sent her running. But when he hadn't confronted her, she realized the way he was acting had nothing to do with Wade.

"Where are you going?" she asked while watching him fly from task to task. "In fact, where have you been all day?"

He shoved her aside and reached for his laptop. "In twenty minutes, I accomplished what you could not do in more than two months."

"What are you talking about? What have you done?"

"I found out where Wade got his financial backing."

Her mouth dropped open. "Where? How?"

"It doesn't matter. I have what I came for, so now I can leave. Stay here and do your fucking job. All you need to do is stick around and babysit these damned fools. I'll see you in October, when you come back to Chicago." He slammed the lid of his computer and shoved it into the slim black case.

Each move Steven made seemed surreal as she processed that he was leaving. She knew she should have felt awful, but Ravenna sighed, relieved. As blood rushed in her ears, she said a little too loudly, "I'm not coming back to Chicago, at least not to you."

"Of course you are. You have an apartment, a job, a life." He finally stopped packing long enough to really look at her.

She took a step back, his features seemed transformed by hate. "Even if I return, my life won't include you."

"You are making a serious mistake, sweetheart," he said as his eyes narrowed.

Pulling her shoulders up, she strained to reach her full five feet three inches. "Trusting you was my only mistake."

Steven barked a laugh and dropped everything to the floor. Stepping into her space, he grabbed her shoulders with a vice-like grip. Towering over Ravenna, he twisted his hand into her ebony hair and bent to claim a final punishing kiss.

She didn't give him the satisfaction of a struggle. But when he tried to pry her lips open with the edge of his tongue, the lips that had just been caressed by Wade, she inched her mouth apart. Her teeth separated enough to find his lower lip and bite it. Hard.

Steven's hand coiled in her hair, pulling her away by the sensitive tendrils at the nape of her neck. In pain's response, her mouth popped open releasing his lip. She licked away the tangy taste of his blood with the tip of her tongue.

"You fucking bitch," he hissed. Steven left, leaving the door swaying on its hinges.

NINETEEN

The constant demand for food kept Iris and her staff busy, but beneath her efficient exterior, her mind spun. She filled orders, poured drinks, and kept her workstation spotlessly clean. Yet, all her planning for this event couldn't prepare her for what she had endured this evening.

She had dashed inside the taproom to borrow napkins from Linnea and restock her dwindling supply. Surrounded by customers, Linnea tipped her head to the far storage room, telling Iris where she could find the extra napkins and plates. Rounding the corner, Iris smiled, looking forward to checking in with Wade. Both were busy and they hadn't found a spare moment to share the joy of his amazing event.

She spotted him talking to Ravenna beneath the shadow of the tall silver tanks. The arm her boyfriend placed across the woman's shoulders appeared friendly at first, but the intimate touch that followed didn't. He seemed enthralled by the slim silver bracelet on Ravenna's arm.

Iris blinked when Wade's lips touched Ravenna's open palm. She ducked into a corner, afraid of what might happen next, but found she couldn't look away. A gap between the tanks gave her a sliver-sized view of Wade taking Ravenna into his embrace. Iris staggered when the arms that had caressed her this morning wrapped around that petite woman.

Betrayal stung. Her mouth went dry as she watched their passion unfold. A kiss like that couldn't possibly be their first taste. No, he had deceived her, but she had also denied the flashing warning signs.

Turning her back to the infidelity, she pressed into the job she'd been hired to do. Over the next few hours, Iris served food to Wade's guests, wearing a smile that hurt while fighting a desperate need to cry.

***

Wade lost focus as the number of guests dropped with the setting sun. The chill of early summer pushed the last holdouts inside the taproom. He helped Foundry take down their sound equipment and load their van. The physical labor kept him from running to find Ravenna. And he couldn't do that, not until he talked to Iris, first.

"The music was awesome, guys. I appreciate you sticking around longer than planned." Wade paid the musicians for their extra time.

"No problem. Give us a call when you need live music again. And hey, thanks for the free brews!" A loud slam secured the door of their van. The parking lot was nearly empty. The only remaining cars belonged to family and close friends.

Iris' little green beetle was parked among the rest in the gravel lot. Wade grinned at the strangely fitting transportation. She emerged from the building carrying the last box of catering gear. He closed the distance, taking the load from her arms. While he followed, Wade slowed his steps and tried to think of the right words. He couldn't go home with Iris tonight.

"Thanks," she said as she opened the trunk of her car. After placing her equipment inside, she slammed the lid and circled to the driver's side door. She leaned her hip against the cool metal. As she brought her eyes to his, he could see that something had changed. Wade hesitated. After today, he couldn't even kiss Iris goodnight, it just felt wrong. Before he got a word out, she looked up. He knew what was coming before the words left her lips.

"I wanted to wait until the grand opening was over ... until life settled down. I enjoyed getting to know you better, Wade. You're exactly the kind of man I admire, but I think we both know we aren't meant to be together for the duration." Her statement stung, even if it let him off the hook.

He exhaled past the tightness in his throat. "Iris, I hoped we could be so much more."

Eyes to the ground, she shook her head. "Huh. So much more?" Her shrug left his words hanging between them on an invisible string, and Wade wondered if she knew what had happened in the brewery.

Iris folded her body gracefully into her car and started the engine. The smell of exhaust filled Wade's lungs, but he didn't feel free to leave. Before she put the car into gear, the electric hum of the window pulled Wade in. He licked his lips, wondering if Iris wanted a final kiss, a last goodbye.

When her green eyes glittered with fire, he knew he'd been wrong. The woman didn't want a kiss, in fact she looked like she wanted to kick him in the nuts.

"I'll box up any of the crap you've left at my place and leave it for you to pick up at Northside's office," she said. "And if anyone bothers to ask, just tell them I was the one who ended this. And that it happened yesterday."

Wade started to ask why, but she reached up and covered his lips with her fingertips. His brows lifted. It was clear to him—she'd spotted him with Ravenna.

***

Iris left a plume of dust as she left Mosquito's parking lot. Wade stared at the gray haze, a sick pit twisting his gut. He knew now, he should have ended it with Iris after meeting Ravenna. Because he'd waited, an amazing woman despised him. He deserved that and hated himself for stringing her along, for bringing her pain.

When a door slammed shut behind him, Wade turned and found his old friend, Leo. "I haven't seen Ravenna in over an hour, and her car is gone. Did she have an errand to run?" Worry etched lines in his face.

"Have you checked her house?" Wade visually searched the lot but didn't spot her Jeep.

"I was headed that way. Watch for her, please. Maybe she's somewhere on the property."

"I'll send a text." He watched Leo jog toward the tiny home. The message he sent didn't get a reply, and he spun to search every part of the brewery.

***

"Why am I always stuck without a car in this damn town?" Ravenna descended into another wave of sobs, feeling stupid and sorry for herself but at the same time, relieved.

She'd gone through an entire box of tissues when the sound of her father's signature knock brought her back to her senses. Crawling down the stairs from the loft, she cracked open the door.

"Ravenna! Why are you crying?" he asked and stepped into her little home. She hung her head, unable to speak. Papa secured her to his chest, and she lost herself in the refuge of his hug.

"Ah, it will be all right," he soothed and waited. Just like her mother, she would talk when she could, once her tears washed away some of the pain.

Several minutes passed before her voice calmed enough to speak. "I've made a mess of things, and I can't see a way to repair the damage."

"We'll fix it. Tell me what happened."

"I betrayed Wade." Her shuttered exhale trapped painfully, guilt squeezing against the bottom of her ribcage.

"That's not possible. You'd never do a thing like that."

Her head sagged, hair falling forward, the long strands concealing her swollen eyes. "Steven used me to steal information. Wade will never trust me again." A ragged sob transformed into a watery laugh. "At least Steven's gone, but I'm afraid he may have taken my career with him."

Papa's steady palm pressed reassurance against her back. "Don't worry, sweet girl, he doesn't have that kind of power." He led her to the couch, and she sat beside him, answering his questions. A faint smile tipped his lips when he heard she had ejected Steven from her life.

A final bout of tears ended on a staggered huff. All cried out, Ravenna only wanted to lie down. "Papa, I'm so tired. Can we talk about this tomorrow morning? Right now, I just want to go to sleep."

He nodded and stood. "If you need anything, I'm right next door."

"I'll be okay. At least Steven's gone." She wiped away the last of her tears, feeling a bit lighter.

With a kiss to her forehead, her father said, "I love you."

"Love you, too." He wouldn't leave until she pasted on a weak smile. Once the door closed, Ravenna sank onto the sofa and replayed the day in her mind. Her emotions swung from pain to anger, and she covered her face with her hands. "I'm such a foolish girl."

The thought of facing Wade turned her stomach. A sudden wave of nausea propelled her to the bathroom where the swollen face in the mirror cured her queasiness with a gasp. She ran cool water on a washcloth and pushed it over her eyes. Her fingers drifted to her lips, and she relived the memory of Wade's unexpected, unbelievable kiss.

***

On a search for Ravenna, Wade crossed the threshold of the taproom. Tense voices hit him, and he took a deep breath. "Shit." Why did his family choose this moment to get tangled in a heated dispute? He'd hoped to pour a beer and bask in the afterglow of the successful grand opening.

Wade shouted over the din, "Hey, I could hear you all from outside."

Every eye shot to his, but Seth's frown disturbed him the most. "Wade, we need to talk."

When he spotted a similar hangdog look on everyone's face, his hands shoveled the air. "What the hell? Am I the only person in the dark?"

Seeming almost too eager to deliver the news, Amanda closed in. "This afternoon I went into Whitewater's office to grab supplies. I found Steven at the computer copying financial files."

Wade's jaw ticked. "Did he do anything to you?"

She tossed away his concern with a flick of her hand. "No, nothing like that."

Seth filled in the remaining details. As each layer of information stacked on the next, Wade's anger grew. "I can't believe this mess. Does Ravenna know? Is she okay?" he worried aloud.

Linnea finally spoke. "We don't know where she is, but I don't think she had any part of this."

Amanda stomped her foot. "You can't be serious! They deceived everyone. Ravenna must have helped Steven steal all those files."

The argument boiled again, voices echoing over one another in a desperate attempt to be heard. When his phone buzzed, Wade stepped back from the snarled conversation. Ravenna had finally responded. *Dad found me. I'm sorry if I worried you. I'm not feeling well and will call it a night.* Wade glanced toward the door, wanting, *needing* Ravenna's touch, but the argument surrounding him kept his feet planted.

Seth managed to reign in the confrontation. "I know we're all concerned, but Wade and I need time to study the stolen files before we decide what to do."

"And I need to talk to Ravenna." Wade's words drew glares from Amanda and Kent, but they seemed to respect him enough to keep their mouths shut.

Linnea spoke with her characteristic calm. "Nothing can be resolved tonight. We open to the public tomorrow. The trouble brewing because of Steven won't change that fact."

Wade clutched the back of his neck. "Can I count on everyone to keep this quiet?" His eyes questioned each person caught in this circle of discontent.

Rick took Linnea's hand and said, "You can count on us."

Amanda nodded, and Wade hoped his cousin would keep her promise. If she didn't this news would spread like wildfire. Kent agreed then left with Amanda, heading next door to lock up Whitewater's office.

As everyone left, Wade remembered that Leo was in his tiny home and he had nowhere to crash for the night. He caught up to Natalie and Seth and asked a favor. "Hey, after I finish here, can I stay at your place tonight?"

"Absolutely, we'd be glad to have you. Would you like to invite Iris?" Natalie asked.

He studied the cracks in the old wooden floorboards. "No. She broke things off." Wade's eyes slid to Seth's—his cousin wasn't surprised.

Natalie stepped closer and gave his arm an encouraging squeeze. "I'm so sorry."

"I'm fine. Go ahead and take off. I'll be a few more hours wrapping up things here at the brewery. Please, don't wait up," he added, "I just might decide to crash on the couch in the office."

Natalie was about to protest, until Seth took her hand and cut in, "Do what you need to do. And don't worry, we'll all work together and make things right."

The pair left, and Wade started gathering empties from the tables in the taproom. Behind the bar, Linnea and Rick moved in unison, stacking T-shirts, and loading the dishwasher with the last of the pints. Seeing them together, Wade smiled, happy his sister had found a man who matched her stride.

When a familiar sound chirped Rick's phone, his sister sighed. Wade recognized the alarm and knew Rick would be heading out quickly. The big guy checked the screen, gently kissed Linnea, and left to handle another call for the volunteer fire department. Once Rick was gone, Wade gave his sister an encouraging hug, promising everything would work out.

After Linnea left for the night, he wandered the brewery alone. The soothing hum of the pumps and coolers tethered him to Mosquito Creek Brewing.

TWENTY

Ravenna woke from her nap, parched. She wondered if all those tears had drained her dry. Even though she'd been surrounded by beer all day in the taproom, she'd never sipped a drop. After the terrible day she'd had she figured she deserved a drink. If nothing else, a nip or two would help her get back to sleep. She climbed the step stool in the kitchen and grinned. Fortunately, Steven had one good quality—he had expensive taste in single malt scotch.

She found his bottle, poured a shot, and downed it. Shocked by the potent vapors, Ravenna struggled to breathe as the fumes leaked into her lungs. Pouring a second, her lips trembled while she slowly sipped the amber liquid. The alcohol loosened her anger and guilt. Alone in the dark, the night absorbed her sadness, helped by a third shot of scotch.

Giggles erupted when she recalled the nasty bite she'd cut into Steven's lower lip. Her tongue grazed her teeth, recalling the taste of his blood. "Yuck."

Angry again, she scowled. "I hope it swells. He's so vain, he'll obsess about that flaw." Another sip of scotch made her smile. "Too bad I didn't bite him harder."

Wanting payback, Ravenna stood, bobbing, weaving. Her fists flew aiming short blows at Steven's phantom face. "Take this." She jabbed, bouncing on her tiptoes. Take that!" she said a little louder. "This will teach you to pick on tiny fierce women." She danced like a prizefighter laying out her opponent in an imaginary round.

***

Wade wandered the perimeter of the buildings, locking the property before leaving for the night. His thorough check brought him to Whitewater's side entrance, and he scrutinized the tiny homes. The interior lights were dark, only the front porch glowed.

He stopped. If Ravenna was asleep, why could he hear her yelling? Her voice sped his steps. She shouted again and he sprinted, worried that Steven had returned. Pushing through her front door, he expected the worst. A squeak in the near dark caught his attention. He found Ravenna on the couch, looking dizzy, disoriented, and confused.

"I didn't think you'd come back." She laughed. Wade stood above her, watching as wild giggles shook her body.

After searching the tiny home, he returned and found her still curled in a heap on the sofa. "What happened? I thought I heard voices."

Ravenna's gaze raked him up and down. "Oh, hello, Wade. Wow, you look so big." Laughter erupted and she covered her mouth with both hands. "Big everywhere I bet," she whispered past her fingers.

His mouth popped open, amused. But his mood shifted when he flicked the lights and saw the stain of tears on her face. "Ravenna, are you okay?"

She didn't answer, only squinted, and sheltered her swollen eyes with her parted fingers. "It's too bright in here. Could you turn down the lights, pretty please?"

After dimming the main switch, he found the light over the stove. "Better?" he asked, while studying her tear-stained face. He hated the man who made her cry and was tempted to wipe Steven's memory from her mind. A kiss might do that, but not tonight.

She patted the couch next to her, encouraging Wade to take a seat. When he took a spot at the far end of the couch, she frowned, a kissable pout. Tempting. She held his gaze while closing the distance between them, her hips wriggling across the cushions. "Have a drink with me, Wade."

Abandoned on the table, he found a glass filled with two fingers of gold liquor. Wade took a taste of the high quality, high-octane scotch. "No wonder," he mumbled with a grin. The rich aroma mingled with Ravenna's scent, so intoxicating. Reaching out, his palm came to rest on her cheek, thumb stroking gently. Ravenna closed her eyes and leaned into his touch.

"Mmm, that feels nice." She hiccupped, giggled, and snorted, then fell back onto the cushions and pulled a pillow under her head. Reclined flat on her back, she bent her knees in a reverse V. Her pink painted toes tickled the edge of his thigh.

A flicker of concern tightened her expression. "I'll fix this mess, I promise," she said without explanation.

"You don't need to fix anything." When she stretched both legs across his lap, her calves brushed his growing arousal. He clenched his teeth, enjoying the sensation.

"I bit him," she blurted.

"Bit who?"

"Steven. I bit him when he tried to kiss me."

Anger pulsed and Wade's fists tightened, wanting to punish Steven. "Did he hurt you, Ravenna?"

"No." She shook her head side to side. Even her irritation looked sexy. "He didn't bite me … *I bit him!*" When she dissolved into giggles again, he laughed, smiling at her determination. He couldn't resist a touch and stroked her feet, ankles, and calves with his fingers.

"Can you believe that dick took my car? Looks like I'm stranded again." A frown puckered her lips, a frown he wanted to tease away with his tongue.

"You can drive one of mine," he offered.

Ravenna took the almost empty glass and downed the last drops of scotch. Rising to pour more, she moved too quickly and grabbed his bicep. "Oh my, the room is getting fuzzy."

"Wait here." He slowly tucked her into the corner of the sofa and smoothed a blanket around her. "Stay. I'll get you some water and something to eat."

"No more scotch?" she asked.

Wade shook his head. "No more scotch." He put the bottle in a high cabinet out of her reach. Finding a tall cup, he filled it with ice and water and brought it to her. "Drink this. I'll make you a grilled cheese."

Two small hands wrapped around the glass. While taking a drink, her eyes followed him as he cooked. She sipped more water as he sliced cheese and buttered bread. Before long, he flipped the sandwich, and a toasty sizzle filled the room.

"Tell me something I don't know about you," Ravenna asked.

Wade spun the spatula in his hand. "Anything at all?"

She squinted. "Yes. But it can't be about brewing."

"Deal. But only if you reveal something, too." Wade found plates and placed them side by side on the counter.

She nodded. "I guess that's fair."

He pulled the sandwiches off the stove to let them cool and met her gaze. "I'm a guitar addict," he confessed.

"Ooohh, how bad?"

"I own twelve. So, pretty bad."

"That's serious. Electric? Acoustic?" she asked as he cut the sandwiches corner to corner.

"Both. I played in a band in Yakima for a while, but it didn't amount to much. We had fun until we decided money was important for survival." Wade carried plates with toasted sandwiches in each hand and reclaimed his spot.

"I want to hear you play. Mm, the cheese smells yummy." She took a bite. Warm cheese hung for a moment between her lips and the sandwich. Her fingers caught the tendril and captured it in her mouth. "Delicious."

Her fingers, her lips, and the slight slur of whiskey in her speech distracted him, bubbling a deep pool of latent lust.

"I took a long break from writing music—but picked it up again right after Vegas." He wondered why he let those words slip. No one knew he still wrote music in his spare time.

"Oh? That's right after we met. Have you written a love song for Iris?" she asked, a little pang of jealousy in her tone.

"No. And I probably won't. She ended it and I don't write nasty breakup songs."

"I'm sorry." She stared at her plate, unable to hide her grin.

"Iris and I are better as friends." He wasn't ready to talk about this. The guilt was still too fresh. Wade finished his sandwich and rose to put away the bread and rinse the pan, now that it was cool. "Your turn, Ravenna. What's your secret? I'm ready to be amazed," he said from the safety of the kitchen.

Still chewing, she held up her hand and thought for a moment. "I know how to ride a unicycle." Her eyes danced and she laughed. "Dorky, right?"

"Why a unicycle?" She was so petite, it wasn't difficult to picture her balanced above one wheel.

"I had a bike and tore around on it inside the brewery. Papa thought I would run over him. He bought me the unicycle to slow me down."

"Sounds dangerous. Did it work?"

"Yeah. Until I broke my arm. Mama had a fit. She worries too much about me. You know I'm an only child, right?" She finished off her sandwich, stood slowly, and took a sideways step toward the kitchen. When she wobbled, he moved to her and reached out a steadying hand, fingers pressing the soft rise of her hip.

After pulling his touch away, he added, "Leo told me years ago, and I know they feel lucky to have you." Wade leaned against the counter grasping the edge to keep his eager hands away from Ravenna.

"There were complications when I was born. Mama doesn't talk about it. But I was never lonely—I'm close to my cousins on both sides." When her body swayed, he steadied her with his hand to her waist. Alcohol slowed her movements and she melted into his touch. A gentle tilt brought Ravenna to his chest. She looked up, and he could tell the alcohol and stress had taken an exhausting toll. "I'm so tired," she said as her eyes drooped.

"Ravenna, why don't you get ready for bed? After I tuck you in, I'll leave." She nodded and wandered into the compact bathroom. He heard the faucet running. The water stayed on while she flushed, and he chuckled—she was shy. By the time she emerged, he'd finished washing the dishes.

Turning from the sink, Wade was surprised to find she'd changed into her pajamas. He hung the dishtowel while his gaze drank in the contours of her body. Sleek legs stretched from her cotton sleep shorts, and her thin tank top revealed dusky nipples. The peaks pebbled the moment his eyes landed on her breasts. She seemed so small, Wade wanted to pick her up and take her anywhere she wished to go. Gazing with vulnerable longing, she reached for his hand, seeking his comforting touch.

He led her toward the stairs to guide her steps to the loft. Following behind, his eyes watched the sway. Her thin sleep shorts revealed that she wore nothing underneath. When she dropped to the mattress and crawled toward her pile of pillows, he mumbled, "Fuck," on a breath. Wade swallowed hard, his cock throbbing against his zipper.

Her eyes, still swollen by recent tears, gazed at him with longing. "Wade, will you lay down with me?"

"Baby," he groaned, "not tonight. But I'll tuck you in and see you tomorrow morning."

The bed was rumpled, and her pillow was damp from her earlier cry. He turned the pillow to a fresh cool side. Humming softly, she settled for him and he pulled the light covers over her, releasing the scent of her lemon perfume. She curled and tucked one hand beneath her cheek.

"You make a mean toasted cheese," she mumbled, "and you make me feel hot and melty, too."

"You're killing me," he whispered, too quiet for her to hear. His fingers smoothed her hair, and she turned a bit, seeking his touch. As he caressed her jaw, each breath became more relaxed. When he was certain she was asleep, he placed a small chaste kiss on her temple.

"Sleep well," he said, and she hummed, satisfied.

Wade locked her door as he left. He took a seat on her front step and shot Seth a text, telling his cousin he'd decided to crash in the office.

TWENTY-ONE

Linnea visually inspected the new Mosquito Creek T-shirt Wade had put on after grabbing it from the shelf. He'd figured she'd guessed he hadn't left the brewery last night.

"Didn't you spend the night at Iris's place?" she asked.

"No. I had too much on my mind." Wade shrugged and stared at his feet, hiding his shame, knowing he'd probably end of confessing all the details to his sister eventually. He started with the basics and said, "Iris and I aren't seeing each other anymore."

"What happened?"

"I guess she figured out I wasn't her forever-guy."

When he shuffled foot to foot, she stilled him with a hand to his shoulder. "I'm sorry—for you and for Iris—and I hope you two can figure out a way to be friends. I like her."

"Don't worry. We'll get there. This town is too small to have it any other way. Hey, I noticed you're spending more time with Rick." He teased and smiled, changing the subject.

Linnea shoved an open palm against his chest. "Really, *Dad*? Way to deflect."

"Dad wouldn't ask questions; he'd just castrate Rick." He laughed, but the humor didn't reach too deep.

Linn rolled her eyes, and Wade knew his comment edged too close to the truth. Shaking her head, she left him to his laughter and began her first standard workday in the taproom. But she never made it behind the bar. A honk of a horn out front caught his sister's attention. She jogged outside and met Natalie who was juggling two trays filled with coffee.

Wade's mouth watered when pink Goldfinch Bakery boxes appeared. A wave of relief swept over him when Linnea left one box in the office and took the other in the direction of the tiny homes. The desire to follow, to check on Ravenna himself, swamped him again. He couldn't. It was just too soon. Fisting his hands, he fought that urge, knowing Natalie and Linnea would have Ravenna feeling better in no time at all.

***

Barely moving, Ravenna needed water—gallons and gallons of water. Her eyes squinted against the dim light that bled past her curtains. She pulled on her soft robe, trying to remain in that half-asleep state for as long as possible.

The tap at her door sounded too tentative to be Papa. She peeked through the window and spotted a friendly face surrounded by a cloud of red wavy hair. Natalie waited on her steps holding a tray of paper coffee cups in her hand.

"Thank God, caffeine. I may live after all," she said before opening the door.

Ravenna knew she looked awful, but the need for caffeine surpassed her pride. Natalie blinked when the door opened, but she smiled instead of reacting to the evidence of Ravenna's terrible night. "Can I come in?" Natalie said. "I've brought caffeine and sugar."

"My two favorite food groups. Come in, but fair warning, I'll be crappy company. I vaguely remember a date with a bottle of scotch last night. Give me just a sec." Ravenna dashed into the bathroom and took her time putting herself back together, but nothing could erase her puffy eyes. By the time she came out, Linnea had joined them.

She took one look at Ravenna and sighed. "Oh, honey, are you okay? If you give me Steven's address, I'll hunt him down and —"

"You don't need to do that." The coffee, the pink box, and the way these women cared swelled a hot balloon of emotion in Ravenna's chest. When her eyes started swimming, she stared at the ceiling and fanned her hands in front of her face. Eventually, she sucked in a breath. "I can't believe I trusted that snake."

"At least he's gone." Linnea shook her head and passed her a tall cup of decadent coffee. The hard set of Linn's mouth let Ravenna know she wasn't the only one who'd been sucked into Steven's vortex. She had to fix this.

The smooth paper cup felt soothing in her hands, and Ravenna hummed with pleasure when her lips took a first careful sip. After another taste, she said, "Last night, before Steven left, he bragged about stealing Wade's financial information. Please, you must know, I had nothing to do with that."

"Our thoughts never went there," Linnea insisted.

"But I invited that dick to Ashwood. It's still my fault."

Natalie leaned in and gave her knee an encouraging squeeze. "Enough about Steven. We're only here to make sure you're okay."

"And we know you cared about Steven. Even if he deceived you, getting over him might take some time," Linnea added with an encouraging smile.

Anger flared again, and Ravenna smacked her coffee cup to the table, dark liquid sloshing over the rim. "No. I don't feel anything. It's like Steven is two different men. I wasted so many kisses on that miserable jerk." Fresh tears skated down her face, and she covered her cheeks with her hands. "God, I hate crying. I've got to stop!"

Natalie and Linnea encased her in a tangle of warm limbs. When enough comfort had seeped into her weary soul, she asked, "Is there any chocolate in that little pink box?"

"Of course, there's chocolate!"

"I love both of you," she said, when Linnea opened the lid to reveal a decadent double chocolate cookie. A smile reached her swollen eyes when she took a bite that magically made her world a little bit better. "And I love Maggie, too."

"We all do," Linnea agreed.

Another cookie disappeared while Ravenna discovered the damage Steven had done during the Grand Opening. Her stomach twisted, yet her temper flared. When she woke this morning, she'd been tempted to hand in her resignation to Coalition. But if that brewing conglomerate was willing to use these tactics, Wade was going to need her help more than ever.

***

Ravenna rushed to her door when she heard her father's signature knock. "Papa! Come in. I've put on a fresh pot of coffee."

Linnea stood. "I hate to leave, but the taproom needs me to unlock the doors."

Her father did not let Linnea escape without a bear-sized hug. "I'll come over to the taproom soon and say my goodbyes." His change of plans struck Ravenna silent.

"Leaving so soon?" Natalie said as she stood to leave Ravenna and her father alone.

He nodded. "Yes. I miss my wife."

Once they were alone, Ravenna sat with her father, and he explained his change of plans. He was only leaving two days earlier than he intended, but she suddenly felt very alone. Knowing he was headed home, made her crave a hug from her mother. "I wonder if I should come home, too."

"Sweetheart, take some time. Make sound decisions. From what I can see your friends need you, and I think you need them just as much." She blushed, wondering if he had noticed the growing connection she had with Wade. Her father tapped the outside of his coffee cup with his fingers. "Having me here, only gets in the way."

"You'd never be in the way." Even though his position on the board of Coalition complicated things, navigating the mess Steven caused would be easier with her father's guidance.

His eyebrows furrowed, and she leaned in to listen carefully, drawn by the intensity in his gaze. "This situation is problematic," he said. "But your place at Coalition is secure. In fact, it may work to your advantage."

"Have you been on the phone with your contacts in the company?" she asked.

"Yes. And I've confirmed what you suspected. Someone appears to have an unusually keen interest in the Michaels' family. It extends beyond the brewery. Be patient, these things have a way of revealing themselves."

Ravenna rose from the couch, thinking clearer as she paced the small kitchen. "You're right. Leaving now would admit failure. It may be difficult, but I need to make sure Mosquito Creek Brewing comes through this, that Wade succeeds."

"That's my girl," he said and chuckled. "Now that I see that twinkle in your eye, I'll need a ride to the airport."

"What? You drove to Ashwood."

"I'm leaving my car here, for you. After I get home, I can drive my trusty old pickup." Leo slapped his hands together, eager to move. "Now, let's see what needs to be done at the brewery. I have a few hours before my flight."

***

Her courage seemed to fly away with her father. Ravenna left the bright lights of Portland and headed back to Ashwood. The road, shrouded by tall evergreens, swallowed her headlights with inky-dark. Her future with Wade was just as obscure. Recent breakups distracted both of them with different brands of hurt.

More complicated, Wade was trapped in a battle with the company that controlled her paychecks. And no one could predict how Steven would use Coalition's power against Mosquito Creek Brewing. Breaking things off with that miserable man was the right choice, but it also cut off a conduit of useful information.

Even with these new complications, her mind tempted her body with vivid fantasies, and every intense scenario ended with her caged in Wade's solid arms. She knew those dreams could shift to nightmares if they fell together tonight. The heat they shared would burn bright but fizzle fast. Wade had to wait. That man was too good to waste on a rebound romance.

She pulled around Whitewater and parked near her tiny house. Next door, she saw Wade's place. A few lights were on, but it looked like he'd already settled in for the night. Before she slipped quietly in her front door, Wade appeared on his porch, and her resolve nearly shattered.

"Ravenna, I'm glad you're back." Rapid steps brought smoldering temptation to her. She held her breath, trying to deny the magnetic draw rolling from his steady gaze.

Blinking away, she said, "Let me put my purse inside. I'll meet you on your front porch so we can talk."

"Talk?" His smile dropped but his untamed gaze remained. "I'll wait right here." His breath gusted, riding a wave of frustration. The man standing on her steps looked ready to lay her on any horizontal surface and claim what they both knew was his.

Leaving him to pace outside, Ravenna closed her door and pulled a bulky sweatshirt over her head, her only armor between herself and temptation. Resolve in place, she followed him to his porch, rocked by the view of his taut ass in snug faded jeans. She sighed, claimed a seat, and looked at the stars instead of his hypnotic eyes. Needing to hide, she concealed her hands inside the cuffs of her sweatshirt and took a steady breath. "Wade, I want to apologize for last night."

"Apologize?" His expression shifted from smoldering to surprised.

She hoped her controlled smile hid her deep craving. "I obviously had too much scotch last night, even before you arrived.

Did I do anything too embarrassing? Parts of last night are still a little fuzzy."

Wade reached for her hand, she slipped her fingers from inside the sweatshirt and accepted his touch. "Ravenna, last night you were beautiful and vulnerable and incredibly tempting. And I loved spending time with you more than I should have ... considering the circumstances. Only one reason kept last night tame—I want you to remember every vivid detail of our first time together."

Heat hit Ravenna, radiating from his touch, settling to her core. She swallowed hard and whimpered, "You do?"

"Yes, I do." He shifted to the edge of his seat. His eyes glittered with intent, and he looked ready to begin those vivid details with her now.

She longed for his hands on her bare skin but recalled her plan and pulled away. "Wait."

Wade's eyebrows shot up and he froze. Before he could close the distance between them, she added, "I want our timing to be right. I don't want to be your rebound any more than you want to be mine. I need time."

"Time?"

"Yes. I think it would be best if we took things slow."

***

Wade erased the mental blueprint he had planned for tonight. No consuming kisses, no possessive touches, no claiming Ravenna as his own.

"Please don't tell me you need a rebound after Steven. The thought of seeing you with another guy makes me fucking insane."

She quickly snapped her head from side to side. "Oh, no. You've misunderstood. Time, I only need time. Can you give me that?"

"Yes. I'll give you anything, and everything." A brush of his thumb at her wrist marked his promise and she squirmed.

176

"Thank you," she said, wriggling away from his touch. She stood quickly, looking ready to bolt.

He couldn't let her leave, not yet. "I just need to confirm one thing," he said. Her gaze followed his as he moved closer, her head tipping back to keep his eyes. "That kiss—the taste of your sweet lips—it haunted me last night. I need to know it wasn't a dream."

He watched with hunger while her tongue swept out to wet her bottom lip, and he knew, she'd dreamed about that kiss, too. Small hands escaped her sweatshirt and smoothed across his chest, grasping his shoulders. "It was the best kind of dream," she whispered.

One calloused hand grasped her slim waist and the other hand caressed the nape of her neck. Wade tipped his head, hesitating millimeters from her mouth. "This may only be a kiss. Still, I need you to know, you're mine."

The connection began with playful nips, so soft she chased his mouth, seeking more. Wade waited for her to commit before exploring the contours, her plump lower lip, her teeth, her eager tongue. When he caressed the back of her neck with his fingertips, she surrendered on a ragged sigh.

Hoping to hear that sound again, he tilted his head and explored. She gave him that cry, gripping him with a hungry passion that would lead to a place he couldn't control. From a well of desire, a low moan hovered between them and his heart jumped. This wasn't infatuation, this wasn't lust, this was more.

With the way her body writhed, seeking his, Wade knew it wouldn't be long before she led him to her bed. He stilled his hands and pulled away, giving her what she had asked for—Time. Time to think about the many ways he intended to satisfy all her future requests. He inched their bodies apart and she trembled, her deep brown eyes glittering and wide.

Taking her hand, he walked Ravenna to her door and gave her another, softer kiss. Her fingers tangled his hair and temptation doubled. One arm held her in place against his chest, while the other hand reached around and turned the knob. Warm air spilled as Wade swung her door wide. He left Ravenna on her doorstep, just in time.

TWENTY-TWO

Wade woke early with a raging hard-on and a fresh fantasy on his mind. For the past two weeks, Ravenna had starred in his dreams. These vivid illusions weren't his fault, and he couldn't control what happened each morning.

She haunted him with exquisite torture. Each night they sat on his porch under the heat lamp and talked, ending their night with a kiss. And those kisses weren't chaste. Their tongues dueled, seeking what their bodies desperately needed, taking pleasure from slick penetration.

Tongue-fucking her mouth ignited endless erotic illusions. He pictured her in the taproom, on the front porch, and tied to the tanks in the brewery. It seemed that there wasn't a single place he could go to escape his vivid fantasies. Distracted as hell, countless cold showers and exhausting runs weren't enough.

The sun climbed the eastern horizon while Wade sucked down strong coffee. He stood on his porch to watch her shadow pass by the curtains in her tiny home. He imagined her naked, maybe dripping and wet from the shower. Cold, with her nipples erect, but not as erect as his straining cock.

Brewing was the farthest thing from his mind. The festival in Denver would be a welcome escape from this torture. He knew he would miss her, but having Ravenna along on the road would break his resolve and shatter his promise to give her *time*. She still wanted more time.

Wade closed his eyes, and the pain in his groin eased. A breeze blew from the brewery toward his porch, and he inhaled the aroma of bitter hops mixing with the sharp scent of evergreen trees. The heady scent took his mind to the farm, where his patented Rusk Hops should now be climbing high on the trellis under the Yakima sun.

After filling his cup with more coffee, he left his tiny house to search for his chief brewer.

"Hey, Wade, have you made a decision?" Erik asked as Wade approached.

"About?"

"The festival in Denver. Do you want me to add those dates to my calendar?"

Wade pulled his hand through his hair while he pivoted away from the distraction that had just appeared in the taproom. He couldn't watch Ravenna wiping down tables and think clearly at the same time. "No, you should stay in Ashwood. Dillon and I will take Colorado. Annie and Vince both have enough experience to help with this festival. You and Trish need a break, anyway. Will you be able to manage both breweries without Dillon?"

"No problem. Ravenna will be around to help, and she knows the new brewery better than I do. So long as Linn can handle the taproom, Trish and I will keep things rolling." Erik's confident smile helped Wade relax.

Once he'd added the trip's details to the calendar on his phone, Wade pivoted and stared back toward the taproom. His mouth watered as his fantasy climbed a ladder, putting her body on display as she reached for swag on the highest shelf.

***

Overlooking the Chicago skyline, Steven ruled his office while he reclined in his calfskin chair. Across the desk, Phil Davis shuffled through the pile of information gathered during Steven's trip to the Northwest.

Phil tossed the printouts onto the polished mahogany and growled. "Jesus, Steven, just tell me what you found. I *pay people* to look at this shit."

"Fine. Once I digested all the information, two details stood out. Unfortunately, Wade's father did not sink any money into Mosquito Creek Brewing. He never has," Steven explained.

"Fuck, so we have no leverage against the hop farm? No way to get our hands on that asset."

"I didn't say *that*." Tilting back, he laced his fingers behind his head, forcing Phil to wait. Eventually, he said past a vile grin, "Wade does have a promising new strain of hops in the ground. I'll find a way to shift that patent to Coalition."

"How will you accomplish that?"

"By sabotaging his ability to reach this year's goals. If he can't produce enough of the Double Deet IPA, we gain control. Then I'll offer him his freedom in return for the patent."

Phil narrowed his gaze. "And how do you intend to pull that off?"

Steven moved forward, put his elbows on his desk, and tapped his fingertips together. "Let me handle the details. Ravenna isn't my only pawn. Her shift in loyalty won't deter me."

Phil's brows furrowed. "I still don't get it. Why the hell would Wade bargain with Mosquito, anyway?"

"His interest in sweet Ravenna will override his common sense. I've become a competitor for some tits and ass. I knew that little woman had more value than the tight spot between her legs."

Hit by the words, Phil tipped away and shook his head. "Steven, remind me to never piss you off."

***

Four trucks baring the Mosquito Creek logo waited nose to tail in a long line. All but the last were loaded, nearly ready to leave for Colorado. Linnea brought Wade a sandwich and two bottles of water. "I heard your stomach growling from inside and thought you might need a bite."

"Thanks, I'm starved." He leaned on the fender of the biggest rig and sank his teeth into the roast beef sandwich.

"How much Sweet Venom did you load?" Linnea asked as he chewed.

"Not enough. Being forced to bring so much Double Deet pisses me off." With the sandwich half-gone, he took a long drink of water, replenishing the sweat that trickled down his back. "It's not my fault Sweet Venom kicks ass," he said while he swiped the crumbs from his mouth with the back of his hand.

"Why did the execs even approve bringing Sweet Venom at all?" his sister asked.

"I don't know," he said with a shrug. "But it will be tricky. I have to pour Sweet Venom at a separate tent, far away from the other Coalition brands. I can't be two places at once, so I'll be stuck with the Coalition crowd serving Double Deet while Vince serves Sweet Venom from a smaller tent at the fringes of the festival."

"What about Dillon and Annie?" Linnea asked.

"Annie's on merchandise and Dillon's gonna float between both tents. With the execs breathing down our necks, I don't want to be the only one pouring at the main venue."

Linnea nodded, her gaze bouncing from truck to truck. "You better move if you want to make the send-off dinner." She hesitated for a long moment. "Is everything cool between you and Iris? If you want, I can pick up pizza from that new place in town. We could have our send-off dinner at the taproom if you'd rather avoid Northside Grill."

Wade winced and shook his head. "Northside's fine, and Iris and I have talked. I don't want to piss her off more than I already have. Did you know she added a second craft brewer to her tap selections?"

"Wow, I'm sorry. Give it time. Maybe she's just sending a message."

"Message received. Mosquito Creek is replaceable. It's awkward, but in time, we'll get back to being friends."

***

Rick and Vince pushed four tables together to accommodate the crew and a few extra friends. As Iris brought out pitchers of beer, Wade had a difficult time not ducking behind the bar to lend a hand. He absorbed the confused looks from her staff. Iris might not look him in the eye, but it appeared that she'd kept the dirty details about their recent break up to herself. When dinner landed on the table, the conversation buzzed with the excitement of the Denver trip.

"Has anyone talked to Dillon?" Erik asked. "He never misses a send-off dinner."

"I'll shoot him another text." Looking at his phone, Wade shook his head when he realized Dillon had never responded to the message he'd sent this morning. This wasn't like Dillon; his friend was rock-solid dependable.

Wade's phone vibrated and he swept the screen to take the call. "Hey, we've got pizza coming. Where are you?"

Immediate concern chased away the grin on Wade's face. "No, that's cool. Get all the rest you need." He listened for a moment. "It's okay. Take it easy, and drink plenty of fluids."

After glancing around the table, Wade shared the news they all seemed to expect. "Dillon's running a fever and has body aches and chills. We're short a driver."

Erik started to move, but Wade held up his hand. "I know you're willing, Erik, but I need you here to keep the brewing on schedule."

Linnea spoke next. "I'll be happy to handle one of the rigs. But I'll need to change the taproom hours—if that's okay." Wade nodded, willing to close the taproom if it meant having his sister's help in Colorado.

Ravenna leaned in, her voice raised over the noise in the bar. "No, Linn. I should be the one to go. Since I represent Coalition, it makes sense for me to take this event."

"Can you handle a truck?" the siblings asked at the same time.

Irritation furrowed Ravenna's brows. "I can handle a rig. Come on, you both know I grew up at a brewery."

Wade regretted the question immediately. Ravenna had cleared every hurdle on her own in a male dominated industry and she deserved respect. "I'm sorry. You're right, I'd value your help in Denver."

She tipped her chin, her eyes sparkling, ready to take on the challenge of the trip. When he stood to order another round of pitchers his hand grazed her shoulder. She shivered beneath his fingertips as he passed.

TWENTY-THREE

Something didn't taste right. The master brewer checked again. Wade was two hundred miles away, and Erik needed to make a judgment call. He shot off a text. *Call when you stop for gas. Got a question for you.*

While he waited, Erik tasted the sample and re-checked the settings on the automated systems that kept the brewhouse humming. It didn't take long before he found the source of the problem.

"Damn it."

"Did you figure out what went wrong?" Trish asked, her hand on his shoulder, soothing his irritation.

"Take a look," he said pointing to the settings.

"The temp was too high when the yeast was pitched. The fermentation happened too rapidly. How is this possible?" she asked.

"I don't know. Anyone else and I'd say human error, but we don't make mistakes like this."

Concerned, she shrugged. "Wade's had a lot on his mind."

"Possible, but we're talking about Wade. I don't think that's the case." Erik checked again, not trusting his eyes. When his phone vibrated, he grimaced.

"Good luck," his wife encouraged as he took the call.

***

Wade stood and stretched next to his rig. "What's up? Is everything okay?"

Erik shared what he found. By the end of the conversation, Wade fought hot anger, but agreed that if the taste was off, the batch of beer had to be tossed. Coalition's demands made any setback a serious concern. If he fell behind on his projected goals, production of Double Deet could move to an outside source. He ran the risk of permanently losing control of Mosquito Creek Brewing.

Wade took immediate action. "Erik, the chance that this was human error is too fucking slim. Someone may be messing with the equipment. I'll call Seth and have him help you install security cameras. Don't tell anyone except Seth and Trish."

"Don't you want me to tell Linnea?" his brewer asked.

"No. I hate to keep my sister out of the loop, but she's too close to Ravenna. I know it sucks to worry about it, but Ravenna's still part of Coalition."

Erik groaned. "Shit. I'll dump this batch tonight, clean the tanks, and do everything I can to keep us on schedule."

Wade kicked the gravel beneath his feet. "I'm glad you're there, no one else would have caught this right away. We could have wasted so much time. Thanks, man. And hey, I know I don't have to say this again, but keep this quiet."

Erik ended the call and Wade stared across the horizon. Without a cloud in the sky, the day would be hot and dry. Ravenna skipped out of the quick-stop and his gut pitched. Doubting her loyalty tightened his stomach. Dressed in cut-off shorts and that damn-cute Mosquito tank, she hurried toward him with a bottled drink in one hand and a bag of pretzels in the other. As the distance shrunk between them, her smile increased.

"I forgot how much I love road trips!" she said as she came to a bouncing halt in front of Wade. "You haven't had time to go inside. Why don't I keep an eye on things out here while you get something to eat?"

He accepted her offer with a nod as her sweet smile doused his suspicions—betrayal from Ravenna was impossible. "I'll just be a minute," Wade said as he left her with the vehicles.

***

Spotting the mushy tread, Wade placed a hurried call. "Hey, Annie, find a safe spot and pull off the road. Your rear tire looks a little low."

All four vehicles lined up in a wide empty gravel lot off the interstate. With the flat, any hope of making it to Salt Lake by nightfall evaporated. Wade got on his phone and found lodging near the Utah border. They limped a few miles down the road and he found a guy who agreed to meet him to repair the damaged tread first thing in the morning.

The rest of his crew slept in while he listened to the time-weathered man explain the slow leak. "From where I'm standin' this looks planned. You got a clean puncture right here on the tire. Too high to be a nail. Looks to be vandalism. Lucky you found it too—this tire was headed for a blowout."

Wade paced a circle and glanced back as the grizzled man repaired the damaged tread. "Can you tell when this happened?"

The mechanic scraped his three-day growth beard. "Hole's small. Two days tops."

Wade nodded. "I appreciate your help."

"That's why I'm here. To keep you rollin' down the road," he said and bent to his task.

It was too damn early, but Wade had to place this call. Wandering to the far edge of the dusty lot, he heard three rings before his friend picked up.

Erik cleared his throat "H-hello?" When Trish murmured something in the background, Erik said, "Babe, go back to sleep. It's Wade."

"Sorry to wake you guys, but I've got a problem."

"What's happened?" Worry replaced Erik's exhaustion.

"At some point in the past forty-eight hours, we had a tire vandalized. At least that's what the mechanic figures."

"How can he tell?"

"The location of the damage and the size of the leak. It could have happened before we left or out here on the road. Do me a favor, get those cameras in soon. Someone close to Mosquito is pulling this shit."

"Already done. Seth and I ran to Portland yesterday and worked 'til three installing some seriously badass hardware. Seth decided to outfit Whitewater Homes at the same time. The entire property is secure."

"Damn, that was fast. How's the system work?"

"I'll send you the log-in and you can check the feeds on your phone. One warning, because you won't let me tell Linnea, you may see more of Rick and your sister than you bargained for." Erik enjoyed a hard laugh at Wade's expense.

"Ah, crap. You didn't need to tell me that!"

"These things are designed to blend in. The damn cameras look exactly like fire suppression sprinklers. I doubt Rick could even tell the difference unless he pays close attention," Erik added with a chuckle.

"Did Seth tell Natalie?"

"Not yet. It seems both Linnea and Natalie have a soft spot for Ravenna. Seth struggled with the decision but chose to keep it from her for now."

Wade grunted in agreement and hated to imagine Ravenna playing both sides. He was too keyed up to get back to sleep. Alone in his room, he played his guitar until the crew woke. After a greasy breakfast, the team was back on the road. The mountains and desert blurred to monochromatic beige. Today's late start put the caravan into Laramie after dark. Hungry, sweaty, and sore from a second day behind the wheel, few words passed between the weary crew.

***

Wade didn't talk at dinner—in fact, Ravenna had barely heard a word from him all day. He stood and mumbled, "I need to get some sleep. We'll meet here for breakfast at seven-thirty." All heads nodded in agreement as he abandoned half of his burger and headed to the register to pay the bill.

His eyes skimmed past Ravenna without stopping. Shoulder slumped—his weary legs carried him outside. Wade left a trail of dust as he shuffled toward the one-story motel that was just across the lot from Ruby's Diner. When he disappeared behind turquoise door number eight, Ravenna sighed. For the first time since she met Wade, he seemed distant. Before the trip they'd talked every night, and his cool disregard stung.

Vince slid from the booth. He grabbed a toothpick and a mint wrapped in foil as he passed the register. Turning, he called over his shoulder, "See you both in the morning."

Annie's gaze skated from Vince to Ravenna. "Damn, Wade seemed to have a bug up his ass. It wasn't anything *I did*," she said with a smirk.

"I'm sure he's just tired." Ravenna picked through the wilted remains of her salad. Hunger far from satisfied, she reached for the dill pickle on Wade's plate. "Do you want this?" she asked.

Annie shuddered. "Ick."

Happy to have something with flavor, Ravenna bit the dill pickle. "Have you helped at past festivals?" she asked to fill the awkward silence.

Annie nodded. "Oh, I've known the Michaels family *forever,* and I worked two local events for Mosquito last summer." She pointed her fork and tilted her head, scrutinizing Ravenna with clumped-mascara eyes. "Just how long do you intend to hang around in Ashwood? It seems to me that we have things handled. That is what you do, right? Help breweries and then move along."

Ravenna bit into her pickle and wished she didn't have to put up with this exhausting girl. "You're right, but Coalition is part owner of Mosquito. So, technically, I'm your employer. And as long as Wade needs me, I'll stay."

Annie's eyebrows lifted. "I wasn't saying you've overstayed your welcome. I only thought some other brewery might *want* what you have to offer."

Tired of the sparring, Ravenna folded her thin paper napkin and placed it over her half-finished salad. "Clearly, we have different opinions. See you in the morning. Sleep well."

Outside, sodium lights buzzed. She glanced back through the diner's dirty window. Annie's fingers flew, sending a message on her phone. Ravenna knew Amanda would be reading a full play-by-play within seconds.

Hidden in her room, she listened to the strumming of Wade's guitar bleeding through the paper-thin motel walls. Ravenna smiled, happy that he had brought his acoustic. The familiar sound comforted her as it had for the past couple of weeks in Ashwood.

The sequence of chords was familiar. His voice modified the melody dependent upon his mood. Tonight, he sounded especially sad, and Ravenna longed to knock on his door and hold him in her arms. A cascade of notes colored the song with a rapid run across the strings. Anticipating the chord changes, she curled to her side on her bed and hummed the harmony.

***

Amanda pushed her phone under Natalie's nose. "Would you *just look* at this text *Annie* sent? I knew Annie would have Wade's back on this trip." She pulled the phone back and tapped a rapid reply to yet another message.

Turning off the computer, Natalie stood. "It's late. I think I've put in enough time today. I'm going to find Seth."

"No problem. I'll see you in the morning." Amanda's eyes never left the screen.

Natalie closed the office door and slumped against it. When she looked up, she found Seth watching. He closed in on her and gave her a kiss. "Will you take me home?" she begged.

"Of course. I gotta put away my tools. Should I meet you at the truck?" he asked. She nodded and escaped, relishing the silence and warmth in the cab of his truck.

When he climbed in, he traced her cheek with his touch and caressed her lips with his. He pulled back and suggested, "Why don't we pick up fried chicken from the deli and take it to the lake? Just you and me and a picnic."

"That sounds perfect."

The sun settled low in the early evening sky. Seth spread their meal across the picnic table that sat on their lakefront property. The rest of the beach was vacant for now, since Ravenna had their tiny home parked in town.

After eating a few bites, Natalie opened up. "Seth, I have an idea, but I'm not sure how you'll feel about it."

"So long as I'm with you, it's all good."

"How would you feel about skipping the wedding and eloping? I just want to head to our honeymoon in Hawaii," she said with a nervous smile.

Seth's chicken drumstick paused in mid-air. "What brought this on, babe?"

"Since the grand opening, Amanda and Linnea haven't really been speaking to each other. Or, when they do, it's awful. Ravenna's helping me with the wedding because Kelsey's too busy with her job. Your dad and his brother aren't exactly happy with each other, since Linnea started dating Rick." For a long moment, she studied her plate. "I feel like we are setting our wedding up to be a

Hatfield-and-McCoy sized family feud. Planning the wedding was difficult before, but now I'm miserable."

When tears welled in her eyes, he got up and moved to her side of the picnic table. "Oh, babe, don't cry. I'm sorry. I haven't been any help at all." His touch offered more support, but that only seemed to make it worse.

Her tears came on full force. "All I want is to be your wife. The wedding ... it's not me. It's just too overwhelming. The engagement party was so wonderful, and everyone had such a marvelous time. Can't that be enough to please the masses?"

Seth scooped Natalie into his arms. "Will you sleep on this decision for one night? Tomorrow morning, if you still want to elope, I'll be happy to hop on a plane and spend as much time in Hawaii as you'd like."

Natalie hummed as he kissed her. Moving to straddle his hips, her hands tangled in his hair. Seth soothed away her tension, revisiting each sensitive spot on her body that drove her wild.

While sliding away her top, he pictured her tanned body wrapped in a bikini on the sand. He imagined palm trees rustling in tropical breezes. As her bra fell away, he smiled and realized the bikini idea was highly overrated.

TWENTY-FOUR

On the first day of the festival everything that could go wrong did. Fucking Everything. Mosquito Creek's mobile card system crashed. Annie gawked, unable to process payments for the swag that waited to roll off the shelves in Denver. Wade had it fixed in less than two hours, but the distraction set him on edge.

Next, the CO_2 changed pressure. More foam was coming from the kegs than beer. An easy fix, yet another irritating distraction. Wade dealt with it and pressed on, hoping his luck would change.

During a rush, Annie dropped a box of glasses. Shards from one dozen shattered pints crunched underfoot. His new employee watched as Ravenna bent to gather the shrapnel. In the process, Ravenna sliced her hand and hurried to wrap it in a towel to slow the bleeding.

Annie's satisfied smirk heated Wade's temper to blistering. Before he had a moment to help with the injury, Ravenna had rushed to the medical tent. He longed to follow, to make certain she was okay, but had to remain pouring beer during another rush.

Wade blamed himself for the chaos. Every decision he made seemed to contribute to the mess. His thick skull pounded. His shoulders ached. "Get your shit together," he mumbled under his breath.

The final rusty nail in his coffin of crap appeared later, clothed in slick black dress pants and a designer shirt. He discovered Steven's smug figure studying the turmoil from the other end of the Coalition tent.

A smirk covered that clean-shaven face, exposing an even row of gleaming white teeth. Steven observed every blunder and fail with open satisfaction. He tipped his head back, laughed aloud, and disappeared into the sea of people.

At least the man was gone when Ravenna returned, pale, with her hand bandaged. Wade coaxed her into a calm corner and asked her to go back to the hotel. She waved him off, secured a rubber glove over her bandaged hand, and wiped down the beer-sloshed counter while ignoring the satisfied smile on Annie's face.

"Annie, I'd like you to go help Vince at the Sweet Venom tent." Wade needed to get this girl out of his sight. If he witnessed another sneer, he'd be tempted to fire her on the spot and fly her directly home, leaving him short a driver.

"But that tent is so slow," she whined with a stamp of her foot, "and we aren't set up to sell any merchandise way over there. Vince probably has it under control." Annie punctuated her defiance with a cold stare.

Wade's glare should have conveyed an undeniable message, but Annie was a little dense. "Clearly, you don't understand who's in charge. If I say you are needed at the other tent that is where you will go," he barked and she shrank away.

"Sorry. It won't happen again." She sulked off mumbling, typing a text as she shuffled away.

Another throng descended, and Wade went back to work, filling glass after glass with his popular Double Deet IPA. More than half an hour passed before he found a moment to pull Ravenna aside. "How's your hand?" he asked.

"Fine, I guess." She wrapped her arm around her middle and swallowed hard, moving to place a keg between them. Her protective stance pressed a hot balloon of guilt against the walls of Wade's chest. He regretted the distance he'd wedged between them over the past few days but didn't know if he had time to fix it.

"They gave me six stitches but it's still numb. I've had worse," she said while staring at the ground. When he shuffled closer, her eyes lifted to his, and she whispered, "Don't forget, I've mastered the unicycle. That toughens a girl." Her quivering laugh edged on an all-out cry.

He carefully cradled her damaged hand and wrapped her in his arms, protecting her small delicate frame. "I'm so sorry, Ravenna. I've been such an ass."

A nod against his chest acknowledged it. "I'll be okay. Papa always tells me that *I am small, but I am mighty.*"

So fragile in his arms, she seemed far from mighty. The need to protect this woman pushed aside all his suspicions. Wade couldn't deny the magnetic pull she'd always had on him, an attraction that reached inside and tugged him to his marrow, attaching to primal instincts. No matter how hard he resisted, each day he lost more of himself to a woman he found wildly attractive, incredibly tempting, and more than he deserved.

***

The evening clean-up stretched into an exhausting night. As they worked, Wade watched Ravenna fade before him, and he longed to keep her to himself. Not long after the last glass was poured, he spotted Annie and Vince as they wandered back toward the collection of Coalition brewers. Since they'd already prepped the Sweet Venom tent, Wade released them for the evening. He gritted his teeth when Annie whooped and high-fived Vince. A wave of relief washed over him as the pair rushed off into the dark.

To close for the night, Wade dropped the white tent fabric and zipped the walls shut, creating a private oasis. A gentle gust of wind shook the canvas sidewall and Ravenna shivered. Grabbing a Mosquito sweatshirt from a tall pile, Wade eased it over her head and stretched the arm to guide her bandaged hand through the narrow sleeve. He traced her shoulders and eased her hair from the neckline of the hoodie. Citrus perfume mingled with hops as she evened the waist of the sweatshirt with her good hand.

Wade led her to a tall seat on the customer side of the now completely enclosed tent. He helped her onto the perched seat and asked, "How do the stitches feel?" He bent his head to take a closer look.

"It started to throb a while ago, but I took Ibuprofen. It should stop soon." A one-armed shrug couldn't hide all the raw emotions she'd suffered all day.

"I'm sorry, today was hell." Wade tried to laugh but the sound came out with a frustrated bark.

"Not everything was bad. Even with the chaos, we had longer lines than any other Coalition brewer."

Wade grinned and tilted his head. "I don't understand how you always find a silver lining, but I'm glad you do."

"I'm a glass-half-full person, I guess." She reached out and squeezed his arm with her good hand.

She'd done it again, without even trying, she'd found another cold spot in his heart and inched up the heat. Degree by degree his icy places were thawing for her. Wade took both of her hands in his and placed them on his chest. Gently, he turned her wrist and kissed the inside of her palm. "Thank you for being my silver lining." He leaned in to taste her lips.

Ravenna clung to the fabric of his shirt and rushed his mouth to hers, setting off an instant chain reaction. He crushed her lips, tasting and nipping. Her tongue heightened the caress. A shared moan shot hot need through his body, accelerating an elemental force that had pulled them together from that moment they met in Vegas.

Gliding his hand beneath the fabric of her shirt, the contrast of her sleek warm skin and his cool rough palm pulled ragged air into Ravenna's lungs. Her sharp intake stole oxygen directly from his frantic exhale, an intimate mingling of breath.

Desperate to feel his warmth, she used one hand to tug his shirt free from his jeans, grazing a plane of rippled muscle. Her fingers smoothed the valley of his pecs and teased the hair dusting his small peaked nipples.

"Take that shirt off, please," she begged. Wade obeyed and peeled away the thin fabric.

When she paused to look, he lifted her to the top of the L-shaped bar, placing Ravenna at eye level. He spread her legs and stepped close. Her unbandage hand danced as her fingernails scraped over each dark nipple. Tracing a path south, she slid her hand down to glide over the prominent ridge of his erection, still encased painfully in his jeans.

A sudden burst of distant laughter reminded Wade that the privacy of the tent was a thin illusion. Only canvas separated them from people still wandering the festival grounds.

"Ravenna, I can't leave here tonight without more of you. Sweetheart, can you be quiet?" he whispered while he trailed a path of warm bites against her neck.

"I can try." Her panted breaths were as desperate as her hands. She fumbled with his belt, needing more.

"Lay back," he said and followed her mouth with his lips. Wade eased her shoulders to the polished wood counter. As she slowly reclined, her glossy black hair tumbled over the wood. She looked like a visual feast, a goddess that froze his feet in place. Every fiber of his being needed to worship the temptress, to bind her to him as he satisfied her unspoken desires. Devoted to her sleek prone form, he skated his hands over her clothes and studied her movement, waiting for her reaction to give him a sign. Her body seemed to want him, but she'd never confirmed that she'd had enough time.

"I need more. We've waited long enough," she whispered on a slow, sexy chuckle. "With the way I'm feeling, we've probably waited too long." A nervous giggle tumbled from her lips as his hands slipped off her shoes and removed her jeans. Reclined on the counter, her sweatshirt protected her from the cool evening air. A thin layer of lace still covering her sex was nothing but a beautiful enticement. Wade lowered his head, nudged the sweatshirt with his cheek, and kissed the rise of her stomach. Sucking the soft skin, he inhaled her arousal. The heady scent spiraled his craving.

A slide of his hand eased the lace down her legs, over her feet, and off. His touch coaxed her knees apart. Nibbling her hip, his fingers teased and entered the paradise between her thighs.

"Good God," she said submitting to the pleasure.

Hearing her words liberated Wade from the last thread of uncertainty. He peppered her belly with nibbles, the hollow between her hipbones with licks, and circled the tip of his tongue against her pearl. Slick arousal eased a finger inside. Her hips rose, increasing his contact. Wade's hair escaped the tie at the nape of his neck. The feathered tickle coaxed a moan from Ravenna. She bit her lower lip, but a few keening sighs managed to break free.

Need pulsed her channel and pulled Wade's fingers inside. He imagined the ripples surrounding his cock and ground against the hard wood of the bar to beat back his insistent need. Widening his tongue, he covered her soft folds with an open-mouthed kiss.

Breath held and body taut, her head arched back. Trembling fingers grasped his hair to hold him in place. He lashed her clit with wicked force as her hips rose to meet the sensation. Rapture whipped her body with waves of ecstasy. She cried his name, not caring who heard the blissed sounds coming through the thin canvas.

Ravenna clamped her hand over her mouth as she rode out the rest of her release against his frantic lips, fingers, and tongue. He tasted her softest spots thoroughly again, before easing his hand away. Through a mess of tousled sun-bleached hair Wade gazed at her and grinned.

The playful smile in her eyes reflected the giggle caught behind her hand. Tossing his hair back, he lifted Ravenna to his chest and mingled her laughter with arousal-flavored kisses. Their uninhibited joy washed away the stress of the day.

"Wait right there." He tickled her bare foot as he eased her panties up her calves.

'Wade?" she asked, questioning his decision to clothe her.

"Not here. And not tonight," he said with resolve. "You already gave me what I needed."

Her eyebrows raised with suspicion. "What if I want more of you?" she asked as he eased her jeans over her calves.

"I'll never have enough of you, but a taste was enough for tonight." His grin warmed her again. Wade eased Ravenna to the floor and helped her shimmy into her jeans. She couldn't manage her shoes one-handed, and he found himself enjoying dressing her as much as he had liked peeling her clothes away.

Once she was covered head to toe, he risked one more taste of her neck, a sweet-salty nibble of her pulse point. Her knees buckled and her breath caught. "Please," she moaned.

He chuckled and straightened. "Back to the hotel," he said with a smile.

She stumbled, but he caught her and laughed. "Ravenna, can you walk?"

"Yes, I can walk. You are potent, but I don't need to be carried back to the hotel over your shoulder."

"Actually, I like that idea. Probably too much." On that thought, he made one final check of the tent. She batted away his hands when he tried to scoop her into his arms. Wade settled for a walk with Ravenna at his side, a two-block stroll back to their hotel.

When the lights of the hotel came into view, she gave his hand a tug. The pain in her eyes stopped his feet. "What's wrong?" he asked.

"Would you mind if we stopped downstairs to grab a bite to eat. The meds are taking a toll on my stomach."

"I'm sorry. I should have thought of that before we—"

She shook her head. "No. *Before* was amazing."

"Let's grab dinner in the lounge," he said, and she nodded, her smile back in place.

The entry of the hotel, slick with marble and chrome, gleamed with synthetic glitz. Their eyes squinted attempting to adjust from dark evening to the bright artificial light. Inside, Wade located a table in a quiet corner where they could talk.

After placing orders, she asked about Wade's family. "Linnea's shared a bit about the hop farm. Why did you decide to leave?"

Sitting back for a moment to gather his thoughts he shrugged. "It might have worked if Dad and I could have found some type of balance, but we're too similar. We're both stubborn and want the final say. Dad wanted me to follow in his footsteps, and I had to find my own path."

"I can't imagine having a father like that. I was sad when Papa sold Silver Raven. And yes, it altered my future but didn't determine it."

"Leo's amazing. I've never met anyone with his combination of humility and brilliance."

Her smile warmed, eyes glistening in the low light. "You're probably not surprised, but I've heard that description of my papa before. I'm lucky, I guess." The gaze that had been watching him carefully, blinked away and then back. "After all this time away from Yakima, does your father still hold out hope that you'll return to run the hop farm?"

"Oh yeah. It's not a hope, it's a demand. One that he brings up every chance he gets." Wade finished off his beer, ready for a second. Talking about his family was taking a toll on his mood.

"Will you go back?"

His head shook. "Never. Brooke, my oldest sister, and her husband Dean put in the time and effort on the farm. They've earned it. I only tolerated that life."

She nodded. "I understand. Knowing how to farm isn't the same as a bone-deep love of the land." After a long moment, a soft sigh escaped her lips. "Some days I feel like a gypsy. When Silver Raven sold, I lost my footing. I've been wandering ever since."

Reaching across the table, he stroked the hand that toyed nervously with her water glass. "You do have a rare gift—helping people realize their dreams. Will you always need to save lost souls?"

With a laugh, she considered his observation. "Lost souls, very dramatic. Maybe I am an enchanted gypsy after all. Papa tells me it's buried in our heritage."

"You found me. And I may be lost without you." Unmasked, Wade hoped to learn how she felt about him and what she desired for their future. Her lips parted, ready to reply. But as she hesitated, the waiter arrived and the moment was lost.

A burst of laughter from Ravenna confused him until she raised her forgotten bandaged hand in an awkward wave and chuckled. "I'm not sure a burger was the best decision."

The server wandered back asking, "Can I get you anything?"

Wade nodded. "Another order of fries, more napkins, and a steak knife please." If he had to cut Ravenna's burger into bite-sized pieces and feed her, he would. Taking care of her basic needs now seemed more important than retracing the steps of the broken conversation.

After dinner, exhaustion caught up with Ravenna. The ride in the elevator sagged her knees while the momentum of the car carried them to the seventh floor. Steadied by Wade's strength, she took comfort leaning against his sturdy frame.

"I'm going to tuck you into bed and head back to my room," he said, needing the words even more than Ravenna.

"Are you sure?" she asked, a fragile whisper.

"Yes. We'll pick up where we left off later."

He barely heard when she agreed and mumbled, "Mm-kay."

The elevator doors swished open, and he led the way to her room. Only able to use one hand, she fumbled with the keycard. He wrapped his fingers around hers to assist. Once inside, it took all his willpower to control his baser instincts. Focused on her deeper needs, he ignored the urge to remove her clothes.

"Brush your teeth. I'll find you something to sleep in," he said as he shut the bathroom door, locking away temptation.

He dug through her suitcase and found what he was after. Her lingerie looked fragile in his large calloused hands. The simple lace-edged top and matching sleep-shorts were nearly translucent. When his cock thickened, he closed his eyes, took a slow breath, and switched off the overhead lights. The lamp by her bed cast the room in a golden, soothing glow. He'd picture her lying here alone, later tonight.

Tapping on the bathroom door, she opened to him as he held out the flimsy garment. "Put this on in there. I want to tuck you in, but if I see too much, I won't be able to leave." Ravenna's sly grin glimmered with desire. Even her smile had power over him. When she emerged from the bathroom, he found passion in her eyes, but the need was mixed with pure exhaustion.

"In bed," he commanded before he touched her. She snuggled under the covers; her dark eyelashes lay against her cheeks. Before he flicked off the light, she looked up with longing in her eyes.

"Could you lie down with me, just for a while, this time? Just until I fall asleep." The request begged for his contact and was laced with trust.

"This time? I thought you had too much whiskey that night to remember anything."

"Not possible. Every minute with you is unforgettable."

His nod agreed—he'd committed every moment with her to memory, too. Wade circled to the other side of the bed and toed off his shoes. He peeled away his shirt but left everything below the waist in place to encase his urgent erection. Settling close, he spooned his body against her warmth. Ravenna accepted his arm around her middle with a sigh. Her hair, soft as silk, smelled like citrus blossoms, sweet and bright. Delicious.

As she fell asleep Wade's exhausted thoughts wandered in two different directions, one glorious and one dangerous. He knew he was falling in love. Yet, he still protected a portion of his heart. Could he trust her?

Seeing Steven at the Coalition exhibit today prickled new suspicions. Part of him wondered if that man could be in Denver to check with Ravenna about Mosquito Creek Brewery. He'd never seen them together, but she wasn't in his sights all of the time.

No. It wasn't possible. There had to be another explanation for all the setbacks. Wade locked his uncertainties into a dark private space. Like a black hole, the unyielding density crushed his doubts and his desires, destroying both for now. He couldn't understand a black hole any better than he understood how he could simultaneously love and doubt Ravenna.

These thoughts warred until he started to fade, knowing if he woke here, with her, they'd both be late for the last day in Denver. Her breathing barely hitched as he eased from the bed, put on his shirt and shoes, and left her sleeping.

Locking her door behind him, he crossed the hall to his room. Yards away, the elevators slid open. Annie's laughter carried as she and Vince exited the elevator. He didn't feel like policing their activities and escaped before they spotted him in the hall. The thick walls did not mask Annie's squeals or the fact that only one door opened and shut.

His respect for Vince diminished. Annie sounded willing but may regret a workplace hookup in the morning. Through the thick walls, Wade could just make out her laughter and the cadence of their conversation in the room next door. He turned on the tv, found a channel, and hoped the low hum of a baseball game would mask their sounds.

TWENTY-FIVE

Natalie scrambled into her window seat while Seth stowed a bag in the overhead bin. "I can't believe we're doing this!" she said as he sat next to her.

"No second thoughts?" Her bright smile gave Seth all the answer he needed.

"Nope, no second thoughts. After I buy a dress, will our hotel handle all the arrangements?" she asked as their fingers entwined.

"From the flowers to the music, the concierge will take care of anything you desire." The plane taxied across the tarmac and her body trembled.

"I'm so happy, Seth. Thank you." He brought her wrist to his lips and placed a gentle kiss against her accelerating pulse. Once they were in the air, the flight attendant offered a glass of champagne while the mainland disappeared into a wide expanse of blue.

***

Erik groaned while Wade detailed the horror that had unfolded over the last couple of days.

"...and after the broken glass mess, Annie showed up late, hungover, and pissed at Vince. She blamed him for letting her sleep late and sulked when he refused to apologize."

"At least it's over, and you're one day closer to home."

"Oh, it's not over. It gets even better. Last night, the first leg of the trip went fine, but this morning when we tried to start the fleet, Ravenna's vehicle was dead."

"You've got to be fucking kidding me?"

"The truck worked great on the leg from Denver to Green River. Then when she spun the key the damn thing wouldn't even turn over. I'm ready to bite someone's head off, so I already sent Annie and

Vince down the road. They'll get back ahead of Ravenna and me—if they don't' kill each other first."

"Shit, Wade. This trip is cursed."

"You're telling me. I've got a mechanic taking a look at the dead truck." He pinched the bridge of his nose and winced. "Have you caught anything on the surveillance cameras?"

"I just checked the security app. Nothing out of the ordinary. Just a healthy family of raccoons looking for a way into the brewery."

"Crap, raccoons. Those creatures can do a shit-ton of damage. Secure the garbage and get the spent grain to farmers."

"Already on it. And the spent grain is already gone. The farmers are competing for the stuff, I guess their cattle love it."

"Good. Hey, I gotta go. Looks like the mechanic found the problem." As Wade approached, the guy from the gas station touched the brim of his orange hat. He hoped the gesture meant good news.

"It's an easy fix—looks like someone pulled a fuse. I'll have you on the road as soon as I run over and pick up a replacement."

"You mean a fuse is blown?" Wade asked.

"Nope, it's gone. Someone tampered with it. Did you leave the truck unlocked overnight? Seems like someone was playing a practical joke. Maybe the competition?" He laughed and readjusted his hat. "You'll be good to go in no time."

As the mechanic jogged to his pickup, Wade glanced around, half-expecting to find Steven lingering in the distance. Eyes unfocused on the horizon, he took a long, labored breath. The choice was his—he could be pissed as hell or thankful that it wasn't a serious mechanical problem. Letting it go wasn't easy—he just wanted to know what the hell was going on.

***

From her seat in the run-down diner, Ravenna watched as Wade paced the parking lot. He paused to talk to the mechanic then resumed his route, his steps leaving a dusty wake.

It looked like he'd be a while, so Ravenna decided to use her time to get something accomplished. When she shifted to get a better look at her laptop, her legs stuck to the cracked vinyl seat in the booth. She squinted her eyes, stared at the screen, and realized she had her own set of problems. Coalition was already demanding rough numbers from the festival.

She didn't know how she should spin the report. In fact, she was tempted to fudge the numbers, because the accurate figures might hurt Wade. Even with the endless frustrations, Mosquito's sales had been far beyond what anyone expected. With profit potential like this, the higher ups at Coalition would only ask for more. Wade had a problem. His beer was so good, he couldn't possibly keep up with the demand.

Still, she couldn't wait to show Wade these figures. The poor man needed some good news after his shit weekend. At least he hadn't overreacted when Steven showed at the Mosquito Creek Brewing tent. When that ass had approached, Wade just stood there, hands in his pockets, and grinned. "Good to see you Steven," he'd said. "What can I do for you today?"

"Just checking in with Coalitions bright rising star. I see that you've had a decent showing in spite of your novice crew. Next time, you should plan ahead. Most of the Coalition brewers know better than to bring green employees to an important event."

Ravenna had suppressed a giggle when Wade had stared at Steven, nodded, and rubbed his chin. "Hmm, I'll take that under advisement, but the way I see it, it's best to keep my experienced staff at the brewery. Even your most brilliant marketing schemes won't sell skunky beer."

Cut by the insult, Steven scowled and left. Wade had enjoyed a good laugh, but Ravenna still could not shake her growing dread. She knew Steven, and the man was ruthless when challenged.

***

Wade approached the diner unable to imagine Ravenna tampering with the truck. What would be the point? Still, someone on this trip must have stolen that fuse.

Questions pulsed through his mind. Perhaps Annie was bitchy enough to sabotage Ravenna's vehicle. Could have been Vince, but he seemed focused on only one thing—escaping Annie's daggered looks. Maybe a competing brewer spotted their fleet and pulled the fuse. Anything was possible.

Closer to the diner he watched Ravenna's fingers glide across the keyboard, dealing with everything Coalition sent her way. Determined to put this trip behind him, Wade decided to bend the truth and tell Ravenna it was a blown fuse. He pushed the door open, and the little bell over the diner door chimed. Her eyes flicked up, heated, and followed him as he settled across from her in the booth.

"Looks like it's a blown fuse," he said with a nod, keeping his eyes on her as he lied.

"What a relief, I was concerned that our truck had been tampered with. I've had a bad feeling from the time we left Ashwood." From the moment she spoke, Wade regretted his deception, but it was too late to come clean.

The waitress rushed over, poured him a cup of steaming coffee, and he declined when she asked to take his order. Ravenna had already finished her meal, and his stomach was in knots. Even with the scent of bacon in the air, he knew he wouldn't be able to eat a bite.

"Unfortunately, this repair means we'll be several hours behind Annie and Vince," he said. "Once the mechanic returns, his repair

208

won't take long. We'll be able to get back on the road and at least make a few hours tonight."

An enticing smile crept across Ravenna's face. Her cheeks flushed as she shared a smoldering idea. "Um, Wade. We have no reason to hurry—I haven't turned in my key."

Her top teeth worried her lower lip, an alluring flash of nerves, and Wade went rock-hard in an instant. "Damn, woman, you're brilliant." On a slow blink his plan gelled. "Wait for me in your room. I'll be there as soon as I can."

A quick giggle shook her body. "I can do that."

"And Ravenna?" He waited for her dark brown eyes to lock on his, needing her undivided attention.

"Yes, Wade?"

"Not one stitch of clothes. I want you laying bare on the sheets, waiting for me." Her face went from pink to a more tempting shade of crimson. "God, I love it when you blush," he said on a low growl.

Ravenna's breath hissed out slowly. "Please, don't take too long."

TWENTY-SIX

The heavy door slammed behind her, a decisive metallic thud. Ravenna rushed, trying to transform the shabby motel room into a dreamy oasis. The lamp in the corner didn't seem quite as glaring as the rest, so she left it on and turned all the others off.

A station scrolling the weather repeated a mix of jazz. She kept the volume low. The dated music was more romantic than complete silence, and the screen tinted the room soft blue. At the last moment, she rigged the lock to give way when Wade pushed the door. Stripped bare, Ravenna grabbed her perfume and spritzed the air above the squeaky bed.

Winded, blushing, and bare, she measured her breathing and tried to slow her racing heart. Her stomach rose and fell. The bluish light hit her olive, sun-kissed skin, enhancing the contrast against the crisp white sheets. Waiting brought a delicious insanity as she listened for Wade's knock.

Breasts tingling and heavy, she trailed a caress over her soft peaks. The cool air rattling from the antiquated air conditioner blew across her aching nipples, and she squeezed the pointed tips. Imagining his touch, she trailed her fingertips lower. A curl of arousal electrified her senses.

A loud knock widened her eyes with a jolt, and she knotted her hands over her tummy. "It's open," she squeaked. The rigged door seemed secure from the outside but easily gave when Wade pushed it.

"Anyone could have walked in." He entered and closed the door behind him. Her mouth went dry seeing the ridge of his length pressed hard against his jeans.

"You would have stopped them," she answered, trust laced in her reply. Ravenna waited for his full reaction as his eyes adjusted to the dimly lit room. His gaze swept, landing on her body.

"Beautiful," he said, as his stance widened at the end of the bed, just beyond the reach of her feet. She watched while a devilish grin tipped his lips, and his gray eyes glinted silver in the dim light. "While you waited, did you tease and touch yourself?" he asked.

"Yes." Her legs inched apart in response to his settling gaze.

In one swift move Wade pulled his shirt over his head. Her mouth went dry at the sight of an intriguing mosquito tattoo. Inked over his rib cage, the art was captivating, masculine, and seriously hot. Ravenna bit her lip and distracted herself with a long visual journey. Hair decorated the skin around his dark nipples, continued past the ridges of his abdomen, and disappeared in a tantalizing line beneath the edge of his jeans.

"Show me." His command brought her eyes back to his.

"Show you?" A sheen of sweat bloomed across her chest.

"Yes, show me how you like to be touched." Wade popped the top button of his jeans and watched her squirm.

Ravenna licked her lips, caressed her breasts, and pulled her nipples to rigid peaks.

"Now lower," he growled. His eyes faded to a darker shade as her fingers teased the wet line of her sex. Wade slid his zipper down at the same rate that she stroked her fingers into her heat.

"I need you," she cried, her legs spreading open, a vulnerable invitation.

"Not yet." Working the top of his pants apart, his cock sprung free and he kicked his clothes to the floor. Ravenna's eyes widened as Wade stroked his hard, proud length.

When a wrinkle of concern clouded her expression, he reassured her and said, "We'll take things slow." Then his lips took on a wicked slant. "Babe, glide your fingers inside, I want to see you glisten."

Her knees fell open, and she canted her hips, dipping two fingers into her pink folds. Her moans increased as she deepened her eager strokes. Her heavy exhales intensified Wade's self-gratifying pulls.

His fingers curled tight around his cock and stroked a cadence that mimicked the beat of her pelvis.

"Don't come, not yet," he warned as her breathing hitched. She inched her fingers from her core, to keep from detonating. Wade prowled, bent forward, and took her wrist in his hand. He brought her fingers to his lips, sucking each one clean. "Your cream is so delicious, so sweet, I need another taste."

Her breath held as she watched him descend. Wade dipped his tongue into the drenched valley her fingers had just teased. With strong hands, he lifted her hips, deepening his tongue's penetration. Desperate fingers tore into the white sheets, as he lapped a long sensuous line to the apex of her sex.

"Don't stop," she begged. He never intended to stop now that he'd found this bliss. He licked and lapped her arousal, starved for her body, drinking in her need. Her keening cries increased but began to edge with frustration. She needed more. Wade slid a finger intimately, and her body pulled him in. He moaned against her center, knowing how satisfying this place would feel around his cock.

With a twist of his fingers and one precise suck, her body detonated. The onslaught on her sensitive nerves rolled, surging waves of hot release. Ravenna barely recognized her voice as she called out Wade's name.

Nibbling her everywhere, he longed to own every inch. He brought her down with caresses to her breasts, clavicle, neck, and mouth as she recovered her breath.

Wade kneeled between her legs, ready to claim what he'd always known was his. The rip of a condom wrapper opened her eyes. He grinned as she peeked through dark lashes to watch him roll the protection over his length. Wade saw a hint of worry and traced her bellybutton with his fingertip. When she hitched a leg around his hip, he knew she was ready. "That was stunning. I want to see you come apart while I'm buried to the hilt."

Her other leg came around, urging him forward. "I want to feel your weight over me, surrounding me when we come," she said. Over her body, he prowled and teased her breasts, sucking each rosebud peak.

At last, he settled against her juncture. Hooking her feet at the bend of his knees, she urged him forward. The wide tip of his rigid cock breached her channel. A fraction in, he eased forward then rocked back again. Repeating the stretch, each pulse buried his length a little more, taking her senses under his control. Braced on his hands, he watched her eyes go wide.

When he was fully seated, she let out a sigh. Then absolute pleasure took over, slick and hot, as she accepted his girth. His breath went ragged and Wade's precision fragmented. Each push inched her up the mattress as he began a slow measured climb that ransacked their senses and entangled their souls in bliss.

Lost in her moans, her scent, and the sight of her dark silky hair draped over the white pillows, his world synchronized to her every move. Ravenna's hips chased the drag of his cock across her inner nerves. With each pass, she squeezed tighter around his length. Her fingernails raked along his back, and he welcomed the sting. Pain mixed with pleasure, he was close to exploding but refused the release.

"Come for me," he gasped as he drove hard and deep. Ravenna's breath came in jagged bursts as her wet heat fisted his cock. Stripped of her senses, her orgasm detonated, a rushing climax that rode her keening cry.

A clench of her pussy sent heat down his spine. White light flashed behind his eyes, and her name merged with incoherent words he had only used in songs. As the last wave of bliss pumped into her body, Wade fell into a euphoria that left him bewitched by her spell. Weight on his elbows, he claimed a kiss that shared her oxygen.

Unwilling to slip from her heat, he spun Ravenna's body over his, and she collapsed against the solid plane of his chest. They heaved in unison, recovering from a place that neither had experienced before.

"Oh my God, Wade, I've never ... that was ... perfect," she said giggling.

Normally laughter would be the wrong response, but he shared her disbelief. "I didn't think anything could be—"

"So powerful," they finished the unison words together. He joined her as she laughed, bodies still pulsing with sated bliss. She lay on his chest as he traced a path down her spine.

His words rumbled against her cheek. "Can I talk you into staying here another night?"

"Mm-hmm," she moaned and nodded, remaining in a sated trance.

"Good. I see no reason to rush back to Ashwood when I have everything I want right here." She shivered when his next touch demonstrated why he needed all day to explore this delirious bliss.

***

Later that evening, she lay in bed ignoring a local news channel as the shower ran. They agreed to escape their sex-cave and find a place in this town to grab a decent meal. If she joined him under the hot spray, they may never leave the room.

While Ravenna had a moment, she replied to a text from Linnea. Vince and Annie had called in with their plan to push home tonight. The thirteen-hour drive would put the pair in town after ten. Evidently, Vince had endured enough of Annie's complaining and wanted to escape her whining as soon as possible.

Ravenna didn't blame the girl for *some* of her behavior. Following their drunken hook-up, Vince had brushed her off quickly. Annie flung the rejection in his face with wicked energy. Even though

Annie was annoying, Ravenna didn't think she deserved to be treated like that.

As the spray of the shower ceased, Ravenna attached her phone to the charger. It immediately chimed with another text. At the same moment, a message buzzed, but this time from Wade's phone. Ravenna's stomach flipped with an instant stab of worry.

"Was that my phone?" Wade asked emerging from the steam-filled bathroom with a towel slung low around his waist. The minuscule, threadbare towel exposed a lean line of muscle that angled at his hips. His long hair glistened with droplets of water hanging on the ends.

Ravenna took a long unashamed look, and he grinned. Flexing for her, he turned and gave her a classic bodybuilder pose. "And to think these hardened muscles come from lifting kegs."

"Whatever you're doing works. Let me trace every inch." She gave into temptation and outlined his mosquito tattoo with her tongue.

His arm came around her, and he whispered close to her ear, "So long as you promise not to ignore the hardest thing on my body." When he pressed the solid length of his erection against her tummy, she moaned and inched away the towel to grasp his hard contours.

With renewed need burning between them, Ravenna ignored the sounds coming from their phones and led him to a chair waiting near a large floor-length mirror. With her man at the perfect height, she fell to her knees to taste his cock. The angle gave Wade a view he would remember.

"Fuck, yes," he growled as her lips teased the plum-colored crown. Her tongue slid over his velvet length and meticulously explored the rigid veins. Curling her fingertips, she grazed his tight balls.

"Shit, that's amazing." His eyes locked on the mirror to relish the erotic show. Wade took control, coiling her hair in his fist. She opened her throat to accommodate his pulsing length. Her saliva dripped, slicking her hand as she fisted his rock-hard shaft.

"God, Ravenna—I'm gonna come," he growled the warning and she took him deeper. Accelerating the pace, she tightened her grip at the base as his seed flooded the back of her throat. She swallowed and sucked while Wade trembled out the last pulse of his release.

"Delicious," she purred, while kissing the muscled contours of his thighs. Wade pulled her to his lap and devoured her swollen mouth with a grateful kiss.

"Babe, that was amazing," he said against her neck. She snuggled in, warm and soft and alluring. He was about to return the favor when the phone pinged again. Frustration laced her sigh as she gave in to the insistent sound.

He was still recovering as she squealed happily. "Oh, my God, look!" Ravenna's fingers touched the screen as she carefully studied each image.

"What's happened?" He grabbed the towel and slung it round his hips before sinking onto the mattress next to her.

"Way to go, Seth," he said, but really wasn't surprised. "I've never seen my cousin look happier. Eloping must have been the right decision."

"It was. Natalie was trying to get the wedding planned, but I could tell she didn't enjoy it. Hawaii looks good on them. Just look at her dress, the flowers in her hair, and that turquoise ocean. Could anything be *more romantic*?"

After sending a text to congratulate the couple, Wade watched as she scrolled carefully through the pictures again. She smiled, commenting on feminine details he never would have noticed—the palms in the background, and Natalie's ring as it glittered in the tropical sun. While Ravenna sent Natalie another message Wade spotted the glisten of a tear in her eye. For a moment, he risked imagining a lifetime with this alluring woman. A future filled with a family, a home, even growing old together. He wondered why those ideas didn't frighten him, in fact nothing had ever felt so right.

TWENTY-SEVEN

Vince rolled in after eleven, about ten minutes ahead of Annie. He was surprised to find Trish and Erik waiting to unload.

"Thanks, guys. I'm sorry we kept you up so late," Vince said, grateful for the help.

"Hey, no worries. Trish and I have been in the same situation more times than we can count—when all you can think about is a bed. Let's finish the essentials and wait on the rest 'til morning." Erik pushed the heavy doors open and grabbed a dolly.

Exhaustion kept words to a minimum as work wrapped up. Annie sped away first, leaving Vince to lock up with Trish and Erik.

"Are you both still staying on-site?" Vince asked as they secured the trucks.

"Yeah. And we'll do this again when Wade arrives. His car trouble will put him at least a day behind you," Trish added.

Vince masked his surprise. He knew an honest mechanic would have found that pulled fuse in about ten minutes. "Wow, it seems like we need to pay more attention to vehicle maintenance," he lied and pondered possible causes for their lengthy delay. This worked in his favor—he only needed a little more time to finish the job.

"See you in the morning," Vince said and stepped toward his car. He watched Erik and Trish wander arm in arm down the path toward the tiny homes.

***

Vince struggled to wake after only two hours sleep, but he wanted this to be over. Steven promised another large cash deposit once he sabotaged another batch of Double Deet IPA. This setback would put Wade far behind his scheduled commitment, trapping him in Coalition's demands.

Tampering with the rigs during the road trip hadn't done much more than heighten tension. At first, Vince thought those little annoyances were worthless, but watching the team come apart in Denver proved his meddling was worth the extra effort.

Finding Annie so willing to hit the sheets, and better still, so emotionally explosive as he toyed with her following the hookup, gave him extra time to put action to his plans. She'd wanted to distance herself from him as soon as possible and eagerly pushed toward home.

Giving up Annie so soon was a regret. She still had *plenty* left to enjoy. But he kept his priorities in line—money was tougher to come by than an easy lay.

Vince killed the headlights before he pulled onto Mosquito Creek's gravel lot. He parked at the shadowed edges, far away from the mill lights and the tiny house where Erik and Trish slept. Using the rear entrance, he crept inside.

The small red light from his headlamp gave the best possible combination of night vision and stealth. He set to work, opening the tank to add burnt malt to the current batch of Double Deet. The scorched key ingredient would taste subtle at first and take days to mature. Ultimately, the entire batch would be ruined.

Once Vince accomplished his task, he slipped out, snuck to his car, and drove away. Now that the mission was complete, he found it easy to sleep. Any threat of guilt had been beaten out of him long ago in prison.

***

Waking in Wade's arms could become a serious addiction. His light nibbles across her breast entered her dreams and left Ravenna panting with need. Pure pleasure accelerated as he drew a pattern down her belly, leaving a trail of heated desire.

"Don't stop, that feels so decadent," she moaned, her eyes still shut to the morning light.

"I need to watch you fall apart with only my touch," he said. "The view is amazing." Her body responded to every glide of his fingers. Each caress pulled a gasp from her lips that hardened his already steely cock. He wondered if he could come by only watching ecstasy play across her expressive face.

Every inch of Ravenna's skin trembled. Her legs scissored on the rumpled sheets until she had kicked off every thread. Laying nude before him, he smiled as she writhed, his to direct and enjoy. Wade took his time, teasing cries from her, circling his fingers and plunging into her depths. She lost herself to his generous touch.

As she arched off the mattress, he knew she was drawing close. It took all his willpower not to lift himself over her body and plunge deep. Watching this joy was too mesmerizing. He simply could not tear himself away from this erotic display. As her climax arced in electric pulses, he was exactly where he wanted to be, controlling each crashing wave as it rolled into the next. She slowly descended and her wet sex grasped his fingers with tight pulses of potent heat.

"So beautiful," he said dotting soothing kisses along her vulnerable neck.

"Mm, good morning, man of mine," she moaned. Wade cherished her possessive words. Meant only for him, Ravenna could never belong to another.

***

Erik loved sleeping in late after making love to his wife. Seven years of marriage only heightened their skills and fortified the relationship. Each time they made love seemed better than the last, especially since she had gone off the pill and they began to hope for a baby.

Giving Trish extra time to sleep, he made a cup of coffee and wandered into the brewery. Erik saw the light was on in the office and knew Linnea had already arrived for the day. The crack of hammers and hum of saws echoed at Whitewater. Carlos, Rick, and Kent worked hard even while Seth and Natalie honeymooned in Hawaii.

Erik went about his routine, finally taking a break to check the previous night's feed with the security app on his phone. It began like every other video, darkened rooms illuminated by the faint glow of a green exit sign. A few security lights reflected across bright tanks, casting silo-shaped shadows that slanted over the plank floor.

His eyes narrowed. A small red light bobbed, moving around the brewhouse. The cameras had a difficult time picking up the details, but a human gait clearly caused some sort of movement.

Erik held his breath when a dark hand crossed the reflective surface of the tank holding Double Deet. Something was dropped into the batch. The hand moved away, and the dark shadow of a barely discernable human form moved out of the frame.

Shit, shit, shit. From this camera angle, Erik could not make out the identity.

Switching to another feed, one that kept watch over the rear entrance, the view was unmistakable. It was Vince—dressed in dark clothes with a red headlamp strapped to his forehead.

Fuck. Fear expanded. He had no idea what was swirling in that batch of Double Deet. It must be dumped immediately. Now that Erik considered the problem thoroughly, everything Vince touched must be sanitized with meticulous care. Damn it, this was not his call, but the risk to the public was too high. And he knew Wade would agree.

Buried in the storage room, away from eyes and ears, he placed the painful call. When Wade picked up, the hum of the diesel engine bled over the connection. Wade was on the road and Ravenna was most likely driving the other rig. Erik swallowed, but couldn't find the right words.

"Hey, good morning, buddy. Ravenna's following me in her truck. We're finally rolling down the road." Wade sounded so happy this morning, Erik hated that he was about to kill that good mood. A sick feeling pitted his stomach as he described, in hideous detail, the events that occurred during the night.

Several seconds of stunned silence preceded Wade's blistering response. "Fuck. Even the kegs that are ready to ship will need to be pulled. This could end Mosquito Creek Brewing."

"We've got time." Erik said, then winced when he heard the slam of Wade's hand against the steering wheel.

"Damn it to hell, I feel like I'm going to puke. Erik, keep this quiet. I need time to think. Tell Trish and Seth, but no one else. We need to find a way out of this fucking shit-storm."

Erik attempted to reassure his friend. "We've got evidence; let's find a way to use it. I'll carry on today as if nothing's changed. Whatever you do, don't give up."

"Not a chance. Maybe I can figure this out from behind the wheel. We'll push home and arrive around midnight."

"See you then. Call me later, and we'll figure this out." While Erik waited for Wade to call back with some sort of solution, he stifled his desire to dump every vessel and clean every tank. He felt like an automaton, completing pointless work that was merely a mask to his churning rage.

***

As the miles passed beneath his wheels, Wade considered every angle. Sweet Venom at Old Mosquito was still marketable. Thank God, Vince had no access to that location.

He knew the taproom needed to close to stop the flow of potentially tainted beer. All it took was one call to the credit card company. When he told the company that handled their system that their account had been hacked on Mosquito's end, they paused the service to give Wade time to investigate the problem.

Linnea called a few minutes later. "Wade, something's wrong. I can't take credit card payments. Do you want me to—"

"Just close the doors for the day."

"Why? We can still take cash."

"Trust me on this Linn. It's for the best. Can you keep this between us for now? Please, just tell everyone we're having computer issues."

"What aren't you telling me?" she begged to know.

"Please, I need time. I swear, you will know everything soon. Nobody, not even family, can know."

"You're scaring me." Fear gave her whisper and edge. "Okay, Wade I'll do whatever you need. I love you."

"Love you too, sis. I'll fix this. I promise."

With ongoing damage contained, he relaxed enough to begin working the problem.

At the next stop for fuel, Wade sped from one gas pump to the next looking past Ravenna toward the fast food spots next door. "After we've filled up, do you mind if we grab a burger and just push home?" he gestured toward the golden arches.

Her smiled faded, but she agreed. "Sure, after last night, I'm anxious to get home and pick up where we left off, too." After he finished filling his rig, she wrapped her arms around his torso, but he couldn't return the warmth and pulled away.

The confusion on her face filled him with guilt, and he held up his hands. "I spilled a little gasoline—I don't want to get fuel on your clothes." He knew the excuse was lame, but at least it put a smile back on her face.

"There's a sub shop inside, why don't I order us a couple of sandwiches while you take care of the second truck?" she suggested.

"That'd be great." He started to reach for his wallet, needing distance between her and the secret he struggled to conceal.

"I'll get lunch today," she said, turned, and skipped away. A few minutes later, she came back with two bags and handed one over.

"I guessed that you wanted roast beef. Do you really want to eat and drive?" He could tell Ravenna had read his impatience, he hoped she couldn't read his mind.

"Yeah. If that's okay with you."

"Well I'm ready, and my truck's fueled." She moved in for a quick peck. Tilting in, he savored the warmth of her lips, unable to resist a more thorough taste. Her sweet lips parted for him, seeking more. On a sigh, she inched apart, and he saw that the smile that he'd stolen was back on her lovely face. Ravenna skipped away, humming, and a thick cloud of guilt surrounded Wade again.

With that smile, that kiss—Wade was *almost* certain she wasn't' involved. Unless. Could it be that Vince took directions from her? Despising himself, he shook his head to erase the errant thought. There was only one way to be sure. He had to find a way to make Vince confess. Miles in the dark gave him just enough time to build a skeletal plan. Unfortunately, success hung on that bastard, Vince.

***

After they crawled to a stop, Trish and Erik joined them to unload the essentials in near silence. Their dollies rolled until the sky took on the purple tint of dawn. Ravenna slipped off to bed long before Wade was ready to sleep. Fear wracked his mind. He knew he'd probably lose her once he revealed his stunning breach of trust.

Huddled in the office, Wade covered the details of his plan with Erik. His friend asked, "Do you think it's a good idea to bring the sheriff here tomorrow? It may cause a firestorm of publicity."

"It's a risk I have to take. Vince needs to feel threatened enough to reveal the source. I'm convinced Steven's involved, but without proof, I'll lose the brewery." Pulling his hands painfully through his hair, stress and exhaustion weighed on him. "We've got to get some sleep if we can. Join me at the sheriff's office tomorrow morning at nine but park behind the building. If word gets out, and Vince slips away before we catch him, we'll be sunk."

Two men walked silently to tiny homes and climbed separate stairs in the early morning light. Sinking in next to Ravenna, inhaling her warmth, Wade never found sleep.

He didn't know how much time he had left with this beautiful woman. She moaned, turned, and curled against his chest. Warm, soft, and sweet, she flooded his senses. He pressed a loving kiss into her hair and surrendered their fate to the unknown.

Too many lives would be ruined if his brewery failed—Seth, Natalie, Linnea, Dillon, Erik, and Trish. Shit, even the small town of Ashwood would suffer. He would sacrifice his future, but not the others—the risk was too high.

He couldn't know how Ravenna would respond until she saw the footage. He tenderly kissed her forehead, closed his eyes, and prayed she would understand.

TWENTY-EIGHT

Vince hovered outside Linnea's office. A traitor's smile tilted the corners of his mouth. Wade balled his fists controlling a deep need to beat the shit out of the guy. Suddenly, the bastard jumped, and Linnea walked into the taproom. Vince leaned against the wall, licked his lips, and followed her movements with his eyes. Wade wondered how he could have missed these sleazy tendencies all along.

Unable to take another moment, Wade slammed a door halting Vince's attention on his sister's curves. The dirtbag spun and adjusted his pants with an awkward sidestep. Their eyes met and Vince tipped his chin. "Hey, boss. Glad your back. Did the mechanic get everything worked out with that engine trouble?" he asked.

"Yeah, it was a minor electrical issue." *You deceitful fuck.* "They had to send for a replacement part."

Vince raised an eyebrow and nodded. "Good thing you found a mechanic you could trust."

Wade blinked away the urge to take his anger out on this asshole, now. "Hey, Vince, can you let Linnea know we're going to have a staff meeting later today."

"Sure, sure, can I help out?"

"Absolutely, we need to go over the Denver trip. I'd appreciate your input about ways we can improve the flow before the next festival." Wade masked his hate with a grin. He'd already met with the sheriff this morning, and the trap for this cockroach was in place.

"What time?" Vince asked, so willing to be helpful.

"After lunch, if that will work for you." He hoped he wasn't acting *too* friendly. A guy like Vince could probably smell deception.

"I'll be there." Vince left to find Linnea and tell her about the staff meeting. Since his sister was a terrible liar, Wade knew he'd been wise to keep her in the dark.

Going through the motions of checking the current batch turned his stomach to acid. Succeed or fail, they'd be dumping every drop of beer tonight. Wade willed this plan to work and prayed that Mosquito would still be his in the morning.

Ravenna walked into the taproom, her arms loaded with a tray of coffee, looking better than anyone should after only a few hours of sleep. "I brought caffeine!" she called. Her bright smile lit the entire room. Gazing at her gentle face gave him hope. *Please let her understand.*

Before the gathering, Erik and Trish brought in burgers for the entire crew. Wade choked his down, feeling like he was eating his last meal. Vince wandered in a little late and smirked at Annie's glare as she ran off with her lunch to clean taps.

The plan moved to phase two when Wade sent the sheriff a text. In minutes, men would block each exit in case Vince tried to bolt.

"Linnea, we can get started whenever you're ready," Wade said calling the group together. She grabbed a pad of paper, intending to take notes about the festival.

A section of video was cued up from a feed on Erik's phone. He had chosen an indiscernible image and paused it on the large screen that covered the wall.

In the center of the taproom, the entire team faced Wade as he took a breath. "Our Denver trip was a little rough," he began, "however, I think we'll find the experience enlightening. Erik has a video to explain the direction we will be taking."

Erik tapped his phone. All eyes watched the strange dark image.

"What is this, Wade?" Linnea asked. "This isn't Denver, it's the inside of the brewery."

The shot looked artistic in the grainy greenish feed. A door opened, and a man walked in. A red headlamp streaked light across the screen.

Vince hissed. "Fuck this, I'm out of here."

"Sit down," Wade commanded. The asshole moved, but Sheriff Holden stepped into the doorway with his hand resting on his hip, a few inches from his sidearm.

Erik's voice echoed in the stunned-silent room. "Seth and I installed security cameras the moment we realized someone was messing with Mosquito's beer."

"Why didn't I know about the security system?" Linnea asked. "Didn't you trust me?" Anxious, Wade's eyes met his sister's. She flicked her gaze away and found Ravenna instead. "I can't believe this." Linnea shook her head, clearly hurt by Wade's lack of confidence.

Ravenna's chin quivered as she whispered, "Don't worry, Linn. He trusted you. Unfortunately, Wade didn't tell you because he couldn't put his faith in me."

Vince shot to his feet again. "I'm not going back to jail!"

From across the room, Annie yelped. "Back to jail? Oh my God! You manipulative bastard," she shrieked and closed in.

As she approached, a snide grin stretched Vince's features. "Hey, babe, I didn't hear you complaining Saturday night."

Her eyes narrowed, and Annie hurled a slap across his face.

Vince bellowed at the statue-like man in the doorway. "Did you see that, Sheriff? That's assault!"

Sobbing, Annie ran next door to Whitewater. Wade hoped she would stay there with Amanda. He still didn't have what he needed to make this nightmare go away.

When the sheriff's expression didn't shift, Vince grew desperate. "It was Steven! He paid me. I have the deposits to prove it." His head snapped back and forth. "Somebody listen! Let me make one call. I can get Steven to admit this was all his fucking idea."

Ravenna cringed and mumbled, "I can't believe it, Steven was just using me all along."

Erik prodded for more. "Tell me, Vince, what did you put in the batch? Did you plan to poison our customers?"

"Don't be an idiot," Vince barked. "Coalition wants control, not a lawsuit. We knew you would never let imperfect beer out your doors. There's nothing dangerous. It just tastes like shit."

Looking at the sheriff for approval, Wade got the nod. "Get Steven on the phone. I want it on speaker. Vince, you've got one shot to prove to me you weren't alone in this."

The room went silent while Vince tapped the screen on his phone. Only the faint mechanized hum of Mosquito Creek Brewery blended with Steven's voice after he picked up. "I'm assuming you've got news?"

"Yeah, it's done. The beer tastes terrible and Erik's dumping it. Wade's scrambling," Vince lied with ease.

"Perfect. Stay in place for a few more days. I have to be sure Wade's backed into a corner. I'll add another five grand for your trouble."

"No problem. I'll be in touch." A satisfied grin revealed that he'd played this game before.

Once he was off the phone, his eyes darted from the sheriff to Wade. "See, I'm cooperating. Whatever you need to get this guy, I'll do it."

Jarrod Holden crossed the room and slipped cuffs around Vince's wrists. A burst of foul language poured from the ex-con as he handed him off to his deputy. "Read him his rights but hold off on his call until I get to the station."

Wade's steady gaze landed on Ravenna, waiting until she raised her eyes to his. Her exposed pain slammed into him, ripping a hole in his heart. "I'm so sorry, Ravenna. I almost told you, so many times. But..."

When she rose from her seat and stepped toward him, a sliver of hope expanded in his chest, but that hope melted away when tears began streaming down her face.

His phone buzzed and he checked the screen. "It's *Steven*. That was fast." He blew out a long breath before answering on speaker, "This is Wade."

Arrogance shot from the phone, "This is Steven. Coalition needs some answers."

"What do you want? We're busy here," Wade said, trying to get Steven talking.

"That's what I hear," he sneered. "Ravenna tells me you're destroying another run."

Ravenna's mouth dropped open. Shaking her head, she buried her face in her hands to smother a cry. The sudden move tangled her delicate raven bracelet in her hair, and she struggled to free it. Linnea moved to her friend and helped without a sound. If Ravenna hadn't collapsed into the safety of Linnea's hug, Wade would have gone to her, even with Steven on the phone.

His arms ached, longing to hold her, but he had to see this through. It pained him to coax everything from Steven, but to do that he had to utter her name. "Ravenna? She's been keeping you up to date on—"

"Everything," Steven cut in. "We know about your employee's food poisoning, the car trouble, and the drama with that little blonde who works for you. Not to mention two failed batches of beer. You're out of options." His chuckle sent shivers down Wades' spine. "But I have a way out. You can buy Mosquito's freedom."

Here it is. Wade held his breath, feeling the first glimmer of relief. "I'm listening."

"Rusk. Your patented hop. We want control of the patent *and* a percentage of the hop farm."

Wade grunted. "I don't own the farm. There's no way my father will give you any part of it."

"Find a way. If you really want your freedom, you will figure out a way to give us part of the hop business."

"Give me two hours," Wade blurted, hoping that would be enough time.

"Move quickly, Wade. You will find I'm not a patient man." With a click, the phone went silent and everyone in the room took a collective breath.

Sheriff Holden pulled out his cell. "I'll give Chicago PD a call. They'll have all they need to hold Steven overnight."

Jarrod Holden asked to speak with Wade in private for a moment then he left to fill out reams of paperwork tied to this uncommon event.

Once he was gone, Wade seized a wisp of hope and decided to beg, "Ravenna, I know Steven was lying. But I hope you can see why I had to keep this from you, from Linnea, from almost everyone. Please can I talk to you? Let me explain."

She shook her head. "No. It's too much. The lies. I'm tired of being used, and I can't take anymore." Small staggered steps carried her wracked body toward the door.

On a move to steady her, Wade pulled her pliant torso to his chest. He whispered, "I'm so sorry. Everything that happened between us means the world to me. Please. I'll do anything."

"You'll do anything but trust me." She sagged against him like a rag doll. Broken, Ravenna tried to shrink away, taking nothing from him and giving him no hope. Her faint whisper met his ears. "Please, Wade, just let me go."

When his arms fell away, she staggered out the door into the bright afternoon sun. He'd won. Mosquito was his. But the victory didn't matter. Wade stood frozen, completely numb. The future belonged to him, but that future didn't include Ravenna.

He startled when Linnea touched his shoulder. "What happened between you two while you were in Denver?" she asked.

A shrug was the only answer he could give his sister. She shook her head and followed Ravenna out. Wade staggered into his office and collapsed on his chair. He pinned his head in his outstretched hands, and said, "I never meant to hurt her," but there was no one in the room to hear his confession.

TWENTY-NINE

Wade didn't know how much time had passed until a sound forced him to move. He fished his phone from his front pocket. Dad's name lit the screen, but he sent the call to voicemail, unable to talk or think. News always spread through the Michaels' family like wildfire in a tinder-dry forest. Reliving the details now might send him over the edge. One memory would haunt him forever, the sight of Ravenna's car leaving Ashwood with her dark hair whipping in the wind.

Shuffled steps propelled him forward. Beyond the office, he made out the sound of liquid gushing from wide-open valves. Joining Erik, Wade lost himself in his work. They cleaned and sanitized every surface Vince touched.

With that task done, he began the heavy lifting. He hefted bag after bag of grain into his truck. The sweat pouring off his back helped to blind his mind. He would do anything to keep from thinking. If he refused to think, he didn't have to feel.

Slipping behind the wheel, he drove to the dump. Even farm animals were too good for grain Vince may have tainted. After cutting open the heavy cloth, he dumped the pungent grain into compost piles. Rot, this all would become a pile of rot.

Soaked with sweat, and sticky with dust, he finally allowed himself to feel. Slashing bags wide open–he welcomed the shredding of his soul. Ravenna would never forgive him. Mosquito Creek Brewing seemed a small consolation prize compared to the loss.

***

The unrelenting pace of fixing Mosquito began to knit his life back together. His sister turned to him before she placed another call. "Are you sure we need to cancel all the festivals for the remainder of the season?" Linnea asked as she checked the calendar.

"Yeah, at least until September. Demand for Sweet Venom is too high. It will take weeks to get back to capacity. Keeping up with our usual customers and the demands of the taproom is already a stretch."

"Okay, I'll keep dialing, but I hate to disappoint our fans."

Wade's phone buzzed and the name Silvestre popped onto the screen. Fingers flying, he couldn't answer fast enough. "Ravenna!" he blurted before hearing a voice.

"Sorry, Wade, I didn't mean to disappoint you. It's Leo, how are you faring?"

Sinking into a nearby chair, Wade asked, "Is she okay? Has something happened to Ravenna?"

Leo hesitated. "She's doing as well as can be expected. Ravenna's made some difficult decisions, but that's not your concern. Not now."

"Tell her I'm sorry. Please."

"I will, and she knows." Leo continued, "Now, the reason for my call. . . I was asked to complete one last official duty when I resigned from the Coalition Craft Board."

"You resigned?"

"Yes." Anger tinted Leo's voice. "I don't want my name associated with Coalition any longer."

"And Silver Raven?" Wade asked.

His old friend huffed. "My label will revert to me." Leo paused and cleared his throat. "Wade, the board decided that if you are willing to sign a confidentiality agreement, Coalition will forgive their investment made in your expansion."

"What?" Wade yelled. "I'm not about to let Steven get away with the mess he caused and live on as if nothing has happened!"

"Oh, no. That, my friend, would not happen while I'm still alive," Leo said with a father's ferocity.

Wade sighed. "Good, that's good." While he had his friend on the phone, Wade tried to mend at least one layer of damage. "Leo, please forgive me for hurting Ravenna," he begged.

"I already have. Steven deceived everyone. But you should have trusted her. Mosquito Creek Brewing clouded your judgment. Your dream meant more to you than my daughter."

Leo was right. Until he'd lost her, Wade didn't realize keeping Mosquito Creek Brewing would mean nothing when he didn't have the woman he loved. He barely heard the rest of the conversation–something about paperwork and lawyers and signatures, then magically the debt he owed to Coalition would be gone. If he could find a way to see Ravenna, to explain, maybe he could find the right words that would make up for all his foolish mistakes.

***

He didn't have a sweet tooth. Goldfinch Bakery was the last place Wade usually spent time. But in the past few weeks, Maggie began test-baking protein bars made from spent grain. With the brewery working at capacity, he had plenty left over grain to go around.

Stepping through her door backward, he pulled the dolly inside. After leaving his weekly delivery, he wandered from the back hoping to find the owner at the customer counter. Hearing his sister's voice saying a familiar name, stopped his feet.

". . . these are Ravenna's favorite."

"Every time a make a batch of the double chocolate cookies I think about her. She called and ordered some the other day, and I mailed a dozen to Klamath Falls." Maggie's words fed him precious clues. Ravenna hadn't left for Chicago.

"Last time we talked she told me she's insanely busy with Silver Raven," Linnea told her friend.

"I can't believe she's taking on that challenge. Have you told Wade?"

"No. I don't want to ruin the progress he's made in the last month. For a while, Wade was barely even eating."

He'd noticed his sister never brought up Ravenna, yet he figured she kept in touch. *Silver Raven.* Wade smiled—that place meant so much to her. The brewery was her second childhood home. The accustomed ache he'd learned to live with eased a bit. Quietly, he slipped through the employee entrance, out the way he came, able to breathe easier knowing Ravenna was happy.

That evening Wade opened his laptop. Keeping to his routine, he scanned the listings, looking to buy a house in Ashwood. Erik and Trish loved Old Mosquito and had leaped at his offer when he asked if they wanted to buy his old place. It was time for him to plant roots and call Ashwood home.

After finding a new home listing, a farm on the edge of town, he jotted down the address then curiously typed *Silver Raven* into the search engine. A modern updated logo filled his screen. She'd patterned it after the bracelet he'd given her for her birthday. Clicking through the pages, he saw links that displayed the brewery's history, featured old favorite brews, and the release date for a new beer.

A click on the *About Us* tab filled his screen with her gorgeous face. The silver raven bracelet glimmered on her wrist. The photo was new, and he could still see a trace of hurt in her eyes. The familiar ache sharpened, and he wondered, *just how long will this pain last?*

A tab for *Employment* caught his eye. She was hiring. Several positions were open. Without forethought, his fingers sailed over the keys filling in the fields. He varied details that might give his real identity away. "Should I send this to you?" he asked her picture.

Click.

"Fate can decide if I have one more chance to change your mind."

***

Leo groaned. "You need to hire some help. You are too small and I am too old to keep up with the physical demands of this place."

Ravenna laughed. "But I'm having too much fun. If I hire someone, it will seem like work. Right now, it's my own delicious workshop."

Soaked in sweat and covered in dust, they shared a satisfied smile. Leo pulled off his gloves and stretched to ease his aching back. "I'm happy with our progress. But I better quit now, because I can't move any farther than my car."

"You better go, or Mama will worry."

"Give me a hug and I'll be off," he said holding his arms wide. She didn't care if he was sweaty. Ravenna hugged him, walked him to his car and waved goodbye.

Renovating the old brewery reflected the changes she was making to herself. Steven, Coalition, and even Wade had demolished different parts of her. Self-restoration took time.

At first, the solitary existence was enough. Lately, she craved more. Ravenna hoped bringing on employees would rebuild her connections to her old hometown. She scrutinized the resumes in her email, made a few calls, and scheduled her first round of interviews. To reward herself, she devoured one of Maggie's double chocolate cookies and sighed.

After dinner, she plopped on the floor and filled a bottom shelf with books. Reaching into a cardboard box, she unwrapped her favorite pottery—an artsy find from a little shop in Portland. Ravenna found a hammer and hung three landscape photographs, gorgeous gifts from Natalie. As she decorated, she hummed the tune that Wade played on his guitar each night in his tiny home.

Her muscles ached. After a long shower, she lay on crisp new sheets and listened to the hum of the brewery. Longing seeped in. Ravenna wanted to share these small details with Wade. He was the missing element. At some point, she'd have to talk to him and complete the last task of her private overhaul, even if closing that final door brought her pain.

At sunrise, an early morning shipment of hops delivered another potent reminder of Wade. Choosing the best, she'd selected hops grown on his Yakima family farm.

Ravenna had forgiven him long ago. All the blame lay entirely on Steven. Fortunately, that snake would pay for his deceit in jail. Now she knew that she and Wade were paying a lonely price, victims of circumstance, distance, and her stubborn pride.

***

Wade checked his email for the third time today. Nothing. Not a word from the new owner of Silver Raven. Should he create another false name and fill out a slightly different application? What type of employee was she looking for?

Ravenna needed someone to do the heavy lifting—that was part of the everyday work in a brewery. What if she'd already found a better man for the job? His jealousy spiked and he yelled at the screen, "Answer my application!"

***

"Thanks for coming in. I'll let you know within a week." She finished the interview with a handshake and another qualified candidate left her little office at Silver Raven.

For some reason, he didn't seem like a good fit. Ravenna had already chosen one employee, but two more slots needed to be filled. As she flipped through the stack of applications, her eyes were drawn again to the guy from Portland. He looked good on paper, almost too good. His cover letter said he was looking for a permanent change to a smaller town. An employee with his qualifications would allow her a bit of freedom.

Fine, why not at least give him a shot. Ravenna hit send as her next appointment knocked on the office door.

When Brandi walked in, she brought in a slew of pleasant high school memories with her. Ravenna recalled Brandi always being friendly, but they hadn't hung out in the same crowd. If nothing else, catching up after the interview would be fun. It turned out Brandi was perfect for the job—willing to learn and a person who displayed all the signs of a hard worker. The interview went so well, Ravenna hired her on the spot.

Finding another employee elevated Ravenna's mood, and she didn't feel like spending another night unpacking in her loft. She slipped into snug jeans, put on a little makeup, and snagged her raven bracelet before grabbing her keys and heading out. Radio on, she sang along and realized she hadn't bothered much with her appearance in a while. It felt good to dress up and go out, even if that meant spending the evening alone at a bar.

Running into Brandi at happy hour kept her from drinking alone. While sitting together, they sipped margaritas as Brandi brought Ravenna up to date on the local gossip. At drink number two, her new hire began asking questions Ravenna had tried to avoid.

"What made you decide to come back? Klamath Falls certainly isn't as exciting as Chicago. I heard you were working for some big, fancy corporation."

She nodded and sucked down a healthy gulp of her tequila-laced drink. It tasted like courage, and she spilled a bit of the truth. "Yeah it was fancy, but that company was too big. And I prefer to be around people I can trust."

Ravenna's belly dipped when Brandi lifted a brow and leaned in. "That sounds like man-made trouble."

She laughed, shrugging away the remains of her strong façade. "There was *a guy* in Chicago. It's a long story, way too long for tonight. I'll just say that his best gift was lying, and it landed him in jail."

"Jail. Shit, Ravenna, are you okay?"

Her hand brushed the air, clearing away the concern. "I'm good. And I'm smarter. At least I learned something about myself. My kryptonite is a strong man who pretends he wants to take care of me."

"Who isn't tempted by a gorgeous alpha male?" Brandi laughed, and Ravenna was glad she'd let her guard down. She'd found more than a great employee today—she'd found a new friend. Ravenna offered to order nachos when a few of Brandi's friends showed. Another round of drinks shifted the night to party-mode. Hours later, she left with cheeks that ached from smiling too much.

On her drive home, she glanced at her raven bracelet, and found that the beautiful reminder of Wade didn't twist her stomach as much. The anger was gone, and the quiet memory of love remained.

***

He missed her and found comfort when his fingers hit the fretboard. The warm, rich sound resonating from his guitar eased the ache in his chest. Wade played until he got the last line of the song he was writing exactly right. He leaned his guitar in its corner and checked his email one last time before going to bed.

"Yes!" he said loud enough to startle the birds nesting in nearby trees.

He could practically hear her lilting voice in the encouraging words he read on the screen. Now he had to come up with the perfect reply, without sounding like a stalker, *Thank you for your offer to meet about the spot at your brewery. I will be available to meet for an interview at Silver Raven next week. Please let me know what day and time works with your schedule. I look forward to meeting you.*

Wade had to keep his fingers from closing the message with *love, Wade.* He re-read the email three times, making sure it didn't sound too desperate or too aloof. Just a few more days. This plan to win her back had to succeed.

***

Awake early, she pulled on her canvas coveralls and made a pot of coffee. While it brewed, Ravenna popped another slice of tart apple into her mouth and checked her email. "Awesome. That guy from Portland replied." With one quick message, they'd set the interview for Monday at two.

Her first cup of coffee tasted perfect, hot and bitter with a dash of cream. This morning, her loft above the brewery smelled like breakfast or baking bread. The aroma wasn't coming from her kitchen, the scent was healthy beer fermenting, bubbling with life nearby. As she planned her day, thoughts of Wade invaded. She knew their movements mirrored one another—taking measurements, tasting, and perfecting another batch of beer.

She closed her eyes for a moment, seeing him at Mosquito. Wade probably had his sandy-blond hair tied back at the nape of his neck, gray eyes focused in concentration. She imagined him chewing on his pencil before he jotted notes on his clipboard.

Someday their paths would cross again—it was bound to happen, maybe at a festival or a conference. The world of craft brewing was growing but remained small enough that she'd certainly see him again. She hoped to have a successful brewery before that inevitable day. At least Silver Raven would give them something to talk about, a safe subject. Anything would be better than admitting that leaving him had been one of her biggest mistakes.

THIRTY

"How many homes have you looked at?" Linnea asked as she followed her brother into a small farmhouse that had just hit the market.

"Four, including this one. There was the old Keller place out by the highway. It was huge. I just don't know if I need three thousand square feet. But it did have a shop." He tapped his chin, thinking about all that tempting space.

Linn harrumphed and rolled her eyes. "What is it with men and shops?"

"Don't even ask." His eyes went wide punctuating his mock-disgust, and she smacked his bicep with her hand. Wade winced, pretending it hurt.

"What? I want to know," she asked, ignoring is apparent pain.

"A boat, snowmobiles, and quads. The shop is all about the promise of filling it with awesome toys."

Linnea shook her head. "Fine, boys and their toys, I get it. What about the other places?"

"I checked out a cabin, but it was too dark. Then I walked through a dated but livable double-wide sitting on seventeen acres. The land is perfect, right on the river. I could build a place while I live in the manufactured home. So far, that's the spot that tempts me the most."

"This farmhouse is nice, but all these outbuildings would be a waste unless you plan on farming," Linn lifted her brows, she already knew his answer.

"Nope, I left Yakima for a reason. I don't ever want to be that tied down again. Oh, I forgot to let you know, I'm going on a road trip tomorrow. Can you keep an eye on things?"

"Where are you headed and for how long?"

He studied his sister and went for the truth. The last time he hid information the consequences were disastrous. "Klamath Falls. But please, Linnea, don't tell anyone."

"Thank God!" she moaned. "I wondered when one of you would swallow your pride, get on the road, and patch things up. Does Ravenna know you're coming?"

Wade shoved his hands into his pockets and stood for a long moment staring at his sister. "You've been expecting me to do this?"

"Hell yes. I'm tired of watching you drag your butt around in a fog of sadness. Ravenna is just as miserable. Oh crap," Linnea covered her mouth with her hand, "pretend you didn't hear that."

"She's miserable?" His smile could not have been wider.

Her hands landed on her hips. "Try not to look so happy about it, Wade." A grin tipped the corners of her mouth. "She's trying to mask how much she misses you with nonstop work."

"Do you think I have a chance? When I planned this, I knew it would be my last desperate Hail Mary attempt to win her back."

"Planned what? Wade, please tell me you aren't deceiving her again."

He winced and backed a step away.

Linnea grabbed his arms and shook him. "What have you done this time?"

When he explained the job, the emails, and his appointment for an interview, his sister's eyes brimmed with tears and she smiled. "Oh my God, that's so romantic! But what if she offers you a job? I mean, if she needs you in Klamath Falls, would you make a change?"

"Absolutely. Her dreams are as important as mine." He'd wrestled with this question. No matter how successful he was, living without Ravenna wasn't a life—it was merely existing.

"I'm hoping she'll help me make a decision on a house. When I saw that land, I could see her with me right on the river. It's perfect.

But when I dream about that home, I always see Ravenna in it. What do you think, Linn, will she forgive me?"

"I'm pretty sure she already has."

***

The industrial part of Klamath Falls looked the same. More than a decade ago, he'd crossed these streets and met Leo Silvestre at Silver Raven Brewery. After meeting Leo, his life had changed. This journey back to southern Oregon gave him hope—maybe the younger Silvestre would alter the trajectory of his life again.

Two hours early, he killed time and circled the streets of town. Driving usually calmed him, but today the wait was torture. He drove past Silver Raven a third time. The car, the one that took her away from Ashwood, was the only vehicle in the lot. Wade hit the brakes, he couldn't wait any longer.

Parking his car next to hers, he stood for a moment to gather what was left of his senses. All the words he intended to say scattered like shards of glass in his fragmented mind. He paced a wide circle then placed both palms flat against the side of his truck—the truck he bought in Vegas after meeting Ravenna. Arms heavy, he leaned into his stance to calm the shaking.

"Don't mess this up." He inhaled a labored breath, pushed out spent air, and moved.

He approached Silver Raven's entrance where a faded *open* sign hung crooked in a white-framed window. With a solid shove, he pushed the door open and walked inside. The heavy door slammed, shaking the panes. Wade winced at the racket. It wasn't the stealthy entrance he'd intended to make.

Following the solid thud, a musical voice rang out, "Hello! I'll be just a minute!"

He followed the sound and waited for Ravenna to appear. When she stepped into view, he inhaled then forgot how to breathe. She didn't move and didn't speak. He took a few solid steps forward and paused. The blank shock on her face scared him more than if she had yelled, or cried, or screamed.

"I'm early," he said.

Puzzled, her brows furrowed, and she only stared.

"For my interview. Ravenna. I couldn't wait another moment to see you. I'm early."

She took a staggered step and a few words broke free. "You're . . . the guy . . . from Portland?"

Rock-hard tension left his shoulders. At least she'd spoken. "Yes. The Portland guy, that's me."

"Wade, I'm confused."

Thank God, when she'd uttered his name, she hadn't winced, or worse, run the other direction. All at once, he needed to feel the warmth of her touch. He closed in on a woman who had never looked so beautiful. Oversized coveralls enveloped her tiny body and leather gloves protected her hands. Almost every inch of her was concealed. Wade desperately needed to feel the heat of her skin.

Speechless, she watched as Wade's fingers removed the worn calfskin gloves from her small shaking hands. When his movement stopped, Ravenna's eyes skipped from her hands, across his chest, to his face. A potent mixture of sadness, fear, and love spilled from her gorgeous features. Wade couldn't hold back his tears.

As his lips parted to speak, she raised to the tips of her toes and slid her fingers possessively around his neck. Ravenna pulled him down to her five-foot-three height. She claimed his mouth and his entire body shook with relief.

"I'm so sorry," he said against her lips. He kissed away their mingled tears and placed his large calloused hands gently on her face, remembering her features with his touch. His thumbs caressed her lashes, her cheeks, and her lush full lips.

"I don't deserve it . . . I don't deserve you, but please. . ." He choked back a sob and pulled away to memorize her beauty again. "Forgive me."

A slight nod tilted her face in his hands. "I forgave you as soon as I drove away from Ashwood, but my pride and my wounded heart needed time," she said, and his lips connected with hers, a chaste touch that soothed the lingering ache.

Forgiveness was a start, but he wanted more. "Sweetheart, I hope the damage I've done can be repaired by the love I have for you. Ravenna, let me try. Let me love you," Wade begged.

Soft and slow, her lips accepted his love. A wisp of smoldering desire flared with renewed combustion. Wade scooped her into his arms and walked toward the door he had just entered. Grabbing the sign in the window, he flipped it over to *closed*. When he locked the door, she tipped her head back and laughed. Wade intended to love her, thoroughly.

Ravenna's legs wrapped around his torso. He supported her butt and rushed through her brewery while his mouth covered her giggles with another kiss. Her small hands caressed away any remnants of his salty tears. Sturdy tanks and tall vessels sped by in a blur. Two at a time, he carried her up the metal stairs to her industrial loft.

"My bed's in there," she whispered with a tilt of her head.

Wade lay Ravenna on the neatly made bed. The open zipper of her coveralls revealed a tiny triangle of flesh that he touched with the tip of his finger. Flushed heat escaped her oversized canvas workwear. The bulky fabric disguised her shapely curves, and he licked his lips, anxious to unwrap this delicious gift.

Her eyes locked on his intense obsidian gaze. Wade's trembling fingers grasped the zipper and slowly eased the closure down. The clicking sound coiled as much tension as climbing the first towering hill of a wooden roller coaster.

His eyebrows lifted as he revealed the scanty clothing choice hidden under the canvas workwear. Amusement tipped the corners of his mouth when he saw her faded Backstreet Boys tank top and slick pink nylon shorts.

"Do you always wear so little under your coveralls?" He chuckled.

"I'm too hot with more."

"Oh, you're about to get much, much hotter," he growled as he lifted her hips to glide the coveralls off her body. Now that his eyes could feast on the banquet of her delicious curves, he didn't know which part he wanted to taste first.

"God, I missed you," he murmured as he prowled to take a kiss. He hovered over her on hands and knees. Their first passionate contact began with her moist full mouth. Every nibble reacquainted his lips with her taste one dash at a time.

Wade had forgotten what her flavor could do to his senses. Like a drug, he consumed. Warm lips partook as she swept her fingers across the light stubble on his jaw. Her hands moved to loosen the leather tie holding his hair, and his wavy mane fell forward, trapping their mingled scent. He lost himself in her mouth, her citrusy perfume, her delicate touch.

Dropping to his elbows, a thousand points of contact pressed her body against his. His chest pressed her breasts, flattening them against his hardened body. The eager movement of her legs propelled his action. Wade nibbled his way down her neck, recalling each exquisite contour. His tongue re-mapped every spot he knew brought a sigh, a moan, or a keening cry of bliss.

What little clothes she wore blocked his path and needed to go immediately. In a blur of fabric, Wade stripped her bare. Time stopped for a moment. He blinked, savoring the woman lying before him. "This time, you're not a dream."

KINNEY SCOTT

Her grin playfully danced, tilting her lips and her eyes. "Wade, in my dreams, you weren't wearing any clothes."

A laugh burst from his chest. "I can fix that."

She put both hands behind her head and her smile flicked to naughty. "Wade, baby, take your clothes off . . . slowly," she directed. A wicked bite teased her bottom lip, adding a sensual glint to her exotic dark eyes.

Beginning with his belt, he moved with powerful precision, measuring his movements against the way her body squirmed. Each stitch of clothing he removed coaxed Ravenna's exploring hands. Wade swallowed hard while she caressed her breasts. His eyes widened when her skin pinkened, radiating impatient heat. Her small hands tickled a path across the rise of her belly and her legs parted. His mouth gaped when Ravenna teased the swollen wet nirvana between her smooth legs. Over the soft linen comforter, she opened like a butterfly in eager invitation.

Removing his clothes at such a slow pace nearly killed him, but he was rewarded with her throaty gasp. His cock sprang free from the confines of his boxers and Ravenna moaned. Her sensual cry pearled a bead of cum from the slit at the tip of his cock. Naked, he dropped to his knees at the edge of the bed.

"I gotta taste you," he growled. His weight curved the mattress when he settled his shoulders between her legs to plunge into her vulnerable offering.

Wade pleased her with his lips and expert fingers. His possessive growl merged with her cries of pleasure. Deep, then shallow, and plunging again, he explored, teasing her off the mattress. His work-calloused hands held her in place as he orchestrated her desire.

Never breaking contact, he pinned his tongue to the spot that begged for his undivided attention and used a curved finger to take over where his mouth had left. Adding a second, his long slow strokes enhanced the pressure as his tongue circled the apex of her sex.

Tugging his hair, Ravenna thrust her hips pursuing an elusive climax.

"Squeeze your nipples for me—I need to feel you fly apart," Wade commanded in a growl and she obeyed. Her hands left his scalp to torture her taut peaks.

From the delicious space between her thighs, his eyes flicked across the sleek rise of her belly. He had never witnessed anything so devastatingly hot. Her fingers tortured her pliant globes while she chased her release.

Dipping his head again, her wet channel tightened around his fingers, and he knew she was moments from ecstasy. In a rhythm matched by his pulsing tongue, he plunged his fingers into her center. She screamed out his name, her head flung back, and her eyes squeezed shut. Her slim body arched from the mattress. Wade feasted on her orgasmic bliss, milking wave after wave of pleasure from her core. Ragged gasps gave way to breathy sighs of sheer satisfaction. He moaned against her center, and finally eased his fingers and lips away.

As she came back to Earth, he drew a ribbon with his tongue from the dip between her hips, moving up the valley and swell of each breast, arriving at last on her lips with a lazy kiss.

"I taste sweet," she said and laughed, low and sexy.

"You have no idea how delicious you are."

"I need you inside me," she begged.

"Mm, that's precisely where I need to be."

Settling over her on his elbows, he watched her expression as he teased the smooth crown of his cock over her wet cleft. She closed her eyes for a moment and his movement stopped. He waited for her gaze. "Watch, please. I need you to see me, Ravenna. I need you to witness my love."

Her mouth parted, but emotion caught her words in her throat. Before she could respond, his hips plunged forward and he sank deep. He possessed her with a simple declaration. "I love you." Her trembling body was better than a worded response. Warm and soft, she gentled beneath him and accepted what he offered.

Her hands and calves rounded his body, clinging to his muscles as Wade fixed his pace. Each plunge drove deeper, and she wrapped passionate tendrils around his soul. Still gazing at her rapt expression, his lips parted. "I love you Ravenna," he declared. "I am yours," he thrust again, "And you are mine."

"I am yours." She repeated his sentiment and shared the same passion. "And you are mine." Her words rushed out on an exhale as he lunged.

He picked up the pace. Pulling entirely out, he paused and plunged again, claiming her with a shattering force that crushed any remaining walls between them.

A low growl pledged again slowly, "I love you."

Together, they echoed fervent whispers, "I am yours."

Merged words repeated, "You are mine."

Connected, invaded, and owned, their bodies forged unbreakable bonds. Wade and Ravenna merged in a climax that connected their souls in breathless euphoria. Cresting and climbing, their ecstasy peaked and finally ebbed into diminishing waves of heady aftershocks.

Slick and panting, Wade caged the woman he cherished in his arms. He rolled her to the top, still sheathed in her intoxicating heat. She collapsed, wholly spent, on his sweat-glistened torso. Wade toyed with her dark hair, humming a soft song while he twisted a tendril around his index finger.

"That melody has haunted me since we've been apart," she admitted.

"What melody?" he asked.

"The song you're humming . . . the one you used to play on your guitar, what is it?"

He hadn't been aware that the tune in his head had made it past his vocal cords. "It's yours. I wrote it for you. I finished it after—" He couldn't say it, the memory of her leaving still stung.

"But you told me you never wrote break-up songs," she said, as she wrapped her knee over his leg.

"I don't. And we didn't. I never gave up on us. From the first moment we met, we seemed . . . inevitable." He placed a kiss on the top of her head. The truth was so easy now. He never wanted anything else.

"I never stopped loving you, Wade," she whispered. The vibration of her voice hummed against his chest. His hands tightened on her hip. She'd spoken that one intoxicating word. *Love.* A confession he didn't hope to hear. Not yet.

Her fingers toyed with the lines of his black and gray mosquito tattoo. "I began loving you when you rescued me by the side of the highway," she admitted.

Wade swallowed, overwhelmed. His words trembled. "I knew I loved you as I drove out of Vegas. No matter how many miles I put between us, I could not get far enough away to break the bands you had fastened around my heart."

"Sounds painful." She soothed and his expression softened.

"Not as painful as losing you. I'm so sorry."

"You don't need my forgiveness. I never blamed you for the tough decisions you were forced to make. I've moved past it and now I'm ready to heal."

"Your father once told me, long ago after we had a few too many drinks, *We cannot control those things that bring us together—*"

They finished the words in unison, "*But we can control if those things tear us apart.*"

Wade's lips met Ravenna's kiss. She wrapped her legs around his hips, her soft words pledged, "I love you. Absolutely nothing will ever tear us apart."

THIRTY-ONE

The scent of ripe hops hung heavy in the damp morning air. Soon, heat would add a sharp dry bite to the piney-citrus aroma. Heavy machinery rumbled away in the distance, moving row to row, cutting vines and hauling hops to the processors.

"Do you think your parents heard us this morning?" Ravenna worried as they walked hand in hand below the towering hop trellises. When she mentioned what they'd done in Wade's old room, his eyes flashed and he pulled her in tight, bunching her shirt in his hands. She clung to him as he bent for a kiss, a plundering of lips that left her dizzy.

He inched away and whispered, "Not a chance. Mom was already downstairs making breakfast. During harvest, I'm not sure Dad sleeps at all."

She'd already noticed that harvest sent everyone into full swing. Ravenna was happy to work alongside his family. She loved the acceptance, the challenge, and the unrelenting schedule.

After one more kiss, Wade released her, then tore a cone off the bine and crushed the papery flower between his fingers. He brought the sticky golden resin to his nose and inhaled.

"Are you happy with the new hop?" she asked.

"Rusk hasn't produced the yield I hoped for, but the quality is outstanding."

"I can almost taste that hint of mango on the air."

He wore his satisfaction on his grin. "Erik and Trish have plans for a fresh hop batch and will stop by to pick up some of the harvest today. It will go into the boil tonight."

"How are they adjusting to running things on their own up at Old Mosquito?" she asked.

"They love the independence, but will need more help—"

She finished his thought, "Now that they are expecting their first baby. I'm so happy for them!" Reaching out, Ravenna knit their fingers together, holding his hand while they walked through the shaded rows. Another vehicle rumbled by, overflowing with deep green hops headed for the processor.

"We better get back or Linnea will hunt us down," Wade said and led Ravenna to the Gator that would speed them back.

Well after dark, exhausted and satisfied from the long day on the farm, the entire family shared a quiet meal. Easing his hand possessively around her shoulder, Wade lowered his head with "I love you," on his lips.

"Love you, too." Her quiet words caught his parent's attention and their eyes connected on knowing smiles. Ravenna blushed as Wade's fingers tightened. He pulled her closer, then a strange sensation swelled behind her ribs, catching her breath. She wondered for a moment if her journey with Wade Michaels had begun long before they met.

*****

Also by Kinney Scott

In Ashwood
Inheriting Trouble
Trouble Brewing
Chasing Trouble
Addicted To Trouble
Trouble Undone

Watch for more at https://kinneyscott.com.

About the Author

Kinney Scott writes contemporary romance from her home near Puget Sound on the rainy side of Washington State. Her steamy heroes and complex heroines feel most at home in the rugged and uniquely romantic environments of the Pacific Northwest. When she has a moment away from her computer, Kinney escapes to her garden or spends a few hours hiking trails near her home.

Want to know more? Visit Kinney at https://kinneyscott.com

Read more at https://kinneyscott.com.

www.ingramcontent.com/pod-product-compliance
Lightning Source LLC
Chambersburg PA
CBHW030125180626
46812CB00002B/557